SO MANY WOMEN

THE LOVE THAT KILLED ME

ROSE CURIEL

CONTENTS

For my sis, Claudia Marie. Miss you beyond words. Acknowledgements to Izzy Samson, MacGarett Pierre, and Gertha Louissaint.

PROLOGUE

I learned from a young age what it was to lose people. I understood that the people you put roots into, the people whom you become attached to, the people that you put your entire heart and soul into, can disappear one day, just like that.

In sixth grade, I learned what it felt like to lose someone I truly connected with. It is always the connections that you make when you have never been more lonely that you remember the most. Fernanda was the first girl in my new school who spoke to me. Even in our youth, when all we were doing was collecting Rainbow Bright stickers or trading lunch box snacks, she had this sort of maternal instinct that meant she took me under her wing. I was shy, and making friends alone seemed like such a difficult challenge. But making one friend in Fernanda meant that I was friends with all of her friends. I had fitted in with impressive ease, and Fernanda introduced me to anyone who had given a cautious stare during my first few days.

On the first day of sixth grade in my new school, I entered the classroom with a pit of anxiety in my stomach. I wanted to disappear. I wanted to be completely unnoticed, to blend in with the walls that hung crappy pictures of the students' arts and crafts. But the teacher had me stand up, introduce myself, then get me to tell the class one fact about where I came from. So, I told the class about my close family and how important cousins and second cousins and third cousins were. Because at this time in my life, the only people I could depend on seeing more than once were my family. I knew for sure that no matter where we lived, we would always find the time and place to see each other. Fernanda had come up to me during the lunch break. She was biting on a red apple; she chewed on a piece and swallowed before speaking to me.

"My family are really close too. I'm going to my little cousin's birthday party this Saturday."

I remember thinking that this was a funny thing to say. But looking back, I think she was trying to make me feel more comfortable after sharing in front of the whole class. Show and Tell had a whole different feel to it when you were the only kid in class who didn't know anybody.

Fernanda and I played in the school playground, had dance competitions with the other girls, and begged the P.E. coach to put us in the same teams, and did the same with the teachers for group projects. In whatever way we could interact with one another during school, we would try and get to do it.

On school picture day, Fernanda looked beautiful. She had a neat bob cut of Jet black hair. She wore a slim red hairband to slick back her bangs. She would say that it's because they got in her way when she was doing schoolwork, but no one could deny how effortlessly pretty she looked. She posed for her photo, and a gold-plated name necklace twinkled into the studio lights and flash. It had been a present given to Fernanda by her abuela. Fernanda's family were from the Dominican Republic and were deeply close, similar to my Haitian family.

When Fernanda saw me staring at her gold necklace, she smiled, then hopped off her stool when the photo session had finished.

"Here. You wear it. Then everyone will know we're best friends."

She smiled down at me because she was a good half-foot taller. I couldn't believe it. She even put it on over my collar just in time for my photo to be taken. I gleamed with pride, feeling the twinkle of light that the necklace was giving me, the feeling of being beautiful and also cared for. Six months ago, I didn't know anyone in the class. And now here I was, wearing my best friend's nameplate in my class photo. They even let us take one together, and we both paid $10 extra for each copy.

It seems funny to write this now, but I always knew that Fernanda was special. She was my introduction to this new town. She was my first example of feeling welcomed in a place that I didn't yet feel like I belonged. This is why she is so prominent to me, even many years later. I had always had the feeling that she was older, wiser, more mature. Well, it turns out she was. She was a year and a half older. Towards the end of the school year, she was taken out of elementary school and put into middle school, where I would never be in a class with her again. My friend that I had made all that effort with, who had made me feel like I belonged in a strange place, was gone.

I remember crying when Fernanda switched schools. Even though we said we were best friends, we were still a bit too young to be trading numbers and arranging to see one another on our own. Besides, Fernanda was one of the most popular girls in sixth grade. No doubt, she would make the same amount of friends in middle school. But I didn't want Fernanda to make new friends. I wanted to be her best friend - her only best friend. Fernanda had written in my school journal "Fernanda and Leila BFFF." I tried to point out to her that this meant "Best Friends Forever Forever." But Fernanda had only smiled, like I had just proven her loyalty and she was pleased. "Exactly. That's what we are. Best Friends Forever Forever."

I didn't yet know that I would meet Fernanda again many years later in my life. For now, her leaving was the deepest pain that I could feel. I cried for days after school, talking about how no one wanted to talk to me anymore now that Fernanda was out of the class. My mother was a single mother, and I had two brothers living with us and a sister five years older than us, so she didn't have as much time as I would have liked for my life's woes. As a child, these woes are the most painful thing to go through. Perhaps as an adult, they don't seem serious. But to me, I didn't know if I would survive without Fernanda. I didn't want to go to school ever again. Perhaps my Haitian resilience got me through it, and I got on with things, surviving and trying to fit in and feeling like I belonged somewhere, like I was understood.

It is no doubt then that in middle school, where I first met Nicholas, he had such an impact on me. Nicholas had given me feelings of belonging, closeness, and sincere friendship, again when I was the new kid. He was well-known in the school, although his emotional and mysterious demeanor meant that he preferred to stay back in the corners and analyze what was going on around us. Nicholas liked to be both within and without. He wanted us to be around people, but when we were, we were so engrossed in each other that it wouldn't have mattered. This sort of romantic lust is welcomed in your teens. Hell, it's essential. And despite all that I know now, I still can't be sure whether I would have stopped myself from meeting Nicholas and even from meeting Fernanda, whom I lost momentarily in childhood. Despite knowing the pain that love causes, it didn't stop me from loving so many people completely, deeply, and honestly. I remember being told that if you aren't struggling and coming up against challenges in life, then you aren't really living.

Well, if nothing else, despite what may happen to me, know that these very words are the markings to prove that I have lived. And I remember everything.

YOUNG LOVE

*M*iddle school had a much faster pace than elementary. Even the classes were beginning to get more difficult. I went in thinking that I would be able to catch Fernanda and maybe see her at lunch break. But the school was swarmed with students, bumping into one another with their heavy school bags filled with books since there weren't enough lockers for everyone.

I hardly ever saw Fernanda. The one time I did see her, she smiled, like she remembered me from somewhere but couldn't quite place where, then continued to show a charm bracelet on her arm to the one blonde girl at the school standing beside her. I didn't like being this exposed to people. I hadn't made close enough friends with people in sixth grade for them to retain any such loyalty to me. The one person whom I had been close to was in an entirely different grade. This is why I chose to lose myself in extracurricular activities. And as a result, this is also where I found myself.

Band was a huge comfort for me, growing up in school. I had played the recorder (laughable) in elementary school, and it was a familiar choice to join the band in middle school. Band was also the place where I formed one of my most important friendships. Nicholas played the trombone. But his talents did not stop there. From the moment I met him, he fascinated me. Nicholas was intelligent; he never seemed to study, yet he would come out with top grades. As I got to know Nicholas more and as we got closer, he soon made me feel like the only girl in existence.

We started off as friends. We would practice every other lunch break, where we ate a quick sandwich by the chairs and squeezed our brass instruments onto our laps and in our hands. We'd play for the whole fifty minutes, taking a short break in between, where Nicholas and I would have broken conversations.

"How long have you played an instrument?"

"Um... since I was a child. This is my first time in Band, though."

"You're really good." He would smile at me. It was a knowing smile, as if he was telling me something about myself that he already knew to be true. I felt like I had met him from somewhere in my life that I did not recall. His energy was magnetic. For the last year in middle school, Nicholas and I had become inseparable. At Band practice, we would no longer care what the teachers thought about us and spent most of our time kissing in the back, whispering sweet nothings into one another's ears.

My relationship with Nicholas grew in strength, and I suddenly had someone to do everything with. He would walk me home, we would have lunch together, we practiced together, and at every school event that required the band or a full orchestra, we would be shacked up in a room, practicing together for hours. So much of our time was spent with each other.

We sat one Tuesday afternoon, lying on the grass in a park about one mile from the school grounds. To get to the park, Nicholas and I would have to jump a high wall and go through another few fields of long grass. Then we would be at the large green patch of park grass. It was a public park next to a lake that had a couple of ducks circling around. Nicholas got into the habit of bringing bits of bread from the cafeteria to feed the ducks with.

We sat amongst them now as Nicholas threw bits of bread into the lake, and I watched it go soggy and then get snapped up by one of the duck's beaks. The air was humid, and it was nearly summer. And being that we were in south Florida, you could feel the heat.

This was also around the time of year that the mosquitos would get you. The eggs would not yet be hatched, but soon, everyone would be burning citronella candles late into the night. This would still be no match for the ever-present mosquitoes that were always to be found around stagnant water. They came in from the seas and the lakes so that you could never find yourself without some sort of insect repellant.

Those who had money could afford to turn on their central air conditioner throughout the summer. But for my mother, we had portable fans in our bedrooms and family room, and we weren't able to use them liberally either. She would often complain about her electricity bill. Once we had finished eating and were getting everything cleared up, there was always a part of the day that my mother would want to turn the fans off since we'd be sleeping with them all night. To survive a summer in this town, you had to be prepared and needed help from exterior resources. But not many people considered how expensive those resources were. It felt as if I had a constant film of sweat around me in the warmer months.

Nicholas and I had nothing with us on this day by the lake with the ducks, except, of course, for the stale bread taken from the cafeteria an hour prior.

Nicholas broke up the bread in his hands and crumbled it by his feet. The ducks quacked loudly in anticipation of their lunch. They waddled close to him but not close enough that they could grab the bread. They would have to wait until he gave it to them. Nicholas seemed deep in thought. I leaned

7

onto my elbows, wondering if he was suddenly getting para-noid about skipping school. Since we mostly did everything together, we bounced all of our insecurities and anxieties back and forth to one another too. This was both a positive and a negative thing in my life. On the one hand, I had Nicholas to help counsel me through my struggles. But I would need to do the same for Nicholas, which of course was satisfying. After all, I was crazy about him. But when there were a lot of issues coming up, time and time again, I began to notice that I was not living my life all of the time. There were parts of it where I was living his life.

Either way, I wanted to see what was wrong with him because if I didn't ask, then there was a chance he could get into some kind of mood with me. Besides, I felt like we should be spending our time making out and not sitting around doing nothing.

I was always eager to speak with Nicholas, and he seemed just as eager to speak with me. Our conversations were deep and authentic and important. He told me things about himself that he had not told anyone else before. I did the same with him. It was my first real intimate relationship with someone who wasn't a direct family member. Nicholas crouched over himself, his black curly hair shadowing his face and thick eyebrows.

"What are you thinking about?" I asked, picking on some of the blades of grass, trying to seem nonchalant.

Nicholas sighed and took something out of his backpack. When I glanced over, I could see that it was a school notebook, and he was looking for a particular page. In it, there seemed to be pages and pages of short poems, not usually going over half a page. He paused on a page that had the title "My Heart." As I saw it, my eyes quickly tried to read the first one or two lines, dying to know what he was saying about me in his poetry notebook. I knew that Nicholas wrote poetry, but until this moment, he had been quite shy about it. He ripped out the piece of paper that he had landed on and I noticed how his hands were shaking as he read from the page, without explaining himself before doing so.

When my heart beats, all I see is you.
In every day,
In every way,
My heart beats for you.
Is this as true for you?
Can you please give me a clue?
How I have fallen, so deeply,
My heart opens widely and discreetly.
Let me carry your heart in mine, my true divine.
My heart, it beats for you.

Nicholas's voice was shaking as well as his hands holding onto the piece of paper as he read out his declaration of love to me, or at least that is what I took it for. Amid this very romantic moment, it was all I could do not to burst out laughing. I don't know what it was that was making me feel so goofy; perhaps it was because I genuinely hadn't expected it. Or perhaps, on a much deeper level, I had never considered how someone could care about me like that. When Nicholas had read out his poem, he had confirmed something in me that I had assumed was imaginary. It was true. At night, before I went to sleep and in the first moment of the morning, it was Nicholas's face that popped into my head.

I smiled at him, laughing slightly, trying to be careful about how I reacted to this very vulnerable outreach from Nicholas. My only response was to hug him, deeply and close to me. As I did, I started to gather my thoughts, to consider what he had just said to me and how it all made me feel. As intense as it was, being in a serious relationship at such a young age, it was also the best proof that I had ever gotten that I was alive and living to the fullest. It was thrilling to think that a boy would love me so much to write poetry about me.

Nicholas pulled me away and looked at me straight into my eyes.

"Leila, I love you." When he said it at first, I swear it was like I couldn't breathe. Here was the guy who had filled the last couple of months of my life up with private moments, intense conversations, and kisses that I would never forget. He kissed me at this moment, and I let my shoulders drop, enjoying it and not letting my anxieties about saying it back straight away get the better of me. This was a moment that Nicholas had planned especially for us. This was the confirmation that I had yearned for, unknowing to myself. The fact that we had always been friends meant that we had resisted defining our relationship and instead had just gradually moved on to doing stuff with one another.

I lay back onto the grass as he leaned on top of me, kissing me still and running his hands through my twisted hair. I could hear the distant quacks of the hungry ducks and the passive buzzing of pond insects or the hopping of a frog, jumping onto the water lilies. The sounds harmonized in this moment as Nicholas kissed me underneath the humid fog of an early summer's day. When I broke away to catch my breath, I was quick to say it back.

"I love you too," I breathed. He smiled like he was glad but not surprised. It felt good to be liberal and say it. It was something that I had been holding on my tongue for weeks now, afraid that it would slip out during one of our make-out sessions. I knew at this moment that there would be no more pretending. Nicholas and I were an item, and we were about to experience the extent of what that would feel like.

When I got home that evening, my face was burned from being outside all afternoon. My mother had looked me up and down as if she knew. But then again, she always looked at us like that, like we were up to no good.

It wasn't normal or acceptable in my culture for a girl my age, at just fifteen years old, to date a guy and have a boyfriend, and my mother liked to remind me of this.

"Now, you better not be doing anything with that boy, you hear me?" For the first year, she only referred to Nicholas as "ti garcon", creole for little boy. I envisioned him as a stray dog that I would let into our house from time to time, the way she said it.

As teenagers, there weren't many places that we could go. Our schedule revolved around when we could be alone together. Band and school were always good opportunities to hang out, but it was stifling. It's not like we could be our complete selves there, and besides, there were always teachers roaming around, telling us to get back to work or to separate.

I chose not to tell my mother much. I never told her that Nicholas was my boyfriend, and I certainly didn't tell her when we started having sex. For a long time, this felt like a burden that I was keeping hidden from my family. My older brothers were as overprotective as you would expect older brothers to be. It's not like they made a point of getting in on my business and keeping tabs on me, but they would certainly cop a second look if they saw Nicholas leaving me at the door and lingering for a good forty-five minutes before saying goodbye.

If my mother were home from work, she would sure as hell linger too. In fact, one time, when we were just lost in conversation, school bags slumped at my front door, my mother banged loudly on the window, then made the gesture for me to come in. Nicholas hadn't realized it at first and started to walk towards my front door. I admired how comfortable he was at my house, even though my mother was skeptical of anyone of the opposite sex that I was hanging out with.

I laughed at him and tried to explain. "I think we should find a better spot to sit and chat when we're walking home from school."

From then on, we used the lake as a sort of meeting place. Sure, it took longer to get to, we had to cross over a couple of fields and jump the high wall, but once we were there, we were completely alone.

Sometimes it's hard for me to place the past Nicholas with

the one in the present. But I remember a lot of kissing, laying on the grass near the lakes, and pontificating about life. We were at that stage where our biggest dreams still seemed possible. We didn't know what it was yet to struggle and have to work. Nicholas was temperamental when it came to school, but part of me knew that he would have his choices when he left. He just picked things up so easily. Even with a new piece in the band, he was always the person to lead our group into the new melody. Suddenly, the trombone seemed like the most important instrument in the group, but that was just the presence Nicholas had.

The poetry continued, and so did the skipping school from time to time, sharing headphones and listening to our favorite songs, swapping Cassette tapes, books, telling stories about our parents, who had both come over to America in the hopes for a better life, what it felt to be the child of an immigrant and an immigrant myself and how much pressure that sometimes put on a person.

Nicholas soon became an escape for me from all of the mundane stresses in life. I knew that my mother was a single mother. I knew that she had to work twice as hard as everyone else and how difficult it must be for her to work in a hotel and not be paid more than $10 an hour. But there was also a small part of me that resented her situation. I resented that she had to struggle so much and that she was always working. Perhaps that is how Nicholas became so central to my life.

My mother would be working a lot, and sometimes his parents would be too. Instead of being minded by our siblings, we could go over to one another's houses and be left alone together. Nicholas and I were so engrossed in each other's company that most people didn't try to separate us. As far as my brothers were concerned, as long as they could still play video games and flipped through playboy magazines that my mom didn't know about, and I didn't come to bother them about much, it was all cool. I guess even they didn't notice the discreet shift in Nicholas when things started to get more serious.

After Nicholas had told me that he loved me, and after I had said it back, there was a strange shift in our relationship. While I was glad that we were moving onto the next level, it only seemed to make Nicholas less secure. If I didn't show up in school, he would go home and call my house to check up and see where I was. I started to notice that the way we fought was emotional and could get out of hand quickly. This could be over something small, like Nicholas thinking that we didn't talk on the phone enough, or perhaps he felt like we didn't see each other as often as we loved and that people were always getting in the way. For me, perhaps there was a part of me that was growing a small bit distant. I had gone straight from being best friends with Fernanda, who was eventually taken from me to dating Nicholas and spending all of my time with him. It was starting to feel a little unwise of me to be concentrating everything on this one relationship. Besides, as much as I tried to ignore it, a part of me still felt paranoid for being in a serious relationship like this when it wasn't normal for my culture.

But Nicholas and I were still a long way away from ending. For now, his bad parts were always overshadowed by his good parts. No one listened to me more or was more attentive to how I was feeling than Nicholas. He listened to every unformed thought that went on in my head, and I did the same for him. Together, we eased the burden of being alive and the mental turmoil that could sometimes come with that.

I knew that sex was going to be next for us. And even though I had been adamant about not losing my virginity too quickly, it seemed like the obvious next step for Nicholas and me. I remember feeling like I was becoming mature, and what if I wasn't ready for all of it? How could I ever know if I would be ready? I thought about bouncing some of these ideas off my mother—you know, if she was not my mother but a complete and total stranger. Because if my mother had known that I was planning on having sex, she would have killed me. The fact that it all had to be done in secret was what made it more appealing. Besides, I had someone that said they loved me. I loved him too. I learned that when you love someone, you want to show them through gestures. And so that is what I did. Nicholas and I lost our virginity to one another shortly after he had confessed that he loved me, and this new element in our relationship made things even more intense. I was slowly forgetting what life was like before I met Nicholas.

2

GETTING HOT AND GETTING CAUGHT

*I*t was a hot and overcast day, and Nicholas was lighting up a joint in my room. The once-innocent Haitian little girl was somewhat amused by this. Here I was, half-naked and lounging around my room with my boyfriend, who was smoking pot out my window when nobody was home.

Nicholas and I always wanted to be together. And once we started having sex, we did it every chance we got. We'd done it at both our parents' house and even his grandmother's house. It was this new and exciting way that we could feel even closer and more intimate with one another, and we couldn't get enough of it.

Nicholas made me feel like I could take greater risks in life. I don't know if I would have bothered to skip school if it wasn't for him. As far as we could see, anything that involved separating us: different classes, home life, responsibilities, was a waste of time. High school was different from middle school in that we got even less attention than before. More students meant more opportunities to slip away unnoticed. Since both of our parents worked during the day, heading back to one of our places at lunch break was the obvious thing to do. It was almost as if we had our own apartment, and we acted with the same boldness as we would have if it actually was our shared apartment. My room had posters of Michael Jackson and Prince that I was already growing out of, a chest of drawers with a vanity mirror, and a string of floral lights wrapped around the curtain pole. Nicholas leaned out the window, smoking his joint as My Prerogative played out of my Cassette player. He had brought the Cassette to school with him and promised that I could borrow it for as long as I liked. It wasn't my usual style of music, but I appreciated it at this moment, in this setting, as I imagined that Nicholas and I were chilling out in our shared studio apartment and not in my teenage bedroom.

Nicholas took a long, thoughtful drag and spoke without looking at me. "You know, the thing about Bobby was that he really didn't care what anybody thought of him. He just did what he wanted, always."

"And what was that? Take a bunch of drugs and go crazy?" I laughed, tugging at my t-shirt and feeling a little exposed, even though my body was basically covered. Getting naked was still very new and strange to me. It's not like I was insecure about my body or anything. I knew even then that I was beautiful. But that didn't mean I wanted to go strutting around my room butt naked.

Nicholas looked at me, quite serious for a moment. "No. The drugs were just a distraction. Imagine holding that sort of genius in your mind. Imagine having all those crazed fans. You'd go crazy too."

He looked back out the window, and I was suddenly jealous of the adoration Nicholas held over Bobby Brown of all people and how I seemingly didn't understand it. I lay back on my pillow and wrapped my twisted hair around my finger, a habit that I had gotten into at an early age.

"Okay, so why do the drugs in the first place? Why not just focus on the creative genius?"

Nicholas looked at me and smirked. "So full of questions

today." He put out his smoke and joined me next to the pillow, looking into my eyes in that intense way he always did. I immediately wanted to look away. I was thinking about the close proximity of my skin, my pores, how he could see all of my imperfections. I wondered if my eyeliner had smudged or if my hair looked messy and unkempt. But it was always the moments where I felt the most exposed or insecure that Nicholas kissed me the most.

Bobby Brown's voice played over us as we were kissing one another all over. Nicholas took off my t-shirt so that all I had on were my panties with no bra. I grabbed the sheets beside me to try and cover some of my exposure, purely out of habit. But Nicholas got on top of me, partly covering me with his chest, then moved the hair from my face.

"You're so beautiful." He said and kissed me softly on the lips. It was as if all of the hesitation and insecurity just melted away with his touch. Soon we were at it again. And I felt so liberated and free, despite the pit of anxiety in my stomach that would stay for the duration of time that we were skipping or sneaking around in one of our houses.

Of course, this anxiety was not coming out of nowhere. Nicholas may have been able to totally lose himself in our relationship. But I was always waiting in anticipation. I was thinking about when my brothers were due home or if my mother had forgotten something or what about the school. What if they had called my mother telling her that this was the second time in a week that I had skipped in the afternoon? Then I would envision the fictionalized beating that would be waiting for me once my mother got home. She would tell me how I was to stay away from "that boy" again and how she would not raise a baby in her household. Part of my mother's anxieties came from my sister becoming a mother at a young age. But she should have known that this wasn't going to happen to me. Nicholas and I used protection. And as far as I was concerned, that was the only thing that really mattered. I loved him, and he loved me. Despite the judgment that this would cause, I believed it was right.

The music was loud, and we were lost in one another. This is why I didn't hear the car pulling up, the keys rattling, the door shutting. Still to this day, I can't believe we were so stupid. But that was just what happened when we were together. We were too busy focusing on one another.

I thought I had imagined a voice calling out to me, and at that moment, I shoved Nicholas off me, anticipating the door opening. But then it was gone, and Nicholas looked at me, confused for my stopping the moment. So we continued. The murmuring could be heard again, but my reaction was not quick enough this time, and Nicholas was on top of me. Before I could catch a breath, my door handle opened, and my uncle walked into the room before gasping and walking out with horror.

"I—uh… you shouldn't be doing that, Leila! What the hell is wrong with you?" My uncle called out from the hall, staggering around and trying to recover from the shock. I pushed Nicholas off me and searched for my t-shirt, feeling disgusted at myself. My face was purple from embarrassment, and I could barely hear anything. It was the worst thing to happen to me.

My brother had caught us once before, which nearly killed me also. It was one thing being ashamed and feeling shy about getting naked with a boyfriend. It is a totally different thing getting caught by the men in your family while having sex. Nothing could be more dishonorable. Considering how my sister got pregnant so young, it certainly made me look quite precarious, messing around with boys at my age.

I couldn't believe it, but Nicholas smiled as he put his boxers and jeans back on. He shook his head. "Times like these, I wish I could climb out your window."

I was still in shock. It was my uncle that caught us—not his uncle or his family member, but mine. That meant that it was me who was at risk of my mother finding out. And that was something that couldn't happen. My only option was to get Nicholas out of the house as soon as possible and try to reconcile things with my uncle. I turned off the music as soon as my t-shirt was back on. When I did, the sudden quietness inside the house, my uncle still murmuring from shock at what he saw, was making me uneasy.

I grabbed some shorts and fixed my hair in an effort to tame it, which wasn't going to happen. Nicholas followed me out, and we found Uncle Daniel sitting on the kitchen table with his arms folded. He got up immediately when he saw the both of us.

"Now, what the hell do you think you guys are doing? You know you're much too young to be doing that—and why aren't you in school, Leila? Who is this boy?"

Uncle Daniel was roaring and carrying on in the exact same way that my mother would have if it was her that caught us. No—in fact, she would be ten times worse. I wanted to calm the situation as best I could. But Nicholas was acting defensively.

"I'm her boyfriend. We're hanging out because we're together. It's what we do." Uncle Daniel looked at Nicholas in shock, then looked at me and back to Nicholas.

"Mwen ta flank ti garcon sa yon kalot! It's not what you do in this house, boy, I can tell you that much. Get out!" My uncle said he wanted to slap the shit out of Nicholas in creole.

Uncle Daniel was sitting, thankfully, so his demand to get Nicholas out of the house wasn't so intimidating, but I still knew that Nicholas wouldn't take too kindly to being told what to do. But I couldn't consider Nicholas and his emotions right now. I gave him a pleading look that said, "Just do as he says!" and thankfully, he picked up the signal.

"I'm sorry, sir, it won't happen again." He nodded his head at Uncle Daniel before giving me a kiss on the cheek and throwing his book bag over his shoulder. Uncle Daniel was barking at him once again, shocked by Nicholas's calm demeanor. Nicholas had lost his damn mind.

"You're damn right it won't! Don't think you can come over here again when her mother ain't home. I'll be making more trips now that I know what you're up to!"

"Please, Uncle, let's talk. I don't want to be in trouble!" I said, sitting down next to him as he shook his head and kept looking out the window, making sure that Nicholas was good and gone.

Uncle Daniel was the youngest of my mother's siblings. They had moved to the same town, and we saw him a lot. He was usually quite casual and easygoing. A self-confessed life-long bachelor, this was probably more parenting than Uncle Daniel had ever intended on signing up for.

I made some cho-ko-la (Haitian hot cocoa) and tried to handle the situation head-on. The most important thing was that my mother didn't know what I was doing. I would travel to the moon, walk to and from Disney World, eat fried cock-roaches for dinner if it meant that my mother didn't find out that I was having sex at sixteen with Nicholas. I knew that if she did find out, he would never be allowed around here again. And my every move would be watched. Despite being in a family with traditional values, I still enjoyed some form of free-dom. After all, most of the time, Nicholas and I could have sex whenever and wherever we wanted. Our lust was getting the better of us, though, and we were slipping up. I didn't like the feeling of slipping up. I didn't want to be categorized as a problem or someone that needed to be fixed.

I poured Uncle Daniel and me some hot cocoa and sat down across from him, sliding a plate of hot buttered Haitian bread over to him as an act of solidarity. I knew that Uncle Daniel loved this bread, and as predicted, he smiled at me before taking a piece of it, but that in no way meant that I was off the hook.

"I need to tell you, Leila, that what you are doing is illegal." He took a bite of his bread before leaning back into his chair and looking at me sternly. I tried to suppress a laugh.

He was right, of course. The consent age in our state was 18.

At just sixteen, I was way too young to be having sex. But you could also say that I was way too young to be in love. And yet, here I was, feeling the most intense emotions that I had ever felt in my life.

"Uncle, please. I really don't want Mommy to know about this. I don't want to upset her."

Uncle Daniel took another bite out of his bread while raising his eyebrows at me. It humored me that he still ate his bread, even though he was clearly outraged and wanted to tell me off.

"And what about God, Leila! Do you care if God knows?"

I sighed. It always had to go back to God.

"Of course I care, and I'm sorry… to God. I'm sorry. But I think that God knows how much I love Nicholas and how I want to be with him forever."

This was mostly true. I wasn't so pushed to put such a major label onto Nicholas and me. Even though we lived in relatively close proximity, I still understood that there was a whole world out there, waiting for me to discover it. Although I was certain I loved Nicholas, perhaps I wasn't certain about that love lasting forever.

"You know, Leila, you're a smart girl. I thought you would have known better than this."

Uncle Daniel looked down at the table, embarrassed to say this to me. It hurt me to think that he was genuinely disappointed in me or thought differently of me now. Uncle Daniel was always my favorite uncle. Mommy had him around the house a lot. Most holidays, we would spend together. And it would always be him and us, taking a flight back and forth to Haiti to visit family. He was as much a part of my life as my brothers were.

But at this moment, my biggest concern was not my uncle and his feelings. It wasn't even my mother—it was Nicholas and me. More than anything else, I couldn't let my mother find out that I was having sex in her home when I was supposed to be in school. There was no way I would survive not being able to see Nicholas. And he sure as hell wouldn't survive not being able to see me.

I had this thought in my head and the sense of urgency that came with it as I pleaded with my uncle to hear my case.

"I know it was wrong."

"And so out of character for you, Leila!" Uncle Daniel raised his eyebrows in disbelief to signify once again how shocked and let down he was by my actions.

"Yes, out of character. I promise I am trying to be good. I will never skip school again, Uncle. But I really love Nicholas. He is a good boy with a good family. I hope that you can trust me and not tell mama that you saw us here."

I had to hear it from his own mouth to be able to trust him. But Uncle Daniel was still fixated on telling me off. He unfolded his arms and pointed his finger at me.

"But it's not just about the sex, Leila. Which, by the way, is illegal!" Uncle Daniel repeatedly telling me that Nicholas and I having sex was illegal was convincing me that I lived in a madhouse.

"It is also this. And I want you to listen carefully to me as I tell you. You may think you are so in love with Nicholas, and I do not doubt that you are! But you cannot deny that a relationship like this is very serious. And the state has recognized that you are, in fact, too young to be engaging in something like this."

Uncle Daniel was thirty-six years old. Before this moment, I had always seen him as young, sort of like one of my brothers. Uncle Daniel never usually told me off, and he hardly ever put on the parental cap. Even when we were away on holidays and me and my siblings would be running around with bare feet, and my mother would be yelling at us to be careful and put some sandals on, Uncle Daniel hardly ever got stressed and told us off. If anything, he would be there playing along with us. I couldn't understand this protective side of his that I was witnessing.

Uncle Daniel looked at me straight in my eyes. "I want you

to be careful, Leila. Be careful with Nicholas, and be careful with your heart." Uncle Daniel pointed to his chest with his index finger. It was the most serious I had ever seen him be.

"Of course, Uncle Daniel. I promise I will." I squeaked, wanting this moment to be over but also wanting to walk away from the situation, feeling like I had gained his loyalty.

Mama didn't get home until later that evening. Uncle Daniel had left with a sad look in his eyes as he walked out the door. The loss of my innocence was upsetting to him. But to me, it all seemed so insane. How could my mother or my uncle or the state, for that matter, decide when I was ready to have sex? It was true what I said. Nicholas and I were practicing safe sex, and I trusted that he loved me. But that didn't matter in my family tradition. It was black and white or not at all.

I rang Nicholas on his home phone as soon as my uncle left. It picked up after one ring.

"Hope you can think of me when you play that Bobby Brown Cassette again and about us getting caught." It had caught me off guard, Nicholas slotting this situation into a fantasy that he could use to turn himself on. I had just been humiliated while also negotiating both of our freedom. I felt like he had no consideration over what I just went through.

"Honestly, after today, sex is the last thing I want to do right now."

Here I was, defending my lack of fragility to my uncle. Only to deny any desire to have sex again to my boyfriend. My mind was definitely confused. For me, getting caught by my uncle had threatened more than mine and Nicholas's relationship. It also threatened my and my uncle's relationship. This was the first time that I had asked Uncle Daniel to omit the truth from my mother, purely for my own gain, over something that he didn't believe in.

"Oh, come on, Leila. We've been caught before—I don't see the big deal."

"The big deal is that both times, it was with my family members! The big deal is that I am a girl, and you are a boy, and people don't have as much to say about you!" I was shouting at this stage, which was not what I had intended. But the entire situation was getting me so angry. Mostly, I was angry at myself for not being careful enough and for considering myself more than my uncle's feelings.

"Fine. If I am such a problem in your life, why don't I just leave you alone?"

Nicholas's voice was exact. Stoic. I knew what was coming. But I didn't have the strength to fight it this evening.

"Nicholas, you know what I mean. That is not what I meant." I spoke the same phrases that had become so frequent lately. It was like Nicholas intended to misunderstand me. Part of me considered whether he just genuinely liked to fight.

"Don't expect to see me in school tomorrow. I won't be going."

Now he was in a mood, and I could either spend the next few hours getting him out of it or choose to ignore it. That evening, it was an easy choice.

"I'm not doing this right now."

I hung up the phone, disassociating myself from the entire afternoon. I felt dirty, considering what had happened. I hated feeling exposed to my family like this. As much as I thought it was ridiculous, the fuss that was being made over Nicholas and I having sex, I equally had never intended on discussing this with them. It was moments like these that I yearned for my sister to live with us. I could always call her. I knew that she would pick up. But part of me wanted to keep the phone line free in case Nicholas rang again, and we continued fighting—at least after I had had some food.

I got in the shower and washed up pretty well, stepping out and getting changed into a fresh pair of clothes, before cleaning up my room and trashing Nicholas's joint remains. By the time my mother was home, I had made dinner and cleaned the kitchen. I gave her a kiss on the cheek when she came in, knowing what had happened under her roof just hours before.

"You made dinner…. I appreciate your help. You're such a good and smart young lady."

I loved feeling her praise, especially in replacement of Nicholas punishing me, which I was certain would come. I also liked how I could still control, to some degree, what my mother thought of me and who she thought I was. Her happiness was important to me. She had enough to deal with without me adding to it.

In school the next day, Nicholas had kept his promise and didn't show up. He didn't show up the next day either, nor the day after that. When I found him standing outside my house on Friday evening, I was not as shocked or surprised as he may have liked. I tried to silence the fast-paced beating of my heart when I spotted him standing at my door. My mother was due to visit family in Haiti this weekend for a couple of weeks. Nicholas and I had, of course, discussed this in detail, as it was a sure amount of time where we would not be supervised except by my brothers.

"Miss me?" He said in a cool manner before slinging his arm around me and walking towards my house. It seemed that our fight was forgotten about, but there was something bigger growing inside my mind. For the first time in our relationship, I felt a tiny seed of doubt take sprout inside my stomach.

3

LOVE IS A DRUG

When my mother was visiting family in Haiti, things got more intense with Nicholas. My uncle finding us didn't scare us off but rather made us even closer. Now, we knew we had something to protect. This brought a sense of urgency into the relationship.

Nicholas practically lived at our house after my mother was gone. More often than not, I would see him sprawled out on the couch, watching TV with my brothers, or we would drive out to the beach since he had gotten a used car. Things were pretty perfect for the start of it. I enjoyed playing house with Nicholas. I loved how intimate things were feeling, how I would take a shower and put on some comfortable clothes, and we would cuddle up on the couch, watching the Fresh Prince of Bel-Air and eating some popcorn. We didn't need much to be happy; we just needed each other.

Now that it was summer, there were even fewer commitments for us to worry about. I waited tables part-time at a nearby restaurant, but that never really got in the way. Nicholas would come by the restaurant too, and we'd chat for an entire shift of mine some days. He had no problem with waiting around for me to finish doing stuff. His family had a little more money than mine. There wasn't a stark difference, but he didn't have an afterschool job, and I did. For that reason, he said he liked helping me and keeping me company while I did mine.

Despite not understanding how overwhelming this close connection was, my body started to react all by itself. One evening, I was walking home from my shift as the sun was setting over a playground, where children laughed as their mothers pushed them on the swing. I smiled, looking over at them and feeling glad and peaceful, happy to be heading home. Then I envisioned Nicholas sitting there, lounging on the couch, watching some show he would insist was incredible and which I had no interest in. I thought about how if I wanted to go out and make myself something to eat, I would have to make Nicholas something to eat too. This would make sense because he and my brothers would be watching a show that I had no interest in. Why would he go and make the food if I didn't want to stay and watch it? The truth was, I didn't want to do anything with Nicholas at that moment. I wanted to go home to my own house, have my brothers grunt a "hi," take a shower, make myself a grilled cheese sandwich, and watch The Cosby Show for the umpteenth time—without my brothers or anyone else in the room. Smiling at customers for five hours every other day was exhausting, especially when said customers were often complaining about their food being cold, the coffee being too hot, or the air conditioning not being strong enough when new customers came in through the door. There was a lot of bullshit that I had to deal with that I rarely told anyone about. What would Nicholas understand about that sort of thing anyway? It's not like he had to work.

So, you could say that I began to resent Nicholas. These were some of the first instances in my life where I learned how some things that were true for me would not be true for Nicholas. I would be scolded by my family for having sex, but Nicholas got away scot-free. I had to work throughout the summer and school year, but Nicholas could kick back and watch TV for seven hours straight. What pissed me off was that Nicholas didn't seem to notice this inequality, which meant that I resented any of the other things I would do for him. Talking to him about his problems at home, catching him up with classes he had missed, making his snacks when we were hanging out in my room late at night. As great as a boyfriend Nicholas could be, I was a damn good girlfriend. I tried my best to treat him with love and kindness, but for Nicholas, it never seemed to be enough. He wanted my undivided attention.

No matter how much I tried to explain to him how much he meant to me, he would always find a way of creating doubt in his mind.

He would say things like: "You're so beautiful," "I don't deserve you," or "You don't love me as much as I love you."

I never understood why Nicholas would say such self-sabotaging things about himself. It really started to get on my nerves that summer. It felt as if he was saying these things to make me feel bad about looking pretty or as a way of manipulating me to stay with him. The thing was, his own insecurities were the very thing that was making me not want to be with him. He was becoming his own worst enemy.

Walking home from the restaurant that evening, I realized that somewhere down the line, I had lost the ability to tell Nicholas when I wanted him to go home and when I wanted him to stay. Sure, I loved having him around some of the time. But that didn't mean day and night, with no room for discussion or boundaries. Even though I loved him, that didn't mean that I wanted to see him every minute. I needed breathing room.

It was a feeling I couldn't shake. And as much as I didn't want to start a fight, I knew that it would be something I had to bring up to him when I got home.

As predicted, Nicholas was sitting on the couch in the dark, watching television, when I got home. My brothers were out, and he had stayed behind. This upset me too. Nicholas didn't have a key to the house, so he would tell me that he was staying so he could greet me when I got home from work. But what was he doing here when no one else was around? I didn't care for him to snoop around my house and my room, looking through my journals and perhaps trying to catch me writing about a boy crush that wasn't him.

"Hey, where'd my brothers go?" I asked, clinking the keys down on the kitchen counter with a little more force than necessary. Nicholas turned his head around, and I spotted his tired eyes.

"They went to a party with some older girl. They invited me to come, but I waited for you, babe." Nicholas mentioning the party to me felt like he was trying to rub it in my face. He could have gone to some older girl's party, and instead, he waited patiently till his girlfriend got home. I should be grateful. Well, I wasn't.

The trash was spilling over, as it always did when I left Nicholas and my brothers in the house for the day, and I pushed down the top of it so that I could tie it closed. Three empty beer cans were tucked in.

"Were you drinking?" I asked, trying not to sound accusatory.

"Uh, yeah, your brothers said I could have a couple beers while I waited."

Nicholas and I really didn't drink much. Neither did my brothers, for that matter. So it irritated me that he chose today to drink instead of cleaning up the house that he was currently living in rent-free. My feet were sore from working, and the zipper on my uniform was scratching off my neck all day. The last thing I wanted to do was take out the trash and clean up after my boyfriend and brothers. My anger must have been palpable because Nicholas walked over to me in a hurry.

"Hey," he said, cupping my chin in his hand. I brushed him off and continued tying up the trash bag.

"I'm tired and hot. What do you want?"

Nicholas didn't like when I brushed him off or stopped his affection somehow. I was annoyed, and it was hard for me to consider acting another way. He followed me out to the trash can.

"Hey, I can do that. How was your day? You wanna watch some TV and chill out? We can get take-out food."

"Well then, why didn't you?" I barked. Nicholas seemed taken aback by this, and to be honest, so was I. It was as if I was reacting before my mind could consider whether this was how I really felt. I knew for sure that I was angry. And it was beginning to feel like I was doing all of the heavy lifting, and Nicholas was just some dude that hung around my house and ate my food. I had shut out these emotions because it didn't suit the arrangement. Nicholas was my boyfriend, and I loved him a lot. Besides, the thought of hurting him was killing me. So now, it was all coming out over an argument about the trash.

"What the hell, Leila? What's your problem? Why are you being so nasty to me?"

I threw the trash into the bigger bin outside. There were lavender bushes growing wild in my neighborhood. They attracted a lot of bees, and they also left the streets scented with their perfume. The heat was finally easing as the sun was going down. I considered how I wanted my evening to go. Why was I feeling such emotional drama at the thought of hanging out with Nicholas this evening? Why couldn't I just let it go and enjoy an evening together?

"I just... I want to be alone tonight."

Nicholas looked at me with shock. He took a step back, practically losing his balance over my request to spend the night without him.

"What's going on?" He asked me, a quizzical look in his eyes.

"Nothing! I'm just so exhausted, Nic. I need some me-time. Even if that entails doing the same things that we would otherwise be doing together. I just need a bit of space."

"Space?" I knew he wouldn't take kindly to that. He was

picking it up as if I wanted space from our relationship in general. But then again, maybe I did.

Nicholas walked around my front driveway, putting his hands up to his head. "I... I don't get it. I waited around for you to be done with work all day. I... you could have told me to go." He looked at me in the eyes when he said this, and I could tell that he was hurt.

Seeing him like that hurt me too. I wondered if something was wrong with me, if I just wasn't as into this as he needed me to be. That was something I couldn't face right now.

"I'm sorry. That's my fault. I should have been more forward." I came up to him as I spoke, putting my hands on his shoulders. He breathed a large sigh and nodded his head.

Just as I thought he was getting the picture, he looked up at me with a weird smile. "Guess I should have gone to the party then." He walked back into the house and started to gather his things. I marched behind him, hating myself for getting mad by what he said and feeling a tinge of jealousy about this fictitious other scenario.

"It's not about that, Nicholas! You don't have to threaten to go off to an older girl's party just because I want to hang out by myself for one night."

"Oh, so now I'm threatening you? How is my saying the obvious, 'I should have made my own plans,' threatening you?"

It was clear what this fight would turn into: us going around and around in circles until we were so exhausted. We would make up and probably have sex, ignoring the issues we were fighting about for another day.

"Look, this isn't a good idea. I just... I need you to leave." I said this without looking at him, worried about what he was thinking. Putting any boundary in place for either of us was strange. For the past two weeks, we had spent almost every waking moment together unless I had been working. If anything, those past two weeks were a sort of test for our relationship. Me telling Nicholas to leave was like telling him he had failed the test. And he wore this devastation all over his face.

"I can't believe you're doing this," he whimpered, tears filling his eyes before he quickly blinked them away, going into the different rooms and retrieving his things that were strewn all over the house.

"Nic, it's just… I don't want to fight," I said, leaning on the door of my bedroom, where he was now picking up his boxers and t-shirts from the floor and stuffing them into one of my sports bags.

"No, I get it. You want space. From me, from us."

"I didn't say that," I whined. This argument was not the first one we had had about this very topic. Whatever way Nicholas was able to love me, I wasn't so sure I could give the same back.

"But you didn't have to say it, Leila. I can already tell." He looked up at me with a fresh set of tears behind his ducts. "Are you seriously making me do this?"

Despite how big of a deal he was making of this, I was adamant. I wanted him out. I could not spend the evening sulking around each other and talking through our fight until we were eventually so exhausted that we fell into an unsettled sleep. Besides, I had to get up early for work the next day.

"Look, just give me some—"

"—Space, yeah. I get it." He stuffed the last of his things in the bag before looking at me and shaking his head, then slumping out the door.

When I closed the door, I breathed a sigh of relief. It was unsettling, feeling so glad to see the back of my boyfriend. But for now, all I wanted to do was eat something and get a good night's sleep.

~

My brothers came home early enough, around 11:30, and I decided to tell them what happened. I never usually spoke to my brothers in this manner. I had a sister who didn't live at home and didn't have to directly deal with mom, so it was safer to tell her things. But it was a lonely and isolating feeling, having kicked my boyfriend out for the night, so I thought I would share with them what was going on.

My brothers were glad that Nicholas had gone home. This unsettled me even more. Now that I knew my brothers felt that no boyfriend should be around all the time, I realized that I would have to put some boundaries in place. But why did I feel such dread when thinking about having to do this?

"Look, Leila, I get it; you're together. But you don't have to be like, together-together all the time. You've got your own lives, you know?" This was what my brother Michael had come out and said. I decided to take his words seriously. If Michael, who was about as laid back as they come, thought that even he would want more space, then I was not crazy.

I lay out on the bed that evening and enjoyed having the night to myself.

~

My 8:00am alarm went off the next morning, and I yawned, opening the curtains above my head. I cracked open the window and could hear the birds chirping in the trees, building their nests. I had to be at the restaurant in an hour, so I thought I'd use this extra time to make myself some breakfast and watch the news.

I dragged my body out of bed and went into the bathroom, rubbing my eyes and getting ready to brush my teeth. As I reached for my toothbrush, my eyes reverted to the bathtub, where a crouched body was curled up and asleep. I gasped, "WTF." It was Nicholas, wearing the same black t-shirt and blue jeans that he had left in.

I leaned flat against the wall. Nicholas somehow had gotten into the house in the middle of the night and fallen asleep in the bathtub. He didn't wake up when I gasped. I held my hand close to my chest, then edged out of the bathroom to wake my brothers up. They were both weary and not impressed at being woken up this early in the morning.

The three of us glanced down at Nicholas, rubbing sleepy eyes, then glancing at one another. We had a quick smirk on our faces at the madness of the situation, but I also think it was clear that this was not normal and something had to be done. It was a bit scary and disturbing.

Michael shrugged at James and me, then shook Nicholas awake. Nicholas groaned, shielding his eyes from the light of the bathroom. I was surprised that he wasn't retracting in complete shock or embarrassment. At first, I thought he must have done this drunk. Perhaps he went home and had chugged down a couple of beers, then climbed into the house. But as he was waking up, he didn't seem phased about the situation. Only sleepy and uncomfortable.

"Oh, hey..." he groaned as he sat up in the bathtub and continued rubbing his eyes.

"Nicholas... What are you doing here?" I asked. I could hear the accusation in my voice, but it was hard to disguise. The fact that he had been sleeping in the bathtub while I was sleeping had creeped me out.

Michael and James looked at each other before stepping out of the bathroom and going into their room. I knew that they were there. And I had informed them of what was going on. I didn't need them to stand there like bodyguards when an obvious fight would break out between Nicholas and me.

Nicholas sat up, looking at me. "I tried calling you. Multiple times. You wouldn't pick up. I couldn't just go home after what had happened! I was devastated!" He put his hands through his hair. I crossed my arms over my pajama top, wondering how I was going to handle this.

"I needed to speak to you. Leila, I can't stand it when we fight. I can't sleep, can't eat. I couldn't think of doing anything else except speaking to you."

"So you broke into my house and slept in my bathtub?" I remarked in a flat tone.

Nicholas paused, unsure as to how to react. He huffed a large sigh and got himself out of the tub. "You see, you don't even fucking care. I'll do anything for you, and still, you don't care."

He was getting upset again, and he marched down the hall. I followed him, feeling frustrated at his inability to see how insane he was acting.

"Nicholas, you can't just break into my house and expect me to be OK with that."

Nicholas spun his head around. "Well, then you can't expect me to just wait around for you while you figure out how much space you need." He practically spat the words at me. I couldn't believe that he was being so obsessive about needing space for one night. It was a warning sign, and I was receiving it, loud and clear.

"Well, if you aren't OK with that, then I don't know what to tell you, Nicholas. But the answer does not end with you sleeping in my bathtub."

"Don't you see what you're doing to me, Leila? You're driving me crazy! While you sort your head out, you're driving me insane and stringing me along." He was getting animated with his hands again as he tried to drill this point into my brain.

The scary part was, maybe Nicholas had a point. Perhaps I was ignoring the uncertainty that I was feeling about him and instead prolonging the inevitable. It was impossible to know because right then, all I wanted was for Nicholas to leave my house. It was black and white. I had reached breaking point, and it was time for us to separate, for a couple of days or perhaps longer. I was adamant about getting this through to him, once and for all.

"OK then. Let me be clearer. I think we need some time apart."

Nicholas gasped a little as I said this like the words were

directly pricking his skin. He moved his hair from his face and fixed his eyebrow, considering what I had just said. He looked at me with his piercing brown eyes before leaving. "I think you're making a mistake."

Then he walked off and out of the driveway, exiting my neighborhood.

My brothers came out of their room not long after and looked outside the front entrance.

"Man... the bathtub, though? That's some crazy shit." Jimmy announced, and Michael laughed. They fixed some bowls for cereal and went about grabbing some orange juice from the fridge. I had to somehow get myself together for my shift that was coming up in 40 minutes.

Nicholas's face was imprinted on my mind, and I feared the possibility of not having him in my life. Most of all, I feared whether that was what I truly wanted.

THE KNIFE

*D*wayne Paul was having a party at his parents' house, three blocks away. I wasn't big into high school parties, but it was the middle of summer, and I hadn't seen many of my classmates since the end of the school year. Nicholas had been taking up all of my time, and it had been three days since the bathtub incident.

As we were taking time apart, and because my brothers had witnessed what had happened, my doubt over whether Nicholas and I should be together was only growing. I had slept uneasily the last few days that my mother wasn't home, and I even started to yearn for her to come back. This was a stark contrast to the anticipation and excitement Nicholas, and I had initially felt about her going away for a couple of weeks.

Going to Dwayne Paul's party was the perfect distraction. My friend Tania had come over to my house, and we were getting ready together. Tania was a girl who lived around the corner, and we had played together since I was about ten years old. When the summers came, we usually spent days selling frozen cups or chalking hopscotch on the pavements. Now that we were older, friend groups and boyfriends had meant that we didn't spend as much time together. Tania had called me the day after I banned Nicholas from my house. We'd gone out to get Milkshakes together, and I ended up telling her the whole story. We somehow managed to laugh about it, and I trusted that she wouldn't tell anyone since we were in different circles anyways. Laughing to a friend about it while still recognizing how weird it was felt like therapy. I knew that as long as I kept people in the know about the situation, nothing could really get out of hand—or at least, that's what I thought.

Tania was rubbing some pink eyeshadow over her lids with her finger. It was a sample she'd gotten in Essence, and it was also the color of the summer season, apparently. I felt guilty for not knowing this sooner.

"Come on, you've gotta try some." She elevated her smeared-pink finger towards me to dust my eyelids the same as hers.

"Um..." She was smearing it on my eyelids before I could protest. I didn't usually wear make-up, but when she was done and I looked at myself in the mirror, I decided that it looked kind of cool and complimented my brown eyes.

I wore a black glitter top with some jeans, and Tania had a pink spaghetti strap tank top on with similar skin-tight jeans. We asked my brothers for a beer each and got our alcohol fix for now before taking one last look in the mirror and heading out to the party.

It took us a while to find the house, but once we got onto the right street, all we had to do was follow the loud music and the noise of people yelling out a yard, water splashing. Dwayne had a pool in his backyard. Only a handful of people had pools in our neighborhoods. I suddenly looked down at my blinged tank top, feeling way too overdressed. It wasn't usual that I even went to parties, so I was already out of my comfort zone.

"Oh, my god. I forgot a bathing suit. I'm going to look like a total idiot!"

Tania panicked, Pulling my arm and marching us towards

the house. "Don't be ridiculous. No one actually swims at a pool party."

Tania was wrong. There were guys and girls, most of whom had beers in their hands, cannonballing into the pool with soaked wet hair. The Girls were afraid to get their hair wet as it would mess up their perms. They wore dark-colored bathing suits, laughed, were carefree, and were checking out the guys. The people inside of the house didn't seem to care what the people outside were doing, either. There was a group of guys hovering over a joint near the shed. A group in the kitchen was playing a competitive game of Go Fish. Others scattered around, chatting, flirting, or dancing. The party was in full swing, and it became quite evident that I could do whatever I wanted, and people wouldn't really care.

Dwayne Paul came over to greet us and Tania neck-hugged him. He eyed me and introduced himself, shaking my hand. Tania put her hand on my shoulders.

"This is Leila. I told her it would be dope if she came."

Dwayne's eyes widened when he saw me, and I couldn't help but recognize the look in his eyes like he was attracted to me. It sounds full of myself to say it, but I think every girl recognizes that look. Besides, Dwayne was swaying a little from the alcohol he had consumed. I'm sure all of the girls looked really good to him at that moment.

"More than dope." His eyes widened some more, and he shook my hand. "Sorry it's a little crazy in here. Ya'll want something to drink?"

"Sure!" Tania answered for both of us, and Dwayne nodded, edging away and grabbing some sodas and beers from the refrigerator. I looked around and instinctively looked for Nicholas. Even though I was totally unsure as to whether I still wanted to date him, I was half-expecting him to show up. Maybe we could talk about things, figure some stuff out.

For now, I did something I usually never did and took a beer from Dwayne. He smiled at me, his brown skin looking good against a white short-sleeved shirt. "Make yourself at home!" He said before fist-bumping another guest and becoming immersed back into the party. I don't know whether it was because I was in a questionable space with Nicholas or whether the party was impressing me, but I decided that Dwayne was a cutie. I didn't let myself go any further with the thought, but I noticed when Tania and I sat down by the pool that I was looking out for where he was and whether he would come and talk to us again.

The music was really loud, and I couldn't believe that the police hadn't been called yet. It seemed like they didn't have as much urgency in disturbances in these neighborhoods. As much as my anxious brain was trying to make me not enjoy myself, I was. It was a nice change from working and going home. A couple of the girls in my classes last year were there, and we talked about exciting topics: going into Junior year, what classes we were taking, upcoming concerts.

Just as the day was cooling down, Dwayne was serving burgers and everyone lined up in front of his impressive barbeque and ate the hell out of those burgers. Dwayne had sat down next to Tania and me by the pool. I was conscious of getting ketchup smeared on the side of my face.

"You're Michael and James's sister, right? Michael's in the same chemistry class as me."

I nodded and swallowed a mouthful of burger. Taking a small sip of my mostly untouched beer, I responded. "Yeah, that's it. They're alright, most of the time."

Dwayne laughed and looked down at his beer bottle. Some guy with black twisted hair, wearing swim shorts with no top on, rushed over to us.

"Alright, you said it's your turn, man. Time to play Go Fish, let's go." The guy dragged Dwayne up so that he was standing, then pushed him over to the table where the guys were playing.

"Wait a minute, whoa, whoa—I'm not playing unless you play with me." To my surprise, Dwayne was pointing and looking at me. The shirtless guy didn't recognize me and looked a little confused.

"Alright, whatever, just come on!"

I was not a regular at card games. I never drank much, and I knew that I would eventually get drunk if I were to drink some more. This was not something that was accepted in my family, and I also didn't like the idea of being out of control. Lucky for me, I was incredible at Go Fish. To my surprise, I was actually starting to enjoy myself. Dwayne and I acted like a fool and high-fived every time we won and I felt a little shot of electricity jolt through my body, every time our palms touched. The whole party was getting involved and cheering for each team. I spotted Tania in the corner, smiling at me fondly. She had brought me to a party on the pretext that I looked normal and cool, and it seemed like I understood the assignment and was doing a good job of it.

It was fun, hanging out with people from my school and feeling like I belonged. Maybe I wasn't so different from them after all. Dwayne put his hand on my shoulder after we won; we hugged as everybody cheered.

People pushed into us as we hugged, and suddenly, someone was tearing us apart.

I turned around to see Nicholas. His arrival had made the group slightly quieter. Nicholas looked at me with hurt in his eyes, then turned his attention to Dwayne.

"You think you can just touch my girlfriend?" He yelled, in an accusatory tone that I hadn't heard from him before this moment.

"Man, back up off me. I didn't know she was your girl-friend." Dwayne put his hands up like Nicholas was a cop breaking up the fun of the party.

I was humiliated. This sort of public display from Nicholas was precisely what I didn't want. Everyone knew that it was not normal in my family for me to be dating around and having sex. And now Nicholas was acting like a total maniac as if we existed in some sort of love triangle. I could see some of the other Haitian girls staring at me strangely as if I had broken an agreement with them.

"What the hell are you doing?" Nicholas said to me, taking in my flashy outfit, the pink eyeshadow, and the drink in my hand. He took the cup and finished it before crumpling it up in his hand and throwing it away. "You don't even drink."

"OK, I think you need to calm down, man." Dwayne stood closer to us, trying to separate me from Nicholas. I knew instantly that Nicholas would hate this.

"Wait a minute..." He chuckled to himself. The party was quiet. Even the music seemed lower than before as everyone sort of half-froze, waiting to see how this was going to unfold. "This is none of your business. This is between my girlfriend and me."

"Nicholas, please. Stop it." I muttered.

Dwayne continued to speak, and I wished he wouldn't. "Why don't we take this outside, man? You obviously have a problem with me."

I was already humiliated enough; I wasn't about to watch my boyfriend fight some guy who'd put his hands on my back. And I hated the way Nicholas kept repeating that he was my boyfriend and that I was his girlfriend. Those titles were starting to feel more and more imprisoning.

As I walked outside, I heard everyone gasp before Dwayne shouted, "What the hell are you doing, man!"

I spun around and saw Nicholas handling a blade knife, close enough towards Dwayne.

"Nicholas, what the hell!" I yelled, and then the rest of the party started yelling before the topless guy swiftly grabbed the knife off of him and shouted at him to leave immediately.

I couldn't believe what was happening. Nicholas looked at me as if to say, "Well, what are you gonna do about it? Are you with me or against me?"

I started to cry, looking over at him. The tears streamed down my face, and I wiped them off with my hands, seeing the pink stains of my eyeshadow on my skin. He ran out the door, and I ran after him like a dumbass. I couldn't let things go before I told him how I really felt.

"What were you thinking?" I screamed, trying to stop him from running all the way home. I continued to cry, loudly and dramatically, not caring about who could hear. He looked back at me, and I could barely make out his face between my tears.

"Looks like you've already moved on." He said in a deep, low voice. I couldn't believe that he was still trapped in a jealous rage after he had just pulled a knife up at some guy. I thought about all the things that had happened recently—my uncle finding us together, the way Nicholas had disregarded how that made me feel. Finding him sleeping in the bathtub, in light of him pulling a knife tonight, had a whole other meaning to it. My feelings of being afraid were clearly justified. It was breaking my heart to admit it to myself, but Nicholas's emotions were getting out of control. The resentment that I was starting to hold for him was coming to a head at this moment, as I considered all that I had been through and all of the stress he had recently caused.

"This is not OK, Nicholas. I'm not doing this anymore."

My voice was calm and cool as I looked at him through my smudged vision. He looked hurt, like he couldn't understand why I was choosing to hurt him like this.

"What are you talking about? What are you doing?! Look at you!" He looked at what I was wearing. "This isn't you. You've changed."

Anything that he said had no importance to me. He had broken a lot of boundaries, and at this moment, I wasn't interested in what he thought or how he was going to twist the situation to make himself look better. I thought about the warning my uncle had left me with that day, how my brothers had looked around the house, trying to figure out which window he had broken into.

"I'm serious. I'm done." There was no other way to go about this. Nicholas had given me no choice.

Without being able to look at him anymore, I walked back

into the house. I could feel his eyes on me as I did so, and as he realized for the first time that he was not going to be my choice.

It was too embarrassing, thinking about heading back into the party, so I asked someone outside to tell Tania that I was going home and waited for five minutes to walk.

I put my headphones in and listened to Nicholas's and my favorite songs, crying the entire way home. I didn't know who I was without Nicholas, what my life would be like. But it seemed as if he was giving me no choice but to find out.

5

SAYING GOODBYE

*T*he end of summer that year dragged on and on until I swore I would never take the cooler months for granted again. Nicholas had taken up so much of my life that it seemed empty and less meaningful without him.

Everyone was shocked about what had happened at the party, and Tania and I had a conversation about it a couple of days afterward. We were sitting on the steps of her apartment block, mulling over the details together. I thanked God that I had a friend in her.

I had lost my best friend to a breakup. To me, Nicholas and I had always been much more than just boyfriend and girl-friend or lovers. We were the best of friends first and foremost. I knew that he had let me down by acting so crazy at the party, but I still loved him deeply, unconditionally. It was a lot for a young teenager to feel at the time. Both Nicholas and I were too grown-up for our own good. We were so young; a relationship and connection as intense as ours were a bit much to ask from anyone entering our final year in high school.

Tania sucked on a popsicle as mine lay limp in my hands, the sticky liquid dripping onto my knuckles.

"Um, you gonna eat that?" Tania asked while balancing a piece on her tongue before swallowing it.

I woke up to reality again. "Oh... nah, I don't think so." I flung the popsicle into the nearby trash can. I had been thinking about Nicholas for a change, how all I wanted to do was call him, ask him to the movies or to go get a cheeseburger, one of our usual activities. Now that the fight had happened at the party, it felt like people were still watching us, and I didn't feel so comfortable asking him to hang out after I had just broken up with him—but keeping my distance was damn near impossible.

"Why do you think he brought the knife out with him anyway?" Tania had asked, knowing full well that my mind was consumed by Nicholas, so we might as well go over every last detail one more time.

"I don't know." I picked up a stick from the ground and drew imaginary circles on the pavement. "You know when you love someone so much that the thought of losing them drives you literally insane?"

Tania looked at me like I had three heads. "No. No, I don't."

Going back to school was far more nerve-wracking than I had anticipated. My mother had braided my hair and bought us all some new plain t-shirts and a backpack to go back to school in. We never had too much money, but then again, neither did most people in our town. So it never felt like we were really out of place. Nicholas and I had some classes together, but we always saw each other in Band, and this year, we were both taking up jazz band. I walked into the first Band practice of that year with my heart racing. To my surprise, Nicholas was at the front, his trombone propped up on his lap, ready to go. We usually sat at the back together, so we could whisper throughout the practice, so he was possibly trying to create some distance between us. Even though I knew that was understandable, it still hurt. I slumped into the back seat and found it difficult to concentrate on playing. My horn sounded out of tune the entire time, and I couldn't seem to retain enough breath to get the sound out that I wanted.

We finished up five minutes early, and I waited outside until Nicholas had packed his things and walked out.

He saw me and half-smiled with sadness in his eyes before walking in the opposite direction.

"Wait!" I called, walking faster to catch up with him. "Hey…"

"Hey." He looked at me and smiled, and I felt a great sense of relief in seeing his face in front of me once again.

"How was the rest of your summer?" I asked with hesitancy, knowing well that the rest of his summer was probably spent being heartbroken and mulling over the fight in his head. Even though Nicholas and I hadn't spoken since the terrible event, I knew him well enough to know that his actions were out of character, and he was probably wearing a great deal of shame over them.

"It was… honestly, I can't remember anything remarkable happening." He was looking straight ahead, his eyes averting me, lest I see the pain etched onto his face.

I followed him over to his locker and leaned on one of them while he opened his, transferring his books from that morning to the mid-afternoon classes. I should have been doing the same, but this was more important to me.

"Look, Nic. I'm sorry how things turned out. I—"

"You have nothing to be sorry about," Nicholas interrupted. "I'm the one who ruined everything. I lost the best thing that's ever happened to me because I was holding onto you too tight." He turned to face me, and his cheeks were wet with tears. My own eyes started to sting at the reaction of seeing him and being face to face with someone whom I had spent so much time loving and being a part of.

"It's OK, Nicholas. I forgive you." I said in a calm and collected voice. Nicholas breathed a sigh of relief, and we embraced each other in the middle of the hall, not caring who saw us. To me, it was only us in that hallway, and I didn't care what anyone else thought.

∼

Gradually over the school year, Nicholas and I got back into a positive space. It was as if the sexual part of our relationship was eliminated for now, but there was still an obvious attraction there. This meant that we were playful with each other without looking for anything in return. It brought innocence and flirtiness and, most of all, genuine friendship back into our relationship, and I was so glad to still have him in my life.

It fascinated me to watch Nicholas navigate our final year of high school. Any class that we had together, we sat in the back, talking about things that went on in the school at the time. And yet, when pop quizzes or tests would come around, Nicholas would always finish with top grades. He had the sort of mind that absorbed information just by being in the same room as the teacher. I knew that he read at home and researched the things he didn't grasp in school, but he was never stressed about studying or worried about not doing well. Academia simply came naturally to him, much more naturally than it came for me.

Thankfully, I had a lot of fun distractions from school work. Everything about high school was fun and enjoyable to me. Especially in 12th grade, I was really starting to feel like I was coming into my own. Playing music was everything to me, and I started to branch out into jazz class by playing the trumpet. Even though I couldn't quite get the hang of the off-beat rhythm, after learning symphonic music earlier on, it was still a joy to be around the music and see it forming together. Nicholas was far more adaptable to the change in rhythm, and he began to get better and better at his trombone. One practice,

I found myself staring at Nicholas as he played. The teacher had written him in a short solo, and he was playing it out to the class for the first time. I felt an immeasurable sense of pride as I watched him get every note written, his eyes closing slightly when he was reaching the higher notes, and how the band was able to play along and compliment him. Nicholas and I had listened to all different types of music together, and I understood how important trombone was to all of the greatest records: Curtis Fuller, J.J. Johnson, Glenn Miller—these were the people that Nicholas had been listening to for years in jazz band, and I could tell that it improved his overall performance.

I found myself musing that day about how if Nicholas were to ever have children, he would probably be extremely attentive towards them, in a similar way that he was to me, always putting me above his own thoughts. Sure, his clinginess had gotten on my nerves sometimes, but I knew that deep down, Nicholas was a good person who was going to be loyal to a woman one day. It troubled me to think of Nicholas with anyone else, even though we were no longer romantically involved.

We maintained our friendship, and I had a chance to get to know some other people throughout the year. The school events always kept me busy, and I made sure to go to most of them. I absolutely loved playing music in school. Songs like "A Mighty Fortress Is Our God," "Oh Danny Boy," "Oh Happy Days," and the horn solos were anthems to the final year of an extremely happy place for me. Sometimes, we had to play for the football team as part of the marching band, which, to be honest, I didn't love, but the buzz at the football matches was electric. Besides, I had friends in the cheer squad, football team, and in the marching band, and we always made sure to make the best of every performance and every game. This is where I saw Travis while attending one of the games.

Travis was a Center who was also in my English Lit class. We had gotten to know each other through the years after the football games, and our friendship continued during the weeks when we would see each other in class. There was something about Travis that reminded me a little bit of Nicholas, which was slightly weird. He had a sensitivity about him, a different vibe to the rest of the football players, which I picked up on right away.

We were reading a short story by James Baldwin in school, the one about the two brothers, "Sonny's Blues." Our teacher Mr. Harmen was a passionate James Baldwin fan and even had a picture of his beaming grin framed and hung up on the classroom wall. Mr. Harmen was going around the class, asking us specific questions about the brotherly relationship and why they had seemingly gone towards such separate paths. Travis and I were sitting next to each other, as we had gotten in the habit of doing for the past couple of weeks. He had intelligent opinions, and I liked having someone to discuss the homework assignments with after they'd been handed out.

"Well, Travis, why do you think Sonny and the narrator went such different paths from each other?"

The class grew noticeably more silent, as they had gotten used to listening to Travis's answers since they were usually measured and critically thought of, unlike some of the others there.

Travis sighed and put down his pencil, thinking for a moment.

"Well, statistically, we know from the poorer communities that addiction is always possible. But I think it's impossible to consider this story without taking into account all of the great jazz musicians who suffered in the same way. Charlie Parker, Billie Holiday, and of course, the brother himself has the namesake of Sonny Rollins, famous sax player and former heroin addict."

The class "mmd" audibly as everyone was hanging onto Travis's last word. From the corner of the classroom, I saw Nicholas roll his eyes and hunch down into his seat, putting his head down so that it looked like he was resting. Mr. Harmen's eyes squinted slightly behind his glasses as he couldn't help but smile, nodding for Travis to continue.

"Well... I think James is making a connection between the pain felt by the black communities, especially those from poorer areas, and the way music can heal that pain, almost transcending it to mean something entirely different. That's how the brothers ultimately reconcile. It is only when Sonny is playing that his status as a musician is confirmed. And the narrator can see who he really is, behind the addiction, behind the poor choices. The music takes over the narration."

A girl with short black hair gasped as Travis finished his sentence, scribbling it down. Mr. Harmen laughed and walked back to his desk. "Just remember to mention all of that in next week's essay."

Nicholas's attendance in school had gotten a little bit worse, despite him always showing up for tests and somehow getting excellent grades. It was a bit of a mystery to me, but I was secretly glad to have some more time getting to know Travis without Nicholas watching. It still felt weird talking to other guys and being asked out on dates. Dates that I couldn't go on with my mom breathing down my neck about our culture and how church, school, and home were the only things a young lady should be involved with. Dating other people was something that Nicholas and I never spoke about in our friendship. This was necessary for us to have a friendship at all. So while Nicholas wasn't in English Lit class, Travis and I became closer friends.

Travis wanted to major in English in college, provided he got a Sports scholarship, and he started to share some poetry that he wrote with me. I didn't know what it was in me that incited these men to write poetry and then hand it to me, but there was nothing I enjoyed more. It was as if these pieces of writing were time capsules that I could hold onto, remembering the connections I had made with people and how their words had made me feel. Travis had a real talent for writing, and sometimes, he would even read the poems out loud to me before class started.

One afternoon after English Lit, we were breaking for lunch, and Travis and I had walked out together, discussing Sylvia Plath's The Bell Jar, which was the book we were studying as part of exams.

"Man, you had warned me before I read it, and you were right. It's pretty depressing." I laughed.

"Yes, but it might be one of the best portrayals of depression that I've read, at least. Plath has such a way of forming an entire mood and tone to her words. I don't know how she does it. I'm still trying to figure that one out." Travis's brow furrowed as he considered this.

"I have no doubt you will." I smiled, and we caught each other's eyes for a moment before looking away.

A group of Juniors was looking at the prom poster and giggling excitedly about dates and dresses. I sighed, rolling my eyes and looking up at Travis to see if he would match my cynicism. But instead, I saw him looking back at the poster with a strange look on his face.

"I cannot believe it's almost time for Prom. This year has flown by, and I am in no way ready."

We stepped out of the school and onto the outdoor fields. Students were moving about, heading to the cafeteria for lunch. Some walked home or others went around to the corner Jamaican restaurants to get food that tasted better than cafeteria lunch.

"I take it that means no one has asked you yet." Travis smiled, looking down at me. He was wearing his Letterman jacket and had a neat low-cut fade. He was a good 6 foot 1 and had the perfect nose that shaped his face.

"Oh, I mean, no. I haven't really thought about it, to be honest." This was partly true. I had always thought that I would go to the prom with Nicholas, but that seemed a little weird now, considering we were no longer romantically involved.

"Well, what do you say? I'll get us tickets. I'll buy you a gardenia flower for your hair instead of a corsage, a quiet nod to The Lady herself."

Travis was referring to Billie Holiday, and I laughed, delighted at his original outlook on going to the prom. There was certainly a spark between the two of us, but more than that, Travis was intellectual and a deep thinker who shared the same love for music and the arts as I did. Besides, there would be no odd looks when we walked into the hall together, like there may have been between Nicholas and me, as people could have speculated that we were back together. Going to Prom with an ex seemed like more of a statement than going to Prom with a friend.

"Alright, sure."

I had fumbled over my words when telling Nicholas that Travis was taking me to the prom, ensuring that we were just friends, even though Nicholas had never asked about the details. His reaction had surprised me, and he had simply laughed, saying: "I wonder if he'll stop talking in his essay-style long enough for you two to get a dance in."

Tania and I had gulped some Kool-Aid in the bathroom and laughed with one another while our dates waited outside. I had found a beautiful strapless purple dress that was half off. As promised, Travis had given me a huge gardenia to wear on my head, which he placed himself when he had come to pick me up at my house, my mother's eyes spying but happy to see such a well-dressed and handsome young man at her door.

We mostly hung out as a big group, and we all laughed at how ridiculous it felt to be dancing in these fancy clothes. Some of the boys snuck out back to get something stronger to drink or smoke some joints. But Travis had stayed dancing and hanging out with Tania and me and her date for the entire time.

Towards the end of the night, streamers exploded down from the ceiling and decorated us in streams of silver and glitter and gold. Travis and I danced together and got closer and closer as the night went on. His hands had started off on my shoulders and eventually had led down to my hips. I leaned my head on his chest since he was too tall for me to reach his shoulders and allowed us to sway back and forth together to Boys 2 Men's "End of the Road."

It wasn't until then that I saw Nicholas sitting at the very back of the hall, a cup of punch in his hand that was probably spiked. He had his tie untied and some of his shirt unbuttoned. As Travis turned me, I lifted my head off of his chest, still staring at Nicholas, who looked back at me and gave me a poignant smile, lifting his plastic cup before downing whatever was inside and stepping out to the hall.

Despite having an incredible night at Prom, the fact that Nicholas and I hadn't gone together felt a little sore for me, and I wondered what he really thought about it. Just before we graduated, I saw Nicholas outside our Calculus class. He hadn't been in in a while, but then again, a lot of Seniors were spending more time at home, preparing for finals. It had been a while since I'd seen him, and I made no efforts to hide my excitement.

I gave him a warm hug, and his body stiffened slightly, which was unusual. When I looked up, I could see that his facial expression was lost, forlorn.

"What's wrong?" I asked.

Nicholas sighed just as the bell rang, and we were supposed to head into class. I took his hand, and we walked around the corner to an empty classroom as I heard what he had to say.

Nicholas leaned on a table with his head down.

"I've made a decision. I don't want you to hear from anyone else, but I need you to know that it's final. It's..." He huffed again, like getting his words out was a great effort.

"What? What is it?" My nerves were getting the better of me, and I was thinking the worst.

Nicholas stood up suddenly, his face stoic. "I'm going to join the Army after graduation. I'm leaving."

"Leaving? Where?" I knew that he meant he would be leaving wherever he was going to be trained. But Nicholas leaving to go anywhere made no sense to me. He had been such a constant in my life since middle school. The idea that he would no longer be in this town, that I wouldn't see him around, was impossible to imagine.

"Missouri. That's where basic training begins. I'll be leaving to get situated in a couple weeks. Pretty much just as school finishes."

Even announcing that he was joining the military was making Nicholas appear more stoic, more assertive. I knew by the way he was speaking that his mind had been made up, but that didn't make it any easier for me to swallow.

"Missouri? But that.. that's like 1,400 miles away." My voice shook a little bit as emotions were rising up within me that I wasn't even aware I still had.

Nicholas's eyes welled up before he continued to speak. "This has been really hard for me, Leila. I'm sorry to tell you. But not spending the year together, seeing you move on... I can't wait around to see any more. It wouldn't be fair on you either, having your ex-boyfriend ruining your fun."

"You're not my ex-boyfriend, Nicholas," I said hurriedly. "I mean... yes, technically. But you're my best friend. I don't want you to leave."

I thought about all of the fun I had had that year. All of the activities that I had immersed myself into, all of the friends I had made, the dances, the new boy interests, the intellectual conversations, screaming at the bleachers for the football team, and then all going out together afterward, drinking wine coolers beside a man-made fire in the winter. It had all been so magical for me, and now, I was realizing that Nicholas had been quietly suffering the entire time. It felt like my fault.

"What am I going to do without you?" I asked, my voice quiet and hollow, like a child's.

Nicholas stiffened a little as he tried to remain dignified, ignoring the tears that were streaming down his cheeks. "You'll be fine, Leila. You don't need me to be here. You're stronger than you think."

After Nicholas had told me that he was joining the military, it felt like there was a ticking time bomb between the end of school and the last day that I would see him for many months. An entire era in my life was ending, and I wasn't sure if I was ready to let it go. I was also unsure about what Nicholas had said. I didn't know what it would be like to be without him, and it was hurting my heart to understand that soon, I would have to find out.

6

FAR FROM HOME

NICHOLAS

$\mathcal{I}$t had been two months since I'd been in Basic training. In those two months, I learned the harsh realities of what it means to train for combat. There were night drills at all hours. Once, the drill sergeant woke up our entire camp at 4:00 in the morning, then ordered us to do 100 push-ups there and then. My bunk partner refused to get up, even after I shook him and shook him. He just lay there sleeping and even said to me, "Just wait till the Sergeant comes around." I knew well not to wait until the sergeant came around. So instead, I dropped to the floor and started doing my push-ups.

When the sergeant saw my roommate, he yelled at him. "WHAT THE HELL DO YOU THINK YOU'RE DOING? GET YOUR ASS UP!" That was enough to get him out of bed, and soon, he was down on the floor right beside me, doing the push-ups at a faster rate than everyone else, the yelling from the sergeant seemingly giving him a hit of adrenaline to work with. We nicknamed my bunk buddy Sleepy, as he was constantly falling asleep during activities or mealtimes. I didn't want him to drag me down and get me noticed for all of the wrong reasons, but I also knew how he felt.

Sleep was something I'd taken for granted. Suddenly, I was being woken up at all hours of the night. It seemed like every second day, we'd woken up for some type of drill. It was rare that I got eight hours of sleep. One day, we got all of our physicals, including our eyes and hearing tests. I found myself practically pleading with God for my eyes and ears exam to result in failure, rendering me unsuitable for the job. But I knew that that wasn't going to happen.

In practically every moment that I was there, I wished to be somewhere else. There were moments of complete despair in which I called Leila and tried to explain to her what it was like, how I had lived in a general state of torment since we broke up. I'd thought the distance would do us good, but I could not seem to get her out of my mind. It was a sickness that I could not seem to recover from.

Speaking of sickness, the eyesight and hearing test ended with us getting shots—five that time in total. The shots were terrible. I barely knew what they were jabbing into us, but I guessed it was mostly immunizations. The penicillin, though, was for a slight infection. That was by far the worst part. To describe it, it is like being injected with toothpaste, as one of my buddies said. The whole thought of that freaked me out so that I was certain my feeling poorly was in my own mind and not from something going wrong with the shots.

But at about 3:00 in the morning, I had to visit the nurse's office since I had a fever of 104 and couldn't sleep. This was supposed to be an evening where we were allowed to go to sleep early after the shots, but my sleep had been disrupted by this developing fever. In my panic, I had assumed that I was allergic to one of the shots and that this reaction was my body slowly being poisoned. I whimpered in my bed for around two hours, tossing and turning before eventually going to the nurse's office. Standing in front of him, I was sure that I was going to pass out, and my head was killing me. I think the panic was really setting in, which was making me feel one hundred times worse. My vision was blurring as I started to panic some more, just as the nurse was asking me to sit down on a chair while they arranged to take me to the Medical Quarantine Unit.

I was put into a pick-up truck, and we traveled over to the MQU unit, where I was given a room that was sectioned off from anyone else in case what I had was contagious. They gave me two IV bags to keep me hydrated and then told me to try and sleep.

I lay in the darkness, hearing the patter of the nurse's feet on duty and the general hums of the hospital machines around me. My heart rate was being monitored as I slept, and I could hear it beeping with every beat. I thought back to my days at home when Leila and I would be by the lake, laying on the grass that had been browned from the sun, hearing the splash of the pond life around us. I cried into my pillow, hating myself for making this decision without fully thinking it through. But most of all, I hated that the 1,400 miles I had put between Leila and me had not put any distance between me and my feelings for her.

The MQU was a lot better than being on duty all the time. For one, I was catching up with all of the sleep I had lost. I had to wash my PT Uniform in the sink of the MQU ward since there wasn't a laundromat. I had also heard from Sleepy, my bunk buddy who had come to visit me once my tests came back normal, that they had been given their Combat Uniforms. I tried not to worry about going back to the Barracks without the correct uniform on, but the loneliness made me panic when I probably didn't need to. I thought about phoning Leila the same way that I always did when I was feeling down and out and regretting my decision to move all the way to Missouri to compete in a grueling training regimen. But I didn't want to drag her down. I knew that she was moving on and trying to get a better life for herself. All I wanted was to be able to do that for her, and as much as I tried, the devastation of not being able to do that was still eating me up inside.

After 72 hours in the MQU, I was released and brought back

to the barracks. The boys were all in excellent moods because the sergeant had told them that we were getting a night off and could go into the town. Personally, I couldn't think of anything worse. I had lost some weight while I was ill, and my body still felt weak, but what was the alternative? Sulking in my bedroom, in the hopes that Leila would phone me? No, I knew that it was better to join the guys and to head out.

We went to a local bar that was supposedly hosting a Ladies Night. I tried to imagine how many military trainees had poured into this little tavern. The boys were in a great mood, and we were all feeling like we had transformed back into the real world momentarily since we were drinking beers and not in uniform. There were a couple of women floating around the bar, but not enough for all of us. I didn't like this chasing game of seeing who would end up with a lady, so I ordered a beer and went outside for a cigarette almost immediately. There was a deck that acted as the smoking area, and I leaned on the wooden banister as I smoked the first of what would probably be many Marlboros.

Smoking was something I had taken up since joining the military training. I had smoked some pot as a teenager, but not enough to get addicted or anything. Most of the boys back home didn't believe you could be addicted to pot, but drugs were something that the military took extremely seriously.

The first full day I spent at camp, everyone had gotten their heads shaved again. It was the shortest haircut I'd ever gotten, and I had sent Leila a picture in the mail to see what she thought. She'd responded a week later, "Country first!" which was her usual poking fun at me for having just joined the military. But she continued with, "You look amazing, smart, and fine as hell!" It was the only recognition I'd needed. Despite Leila having mixed feelings about my joining the military, her approving the new haircut was probably the first positive thing she had said about it.

But I didn't want to think of Leila that night. I had spent the last couple of years of my life thinking about her. Part of coming here was trying to get out of that habit. As I took the first sip of my beer and a drag of my cigarette, a woman with dark, bouncy hair walked over to me.

She smiled and gestured for a cigarette. I fumbled with my packet and handed her one, which she put in her mouth—a mouth painted a light peach color—and then waited till I lit it for her.

"You're not joining the rest of the hound dogs in there?" she asked, a slight Southern drawl to her voice. She had beautiful caramel brown skin and looked Hispanic. I found myself wondering where she came from, what her story was.

"I'm not so into hound-dogging," I said, smiling. This was the first woman I had spoken to in months, and it was surprisingly easy. Some of the men had women at home, some were already married. But a lot of us were fresh out of school with little to no life experience. I still think I was better at speaking to women than most of the other guys in there. Being overbearing was not my style.

"You know, we've been waiting for the new training team to come out and show their faces." She looked inside to the crowd of boys fighting for the attention of the other five or so women in there.

"Is that so?" I asked, making eye contact with her. I knew that my dark eyes were one of my best features, and this woman had come up to me, after all. She must have liked what she saw. And so did I.

She was wearing a flimsy white off-shoulder top that showed off her slender collarbone and shoulders. She wore gold shimmer on her cheekbones and had a curvy hourglass figure, despite only being about 5 foot 4. I stiffened a little, realizing for the first time that I was attracted to her, then took a bigger swig out of my beer, deciding that this was fine, as long as I was slightly drunk.

"I'm Nicholas. I moved here from Florida," I explained. She raised her eyebrows at me.

"Florida? Oh, you're not so far from home." Then she

turned away as if this disappointed her a little. If this was a process that she was used to: that is, dating men who were not going to be around for much longer than the night (we didn't get much time off), I had to make it as exciting for her as possible.

"Well, I'm from the Dominican Republic originally," I explained, and her eyes lit up as she looked back at me.

"I'm Natalia. My parents are from Bolivia." She pronounced Bolivia the way only Bolivians know how to. "Boliiivia." Then I gave her the same reaction she had given me, eyes lit up with delight as if her confirming her otherness made her more unique and mystifying.

We spoke together in Spanish for some time, her leaning into me with every story she told and every drink we had. Soon, we had switched to Tequila, and I ordered two drinks at a time to avoid the jeers and overreaction from the other guys. We walked in, and half of their faces dropped, disgusted that they hadn't seen her for themselves. I wasn't even sure if Natalia had entered the bar before we had gone in to order drinks. It was as if she had come straight to the dock as soon as she arrived, and I had happened to be there. Perhaps she wasn't so into the chase either.

We snuck away from the bar about three tequilas in and walked along a winding road that seemed to lead to nowhere, but Natalia promised she lived just five minutes from the bar. I couldn't understand what a girl like her—young, single, and beautiful—was doing in a dead-end town that had nothing but military training. She had shrugged this off in the bar, claiming that she was a primary school teacher who grew up in the town and that the rent was nice and cheap. Besides, she said, she'd never really know anything else.

A part of me envied her familiarity with her homeplace. Having come from the DR, I felt a lot more misplaced in America. I was both within and without, both identifying as a Floridan and a Dominican. Even though we enjoyed a large family that was easy to visit, there was always this confusion hanging over me about where I really came from, what home had meant to me. I used to think that home was with Leila, but I'd had to let go of that view when we broke up.

Natalia had a ground-floor bungalow that had a large garden with some brown and green patches of grass. She had funky sofas that were 70s style. She told me she'd gotten them in a thrift store for half the price they'd originally gone for. They were a pastel green color and almost had the shape of a mussel shell.

She poured us some wine, and I was beginning to regret all that I had drunk, knowing that we would be doing drills and an obstacle course tomorrow. This was a habit of mine—I had a way of spoiling the present moment by thinking of the responsibilities waiting for me in the future. But not tonight. If anything, I should have been feeling extremely proud of myself. Here I was, sitting on the couch of a beautiful woman's apartment, while ten of the guys were probably fighting for the attention of one lady right about now. There was only one reason why Natalia and I had gone back to her apartment, and it was not to talk about my drills and obstacle course tomorrow morning.

She sat closer to me on the couch, and I could smell her perfume, a strong scent of vanilla and nectarine. The apartment and sofas retained a similar scent, and I suddenly imagined her naked body bathing in oils and perfumes in a luxurious bath. Without overthinking it, I leaned in and kissed her perfect lips. She kissed me back with hunger, and we suddenly were letting go of any pre-shyness.

I leaned over her on the couch, and she lay back, balancing her head on the couch rest. I pushed myself on top of her, and she whipped her head back, instructing me to kiss her neck then her breast. It started to dawn on me that we were definitely going to have sex tonight and that this woman was probably not so shy in telling me exactly what she wanted. I refused to let myself think of anything else at that moment. All of the emotion and the loneliness that had been built up over the past few months was coming out of me now with a hungry sensation for pleasure and to give pleasure.

I lifted my head. "Can... can we? Should we go to your bedroom?"

She gave me a sultry look, her brown locks falling perfectly over her shoulders, and I caressed the trace of her collar bone, feeling her breasts underneath her top.

"Yes."

She took my hand, and we walked into a humble but normal-sized room with a double bed, a bundle of pillows on top. She pushed some aside and then forced me onto the bed, climbing on top of me.

Then she took my head into her hands, looking at me intensely for a moment. "I'm going to make you remember this." She said before kissing me with a wildness that I hadn't known since I was a teenager, hungry to experience sex for the first time.

Sleep was not in the cards for us that night. The idea that we would probably never see each other again brought forth feelings that were both erotic and euphoric. I placed my hand in between her thighs as I began my ascension to heaven. The closer I got up there, the more she moaned and groaned uncontrollably.

She suddenly grabbed my hand with vigor. Before I could finish exhaling the deep breath I had taken, she was under the sheets. She began to do things with her mouth to me that not only held my breath hostage, but my soul begged for freedom that I wanted to be denied.

I quickly flung her over. She rolled onto her stomach with intentions she knew were understood. What began as slow seductive strokes became powerful thrusts with meaningful intentions. She looked up at me, pressing her hands onto the mattress, and I watched her face crease with pleasure as I thrust inside her. She then climbed over me, and I watched as beads of sweat dripped down her toned brown body. She had flung her head back and groaned loudly, clearly taking advantage of the fact that she lived alone and in the middle of nowhere.

Her motions caused me to swell even more; she too began to pulsate. As euphoria and eroticism met in a head-on collision, we both collapsed at the finish line like two Olympians who had just won gold.

I thought about the military men that had entered her bed and had felt her touch. It made me want her again; I wanted to prove my worthiness to her, and I held onto the back of her small waist as she kept thrusting herself onto me before we finally collapsed into each other's arms hours later.

By the morning time, we lay together, in the same intimate way as long-term lovers do. Even though it was partly performed—that is, neither of us were in love with each other —I let myself pretend at that moment. I saw the silhouette of her curves formed into the white bedsheets. Glancing over at the alarm clock, it told me it was 4:15 am. This was only half an hour later than when the sergeants usually woke us up. Sleep was a luxury that I was no longer used to.

Natalia stirred and mumbled something in her sleep, nuzzling her head into my neck and flinging her arm over my chest. I took her thigh and moved it over my body, and she smiled and sighed. Both of us still had a film of sweat on our bodies from the sleepless night, and the bedsheets still felt a little damp underneath us. I kissed her on the forehead, almost out of habit. It was only at that moment that I thought of Leila.

I imagined her dark skin flung over my body, exhausted from a night of lovemaking. I thought about how we would spend the day if it had been her. We'd go swimming in the bank, and I'd wrap her legs around me underneath the water. Then we'd lay on the banks and let our bodies dry naturally before leaving to pick up some food and laugh about something dumb we saw on TV.

Everything with Leila had been so natural. Everything about her reminded me of a sense of belonging. How could it be, after all this time, that when I thought of home, I saw her face, clear as day?

I managed to get out of the apartment without Natalia waking. I wanted to make sure I was on site in time for breakfast. But more than that, I didn't want to say goodbye. I was never the type to have one-night stands, and I wanted to avoid any feeling of loneliness that might arise from it. But I decided not to make something bad out of a good situation.

"I'm going to make you remember this," she'd said. And in that, she had definitely succeeded.

7

MOVING ON

*I*t was easier to separate myself from Nicholas now that he had moved out of town, even though we still spoke on the phone every other day after his basic training. Nicholas being out of town helped me create a life of my own, separate from the one we had growing up. His training would last four years, and he didn't make a habit of coming home too much, although I always really anticipated when he did.

During the rest of the time, I started dating again. I was meeting eligible bachelors and rarely found myself without a date. My girlfriends and I would group date, going to the movies or out to shoot some pool, or out to get some food. We were young, attractive, and earning our first bit of money. And although it wasn't enough and the hours were borderline abusive, we were having the time of our lives.

Working in the law firm and going to college also meant meeting a different type of bachelor. Gone were the spotty teenagers, and in replacement of them, here were these deliciously handsome, well-dressed, often mature young men who are stable and have even better manners. Harrison was an aviation major who was earning his second degree. He was already employed as a police officer. Harrison was adored by everyone. Going out with him, it seemed like even the waitresses at the restaurants wanted to take him home. He was tall, dark, and handsome and had enough charisma to light up an entire room. I often considered how he had all his money and assumed that he was born into wealth. The way he conducted himself certainly matched that description.

But Harrison was also eleven years my senior, which made it even more exciting. This meant that he had been married and was divorced with one child named Julian. Harrison often spoke of how he wished he could be more involved in his son's life but that his wife would not let him see Julian. Their relationship was fractured, and he did not believe there was much possibility of change there. Being in my early 20s, I was thankful that Harrison didn't have many responsibilities and could focus on dating me.

It was very difficult, hiding this newfound glamorous dating life and not being able to share any of it with Nicholas. Of course, I am sure he wouldn't have really minded. But it was never a thing we got into the habit of sharing. Whether the other person dated, our friendship did not need to know about it. It was as if bringing up such a thing would suggest that there was still romantic involvement in our relationship. And that was a can of worms that neither of us really wanted to get into.

As I became closer to Harrison, my relationship with Nicholas became more distant. Time apart from one another also set a sort of distant yearning inside of me, to see him and to feel his face, just to know that he was still there. But since Nicholas wasn't around and wouldn't be for the foreseeable future, I put most of my focus onto Harrison.

On the few occasions that we rang, Nicholas would tell me how much he was struggling with military training, the physical and mental turmoil coming up for him, and how he missed me terribly. It made me sad to think of Nicholas, isolated and alone with no female encounters. But then again, he did tell me that they got out sometimes. I sort of figured that he had a couple of girlfriends and liked to cry on the phone to me, alluding to the opposite.

There were times that Nicholas phoned me drunk, explaining how he had only gone to the military because he was so heartbroken over our relationship ending. He would cry on those nights when he had drunk too much, asking me why I had broken up with him those years ago. But these were few and far between, and when I started dating Harrison, our phone calls lessened.

I respected Harrison so much for undergoing even more schooling, despite having gone through the police academy and working as a full-time cop. His job and his studies were extremely important to him, and he would travel to and from the Bahamas as part of his flying hours that would eventually get him his aviation license.

Any moment that Harrison wasn't either traveling, seeing his son, or working, we would spend it together. He was living in a duplex joined to a house where a woman named Belle lived alone. Belle was battling stage four cancer, and I couldn't help but wonder what was ahead of me in eleven years. It seemed that wherever Harrison went and whoever we met, his friends had such colorful lives, and the connection between them and me was often instantaneous. I adored Belle. She was a kind and quiet woman, and she had never asked for anything, despite only having a nurse come to visit her home twice per week and then attending the hospital every Monday for chemo.

We spent a lot of our time sitting together, drinking hot tea on her porch as she told me stories about her life before either of us knew her. Harrison was incredibly kind to Belle. He insisted on doing her grocery shopping and often made her dinners. He was an excellent cook. I loved watching him in the kitchen. In fact, I loved watching everything that Harrison did.

After a couple of meaningless flings, I wanted to take things slowly with Harrison, even though his body was to die for and was making me melt. We enjoyed passionate kisses after dinner that sometimes led to us almost going crazy and giving in to our wants. But so far, there was no sex.

One evening, Harrison was unloading Belle's groceries for her, and she and I were sitting on the porch, having a chat about nothing in particular. I was fixing Belle a blanket so that she could sit outside without getting cold, and I had brewed some tea for us, knowing that she never wanted anything else after a day of chemo. I was happy that she was sitting up and had not asked to be put to bed. We spoke about her cancer, and she mulled over the facts dispassionately to us. But on this particular evening, I knew not to pry. It had been exactly three years since Belle's diagnosis, and she was now at the terminal stage. As far as she was concerned, enough of her life was made up of hospital visits and bad news. Sometimes, all she wanted to do was sit on the porch and gossip.

"Now tell me, child." She patted down the blanket on top of her and sunk into her pillowed rocking chair. "Have you done the nasty yet?" She looked over at me with a grin, and I burst out laughing, looking behind me and making sure Harrison was a comfortable distance away from us.

"Belle, have I gotta wash your mouth out with soap again?" I cried, and she chuckled, lifting her mug up to her mouth and smelling the lemongrass, mint, and cinnamon aromas. I had bought her a special teapot that was made for loose tea leaves. "Girl, that's too uppity for me!" Belle had cried. I explained to her how I had found it for $10 at the hardware store, of all places. The loose tea leaves were being sold for cheap in a small tea shop that had opened up in our district a couple of weeks ago by a local Indian family.

"Now, how in the hell am I gonna get over there?" she exclaimed before I propped three large bags of loose tea leaves in front of her. I saw a smile gathered around her lips, and she hugged me while staying in her chair.

Belle really didn't have a lot going on except for her illness, so it was important to consume her mind with something else, even if it was at my expense. She knew not to press me for information, but I sighed and looked behind at Harrison, who was whistling to himself and cutting up some chicken for Belle's dinner later on.

"God, I love him," I said out loud, at which Belle's eyes grew large.

"Oh, love? Now, you didn't tell me we were talking about love."

It was true. There was so much to love about Harrison. Here was this man who already had a great career and aspirations, looking after the sick woman whose house he rented. He even had a son and understood what it was to be a father. My own father had left when we were very little, too little to remember anything of personal importance. This left a gap in all of our lives. I couldn't help but feel like that gap was closed just a little when I was around Harrison. I knew I could trust him, that he was a good and honorable man. He was dreamy and had the sexiest physique—and he had a predictable income, one that could possibly support a family one day. Perhaps I was getting a bit ahead of myself, but I was just so excited to have met someone that seemed to check all the boxes.

"Well, Lord knows I want to, Belle. But Harrison, he's a little shy. I don't know how to give him that push he needs to take us to the next level."

I was never this vocal about my sexual escapades, but there was a frankness to Belle that was infectious. I knew she expected a certain level of honesty from me because she would give me the same level of honesty back. Besides, when someone is dying from stage four cancer, they don't have enough time for people to beat around the bush. Speaking like this to an older lady was so refreshing. I was used to my mother telling me that I would go to hell if I had premarital sex. I didn't have the heart to tell her that it was already too late for that.

"Girl, the only push he needs is to see you in a fancy, silk lingerie number." She cackled, taking a sip from her tea and showing me her gap-tooth grin. "Trust me, it works every time."

"What are you two plotting?" Harrison came out, holding two bowls of watermelon, mint, and feta salad. He always prepared the same salad for Belle when she came home from chemo. My heart skipped a beat as he handed me mine, feeling intensely close to him in our shared concern and care for Belle.

"Oh, don't you worry your little head about what us gals talk about," Bella answered. "It don't concern you."

That evening, I thought about what Belle had told me, how I needed to make the first move, approach Harrison in something sexy. I found a simple black slip in the bottom of the wardrobe of my studio apartment. I had been living alone for the past six months, although I may as well have been renting with Harrison since I spent most of my time there. Even when he had to travel to the Bahamas for work, it made more sense for me to stay there and help keep an eye on Belle if she needed anything.

I tried on the black slip and laughed a little, fingering the lace that lined it and the slit that came up at the left thigh. Lord knows when I'd bought it or who I'd bought it for. I thought I remembered spotting it in a thrift store, but it would do.

Harrison was doing everything but sit down beside me that evening. He was cooking us homemade burgers—"My specialty!" he kept saying as if burgers had ever been considered a specialty.

I waited around, drinking some soda on the couch, wondering when would be the most appropriate time to change into the silk number. I could hardly wear it when my mouth was full of hamburger. As we ate, I encouraged Harrison to sit close beside me, and we kissed for half a minute before he pulled away and insisted that we eat before the burger got cold. "It's very important!" He said, taking a large bite and letting the sauce dribble down his chin.

To me, he still looked sexy, even when he was stuffing his face. His shoulders were broad, and he kept his hair short and shaved, saying it was more suitable for the job. He had large cheekbones and chocolate brown skin that was smooth and expertly toned. I loved feeling his muscular arms around me. Training for his job as a policeman and an aviation specialist meant that his body was kept trimmed and muscular.

We ate quickly, and I insisted on cleaning up, which gave me some time to freshen up in the bathroom before changing into something more comfortable. I brushed my teeth and slicked back my hair since I had recently permed it. Surprisingly, I was a little nervous. I thought about what Belle had said earlier in the week. "I didn't know we were talking about love." Neither had I until I'd considered it.

Talking to Nicholas every so often and even discussing seeing each other when he was home was a tie I hadn't realized I was still holding onto. Nicholas and I were best friends, and nothing would change that. But I had seen the way Harrison's eyes had blinked when I spoke about Nicholas and how he was getting on in the military. Part of me had even expected the two to get on, considering their shared job interests. But I knew that this was just wishful thinking on my part. Maybe part of me moving to the next stage with Harrison was the right thing to do. Despite my eternal affections for Nicholas, maybe the next stage was only possible if Nicholas and I grew apart a little. After all, Harrison was so loyal and devoted to me. The least I could do was show him the same loyalty and devotion back. And tonight, that was precisely my plan.

I waited for Harrison to come into the bedroom and put somebody butter on my legs so that they shone and had a gloss to them that would make my skin feel supple and silky next to his body. Not to mention I had ashy skin. So I desperately needed that. I wasn't overly obsessed with adhering to female beauty standards. But I was slim, slender, and naturally pretty. So by proxy, I guess I was adhering. I never worried too much about jewelry or getting my hair done or anything like that. I had worn some makeup tonight, though, and I felt proud of my sleek, curvy figure that was hugging the silk and sexy lingerie.

Harrison walked in with a kitchen towel still in his hand. His jaw dropped when he saw me, and a huge smile broke out all over his face. "Come here, baby."

I stripped off his clothes, his polo shirt, and dark blue jeans: he always dressed a bit like Carlton from Fresh Prince, but he couldn't hide his exceptional body. We'd gone swimming together before when I'd seen him in swimming trunks. He was like a large stick of chocolate. I'd never been with someone who had such a fine physique before, and I couldn't wait to know what it felt like.

Harrison was rummaging in his dresser for a condom while I was trying to place myself sexily on top of his pillows. His sheets were thick and crisp, and he always kept them spotlessly clean. I was worried that some of my body butter would leave a mark. Harrison didn't even let us eat in bed. I was surprised he was so ok with having sex there. I had half-expected him to take off the pillows and sheets one by one and put down a towel.

He'd turned his back to me while he was putting on a condom, and I was curious for him to turn around. When he finally revealed what he was packing, I gasped a little. Harrison was generously well endowed, and he almost seemed a bit bashful about it. I giggled, unable to contain my hyperness —but also because the best sort of sex was the times where you could be yourself. He came towards me, and we kissed softly at first. He was patient and was kissing my neck, my shoulders, my face, all over my body. I could feel his kisses. I moaned in response and was thrilled at the idea of making love to the man that had stolen my heart those past few months.

He entered me, and I made a larger gasp as he slowly moved up and down, a little awkward at first, sort of like he wasn't so sure which side of me he wanted to lean on—the left or the right. So, he kept switching it up and, a few times, missed the opening.

"Oh... I—" I leaned back into the pillow, my neck forming a double chin as I tried to look underneath us and put him back to where he was supposed to be. But Harrison acted as if it hadn't happened, still kissing me madly and thrusting—even though he was not inside!

"Oh, yeah, baby. Oh, you like this big dick? You like when I put it inside you like this, huh?" Harrison was holding himself up with one arm while he fumbled around his groin, making sure that the condom hadn't slipped and clumsily trying to get back inside me. I didn't understand why he was talking dirty when we had barely even started. But then he slotted back into place, and I breathed a sigh of pleasure, ready to get really into it.

Apparently, Harrison was ready too, as he continued to tell me. "Oh, yeah baby. Oh, baby, baby, baby, just like that. I know I drive you wild; you like this big man inside you, huh? Huh? Tell me you love it, baby, come on. Tell me you love it."

I made a face to myself from behind his shoulder and rolled my eyes in disapproval. Harrison wouldn't shut up. All the while, he kept fumbling around and thrusting like a fish out of water. The fact that there had been absolutely no foreplay was even more disturbing.

I didn't get it. This shit couldn't be happening! I wanted to laugh even. How could this handsome chunk of chocolate be so terrible in bed? The universe must have been messing with me. Usually, it was hard for me to come during penetrative sex— and I sure as hell had no chance as long as he was yapping away before I'd even gotten close. But nothing would shut him up.

"Uhh, yeah, who's your daddy? You're my nasty little girl, huh? Bad, bad, bold girl, what are you gonna do about it, huh? You like how I fuck you? Come on, baby, tell me you love it. Oh, yeah, I wanna hear you scream. I wanna hear you scream, come on. Come on, give it to me. Scream for me, baby. I can't hear you. Are you a little shy? Come on, scream—"

I shoved him off of me. "Harrison, I'm going to scream in a minute if you don't shut the hell up!" He gasped, shocked at my outburst, and actually, so was I.

He leaned on his side, the condom still in place on his depleting erection. Great, now I had really gone and killed the mood.

"What? Dirty talk turns me on."

"Well, it turns me off. Sorry, I just... I can't hear myself think."

Harrison stopped panting for a moment and considered what I had just said. "Think? What is there to think about? We're supposed to be in the present moment."

He had a point there. The mood had pretty much altered by then. He took the condom off and laid back in bed, looking up at the ceiling. I had clearly upset him, so I kissed his neck and touched in between his thighs, trying to get him up again and at least finish off what we started. I ended up giving him a hand job and finishing myself off, during which he kissed me and did some more dirty talking. Instead of shouting at him to shut up again, I imagined how coming was the only thing that would stop him from talking—and that was the thought which I eventually climaxed to.

8

BETRAYAL

*H*arrison and I continued dating, and despite the semi-awkward sex life, we continued to get closer and closer. I didn't really know what it was about Harrison and sex. At first, it bothered me that we didn't appear to have a sensual connection. This had never been a problem for me before. But then again, Harrison was eleven years my senior. Maybe he hadn't dated someone as young as me before. Maybe he thought that was what people my age liked. But the stupid talk and instructions had to stop; that was one thing I was certain of.

I eventually approached this with him at a dinner date. We went to a Haitian restaurant and had just ordered some legumes and fried fish.

"So you know the way... You know the way I'm not like...really into the whole.."

Harrison had some legume on the side of his mouth, to which I signaled, and he wiped away.

"Hmm?" he promoted me.

"The whole dirty talk. I'm not into it."

He swallowed. Raised his eyebrows then nodded while taking a drink of his jus grenadia. "Oh."

We sat in silence for a moment, and all that could be heard were the scraping forks and knives of the customers around us, assumingly not discussing their kinks—or anti-kinks—over dinner.

"Sorry, I just… I find it hard to concentrate. Maybe we could try it without?"

Harrison shrugged as if it was no big deal either way, and he wanted to move on from the subject so that he could save face.

"Sure, let's try it." Then he went back to eating his legumes, seemingly unbothered.

I kind of appreciated how Harrison took my request on the chin like that. It could have been a really awkward conversation, and instead, it had felt like I asked him if we could switch from diet to regular soda. There was all of this built-up tension in my head that night as we went home, however. And I got ready for what could be a really awkward sex night where we were back at square one, and Harrison was acting as if he hadn't been with a woman before and was doing all of the wrong things. But instead, we didn't even end up having sex.

I remember that night, feeling slightly disappointed about how it had all gone. I didn't feel guilty for admitting to him how I felt because I knew that was necessary. But I certainly didn't want to lose him or make him believe that there was something wrong with me. It was a strange thing, feeling so emotionally connected to someone and so physically attracted to them but not having that instant chemistry and spark lighting up the bedroom.

Sex has always been an important part of a relationship with me. Nicholas was fiery and passionate in the bedroom. We had an incredible sex life which was part of the reason why I had had sex at such a younger age than I would have done had I not met him. Nicholas and I had such sexual chemistry with one another, and I wanted to feel the same way with Harrison. I remember feeling like a failure that night when I went to sleep. Harrison had put in his earplugs and didn't spoon me for long enough, claiming that he got an ache in his arm.

Besides the awkward sex life, I adored so much about Harrison: he had a brilliant mind and would tell me about the unique situations his life as a cop, and an aviation flyer had gotten him into. He spoke about the heartache of losing his family in the divorce and how he wished he could see his son more often. He was stylish, always well dressed, and loved to treat me well. We went on vacations together, out to fancy parties and restaurants, concerts, and all sorts of exciting events. He was a well-rounded gentleman. His position as a cop had made him well known throughout the tri-county areas. That was always fun to experience.

Recently, Harrison and I had even viewed an apartment together. He had acted like it was no big deal. We were due to meet up, and he insisted that we go a different route and see a place on the way.

"A place?" I'd asked.

"Yeah, like a house."

I tried to still my beating heart, but it was hard not to get instantly excited. It made complete sense for Harrison and me to move in together. Belle was soon to be going into a Hospice where she would have 24-hour care. And the side of her duplex was starting to feel a little cramped. We spent all of our free time together. It bothered me, waking up in his and forgetting something from my overnight bag or make-up bag, then feeling like I was living out of my car—from college to work and then straight over to Harrison's.

I thought it a little strange that he hadn't wanted to discuss it, but then again, Harrison was a bit like that. He showed his love with actions. This was his way of telling me that he was ready to go to the next level. Now, all I had to do was decide if I felt the same.

When we stepped into the house, it took my breath away. At the front, there was an over-spillage of flowers in bloom, perfuming the entire entrance. It was a bungalow but still spacious. They had done it quite open-planned, which was unique for the area. There was a high ceiling and a large sitting room with the kitchen on the other side of the room. Tucked in the corner, up a couple of steps, there was a double bed and a large window on the side, looking out to the garden. I gasped when I saw the view. The garden was full of fruit trees: mangos, avocados, and limes. The realtor brought us out to see it, explaining that one half of the garden would be ours and the other half belonged to the residents next door. There was a large garden table on our half, with enough seats to host an entire dinner party. To my surprise, the realtor then brought us around to another corner of the building, where two more rooms connected to the small bungalow. One of the rooms had an ensuite, making it a two bathroom and three-bedroom house of about 1,200 square feet. This was when I really got excited.

Not only was Harrison interested in buying a house together, but he was buying a house with enough rooms for us to have children. Was it possible that he was considering asking me to marry him? Speaking about Harrison's son had always been a bit of a no-go subject. I knew it really upset Harrison that he couldn't be a conventional dad, one who got to go to every soccer practice or who showed up at the same time for dinner every day. There was a part of me that was confused by his interest in this family home. How could he think about buying a family home with his girlfriend when we didn't yet have a family? That's when it dawned on me. Harrison must have been planning on proposing.

I walked around the house, putting my fingerprints on the walls and trying to paint our stories into the rooms. There was a kitchen with a filter tap and a huge garden that looked onto the yard. There, I could call the children and the dog for dinner. We could gather around the oak dining table, and I could cook for four of us, with how big the oven was. I had plenty of space to chop vegetables and meats. I would make spaghetti and boulette. In my daydream, Harrison had come home with garlic bread and red wine and kissed me on the cheek. Then, we would put the kids to bed and enjoy a night together, where I could speak to him about his job. By then, he would probably be promoted, and judging from the money that he seemed to take home so far, I may not even need to work.

The garden had plenty of room for planting vegetables and fruits, something I had always wanted to do. I never understood why not enough people took advantage of the tropical weather in Florida and its ability to grow there. I considered what my life would be like inside of these four walls, and I decided that even though Harrison and I may not have the wildest sex lives of all time, we could still really enjoy each other and make a good team. I even let myself imagine Belle making it through her last stage of treatment, wowing all of the doctors and coming over for dinner every other Sunday. I imagined her cackling laughing as we invited guests over, and she would be able to retell over and over again how Harrison used to live in the side of her house. "And look at them now! True love prevails!"

"Excuse me, ma'am, do you have any other thoughts? Perhaps you and your partner want to talk it over?" The real estate agent had found me and was now looking for my vote on the house, except I had no idea what was going on. Harrison had left me entirely in the dark with this whole thing. My daydream zapped out of my mind, and I felt a bit foolish for letting myself get carried away.

Before we left, I wondered whether Harrison would turn around and ask me for my opinion or what would happen next. I hadn't bought my own apartment yet, and the very idea of it all was making me extremely hyper, like I was finally growing up and starting to do all of the things that I had been promised I could do. I wondered how it would feel to get through college without worrying about working at the law firm and how much quicker I would get my education. The fact that he was eleven years my senior had always given him a protective air so that I believed he was consistently planning for what was right for us. And I loved that about him. He was one of the first guys in my life, besides my brothers, who put me first and promised me a better life—one where I would be supported and happy with a man I loved.

The realtor shut the doors and smiled at both of us. "Well, I trust that you two have a lot to talk over. But please, let me know as soon as possible if you'd like to put an offer down on the house. We have a lot of interested clients."

"Certainly. Thank you for your time." Harrison bowed slightly before walking towards his Truck and opening the side passenger door for me.

We drove home to the small duplex in silence. The radio was playing old-time favorites, and Marvin Gaye was buzzing out of the stereo. I held my purse in my lap tightly. I didn't have the kind of money to buy a house, so I didn't really understand what more had to be said. But the lady had told us to let her know as soon as possible, so it was a little strange that Harrison wasn't discussing what we were going to do next.

I pushed him. "Well? What did you think?"

"What, the house? Oh, beautiful. Clearly."

He took a sharp turn left and put his eyes back on the road, seemingly unphased about discussing any more.

I waited for a moment before continuing. "Well, don't you think we ought to discuss it together?"

"Discuss what?" Harrison looked genuinely confused as to what I was referring to.

"The house, Harrison. Whether we're going to get it or not. Isn't that what's going on here?" I became paranoid for just a moment. Letting my insecurities get the better of me and considering what I would do if Harrison had utterly no intentions of moving in with me and was, for some reason, buying a three-bedroom house simply because he could.

He lifted his brow a little. "Oh, yeah... Yeah, yeah, of course. Don't worry about that, baby. I'll take care of it."

He took a turn to go towards his police station, and I ended up waiting in his car for over twenty-five minutes while he figured some things out in the office. Harrison could be both so present and so disengaged at times. I knew things had been extremely hectic at work for him, though, so I wanted to let it slide. As a cop, it was difficult to give him any crap about work. After all, he was out there trying to make society a better place, or so I thought. When you really love someone, I have come to learn, you can get really good at missing warning signs and making up excuses.

∼

Despite there being no real movement about house hunting, Harrison and I continued to spend a lot of time together. We had developed in more ways than one. Belle had moved out of her part of the house, and Harrison had held me as I cried into his shoulders, and we lay on the sofa feeling what would be the first stages of our grief for her.

Our sex life had also improved. Now that Harrison and I had discussed, at least a little bit, my dislike for his version of sexy talk, things were getting better. It wasn't so much Harrison trying to control the mood with a "dirty girl" narrative, and more so, both of us connecting in a sensual way— although he was still not as natural at this as other romantic partners may be. I was willing to look past this because there were so many other features of his personality that I loved.

Weeks went by, and not much had changed. I was busy working on college assignments and trying to get enough shifts in to pay for the actual college. Some high school girls were already having children and getting married. It all seemed a little strange to me. Even though Harrison and I were serious, I wasn't so sure I was ready for all of that yet.

But as I have often learned, the Universe had different plans. It was a Tuesday afternoon, and I was late. This was not the first pregnancy test I had ever taken. Harrison and I were mostly safe, but having been together for so long, there had been a few slip-ups. The month before was one of those slip-ups.

Before meeting him later that evening, I took a pregnancy test just to keep my anxieties at bay. My mind was somewhere else. You'd think that when I am alone in a bathroom and taking a pregnancy test, I would be considering my current situation. But as I waited for the pee on the stick to tell me my fate, other things were going on in my head. Harrison still hadn't confirmed whether we were going to buy the house but had been signing some papers and taking some phone calls that made it seem like he was sorting something out. He was a generous boyfriend, and there had been a good few occasions where he had surprised me with gifts or a new dress or a fancy dinner. But still. There was a lot to be discussed if we were actually going to take that next step and buy property together. Also, I had to think about what my mother would think of me, moving into a house with a man before we were married.

"Ko Manman!" I looked down at the test tube and saw two blue lines. That couldn't be right.

I took a look at the back of the pack, my pants still down on the toilet seat, and got confirmation that the pee stick was telling me I was pregnant—or at least that's what my pee had indicated. My heart started to lightly flutter underneath my work uniform. I was in the middle of a shift. Peeking into the box, I looked for another test, but there didn't seem to be one.

"Huh." I thought to myself for a moment. Could this really be? Weren't there countless occasions where women peed on sticks and thought they were pregnant, only to do another two tests and find out they weren't?

There was no need to freak out just yet, but I knew I had to get another test. The adrenaline of the unknown was starting to kick in. Was this something that I'd have to deal with? Was this quick little test going to become a major life decision for Harrison and me?

I walked out of the bathroom in a hurry and held onto my stomach, which at this stage, was cramping with anxiety. My boss had frowned, telling me that I'd need to make up the time but believing my stomach ache enough to let me go for the rest of the day.

The same pharmacist served me, and I asked for another two tests, at which she frowned and gave me a multipack. "You know, honey, it's 99%." I assumed she meant the accuracy. Even still, I wasn't going to take any chances.

I couldn't return to work, so I stuffed the test into my bag and hurried down the street. There was a coffee shop around the corner the staff usually got our lunches at. That had to be avoided because the last thing I needed was to see co-workers on their breaks after I had bailed on the remaining five hours of my shift.

At the bottom of the road, an old bar housed the majority of the drunks in the neighborhood. It was in the sticky bathroom toilet cubicle that I did my second and third tests. Two tests with the same pee couldn't be wrong. Waiting for the stick to show up the one or two bars this time was more intense.

Again, I found myself thinking about Harrison. But this time, I was thinking about him, us, our relationship, and what a baby might do to us. I knew that Harrison had a son and that he really yearned to be closer to him. The fact that he had a lot more life experience than me made me feel as if I couldn't comment or judge what he'd been through. I didn't know what it felt like to be divorced and not get along with the partner I'd had a child with. But deep down, I think it bothered me a little that he didn't see his child. After all, he was going to be an official pilot. He was flying to the Bahamas and took some trips for his studies quite frequently. Also, he had enough money. I didn't understand the arrangements that he had with his ex-wife, or if he had any at all. I just thought that he would have told me if he was paying child support. And the absence of this information was confusing.

Still, I was sure there was plenty about Harrison's life that I didn't know all the details about. That's why it was important for us to decide once and for all what the next stage of our relationship would be.

And it looked like my body had decided that for us: both tests showed two perfectly straight lines. Three tests all told me that I was pregnant.

I felt my shoes stick to the surface of the floor, but my face was beaming. I had surprised myself in my own calmness. Something in me was telling me that this was meant to be and that it was going to work out. Even though it had been unexpected, I loved Harrison, and I knew he loved me. Besides, he would be happy to have a child whose life he could be involved in. There was no real reason why a baby would tear us apart or be a disaster.

A baby. I laughed to myself, flushing the toilet and walking out of there, deciding to walk all the way home as I gathered myself. It all felt quite fictional.

A baby. Harrison's baby. Harrison and my baby. For a second, Nicholas's face flashed into my eyes and I had to blink it away to get back into the present moment. What was I still thinking about Nicholas for? Here I was, walking home from work, imagining a stomach ache when in actual fact, I had a baby ache. What did Nicholas have to do with that? There was this strong urge inside of me to call him, to tell him the news. Before I phoned my friends, before I spoke with Harrison, before I told my mother, Nicholas was the one I wanted to speak to.

I guess in a lot of ways, I had always imagined that we would have a baby together. But Nicholas and I had already tried being together, and besides, he was off on duty. That would probably be his life now. He was intelligent and a go-getter, so he could end up being a Sergeant one day and settling out in another state or country somewhere with a woman who bore four children to him. Still, there was a sense of knowing that he would be there for me and that he would help me get through what lay ahead in the next nine months, even if it broke his heart.

Everything about my body was starting to feel foreign, like it didn't belong to me anymore. I was hyper-aware of the fact that there was a tiny pea-sized something that was going to begin to dictate my every move and decision. But here I was, in a happy relationship with a man who loved me. We had even discussed these things together in bed. Sure, it was loose and nothing serious, but it never felt too out of reach. Dating someone with an age gap instantly made things like that bit more serious. If you're going to bother putting up with the judgment from people when they see you're with a slightly older partner, you have to be prepared to fight for the relationship and make sure it's worth fighting for.

I sipped on water while I was getting ready, laughing to myself at the absurdity of how fast life can go sometimes. A couple of weeks ago, none of these serious notions between Harrison and I had really crossed my mind. But now, in a very short time, we were looking at houses together, and I had become pregnant. I so hoped that Harrison would react the way I thought he would.

~

Harrison was in an excellent mood when I met up with him that evening at the beach boardwalk. We had a drawn-out dinner, and I had declined to look at the wine list. Harrison had looked at me strangely, knowing that I enjoyed dining out with him and drinking wine together, but he went ahead and ordered himself a beer, not noticing.

We walked hand in hand on the boardwalk afterward, and I nuzzled myself into his side. He held onto me tighter and kissed my head. We were watching as the sky was turning a peachy pink glow. It was painting out all of the beautiful colors of the sky right in front of us as if to help celebrate the new creation that was growing inside of me. I couldn't believe it. Was I really about to get everything that I had ever dreamed of?

We found an ice cream place at the end, and I ordered a double chocolate ice cream cone with sprinkles and two scoops of chocolate. We shared it together, the way we always did. Any way we could be affectionate with one another, we took the opportunity and ran with it. I am sure people thought we were horribly annoying to be around. But this might explain why I wasn't so phased about the actual sexual intercourse. We had a much greater connection of love and affection, and when we were together, we took many opportunities to express it together.

Harrison was holding the ice cream cone, and we were laughing as I was trying to catch the drips that dripped down his knuckles. I smiled up at him as I did this, and we burst out laughing again. This was often the way between the two of us. Part of the reason why we didn't get so in-depth into the more serious topics on our relationship was that we were having too much fun. A lot of our time together was spent laughing and joking around. Sometimes it felt like the mood would change if I were to push on some movement with the house or urge him to take the next step.

Even still, as we sat and ate our ice cream together, giggling like school children, and as the sun was setting in front of us, I knew that this would be the perfect moment to tell Harrison my news. It all felt so serendipitous. I was young and didn't have a clue about babies or how to raise them, but I knew that I loved Harrison and that he loved me. For now, that was more than enough. Besides, we would have nine months to get ourselves prepared. The only thing that mattered was that we communicated together and stayed close. I had to be strong and get us there. Even though I was early along in my pregnancy, I knew it was the right time to let Harrison know.

Wiping the remaining melted ice cream off of his knuckles with a paper napkin, I spoke.

"So, I have some news. Some important news," I said.

"Oh? That's funny. So do I." Harrison looked at me suspiciously, and I laughed again, nervous about what was about to happen. Since I adored him so much, my mind instantly got distracted over what he would say to me. Had he put a number down on the house? Was he going to ask me to put my name on the lease or mortgage? Could he possibly be ready to propose to me? I had never thought that all of those things: home, love, baby, marriage, could be given to me at one moment's notice. And now, here I was, laughing with my soon-to-be fiance about the next steps we were about to take.

"Me first, please," I said, feeling giddy at the idea of our news perfectly complementing each other: 'I'm pregnant!' 'I got us the house!' We embrace, we kiss, we remember the moment forever.

I was right about only one thing at that moment—I would certainly remember this moment forever.

"I'm going to... I mean, we're going to..." I found myself nervous at the anticipation of his reaction. He looked at me curiously, like he had no idea what I was trying to say. So then, I simply had to come out straight and say it.

"We're pregnant!" I blurted.

Then I waited. And waited. And waited.

Harrison looked back at me as if I were speaking a foreign language. Don't worry, I instantly started to reassure myself. He's shocked. Plenty of men are shocked when they first hear this news. It's your job to get him back to a place of security. So I tried to fill the silence.

"I just found out today. It's not like I was keeping this from you or anything."

Harrison started to shake his head. He was wearing a look of actual horror on his face. I couldn't believe it. Then he put his head into his hands, muttering "no, no, no" over and over. I didn't care anymore how he thought he felt. This was some bullshit. This was selfish of him. I was the one who had dealt with this news all alone in some grimy bar toilet. I was the one who was carrying the baby. I was the one who would have to go through all of the changes and quit drinking alcohol and coffee and basically everything that is fun. So Harrison making this all about him was pretty insulting, as well as surprising.

"What's the problem?" I asked. "What are you so worried about?"

He looked up at me for a moment. His face was meek, and it almost seemed like he was going to throw up. I couldn't believe how he was acting. Eleven years older than me and someone who already had a kid. I didn't get it.

"You don't understand, Leila," he finally said, hanging his head down low. "I can't do this."

At this point, I started to panic. At the moment when I needed him most, Harrison was acting like a schoolboy. I couldn't raise this baby alone—and nor should I have to! I was in a serious relationship with a man who had money, a great job, and who said he loved me. What was the missing piece?

"No, please. Harrison, you have to do this! We have to! Look, I know it's not perfect timing, but we were viewing houses—the house with the three bedrooms—"

"Oh, for Christ's sake, Leila. That wasn't for us. That was for me and my family. Me and my wife, Sue!" He spat this out at me and immediately got up from the bench, walking up towards the pier.

I sat there, my palms in my lap, watching as my entire world was moving through my fingers like sand.

He had a wife. How could he have a wife?

I was crying now. This was not going to go down the way I thought it would. This was not my fairytale beginning but my nightmare. And Harrison, whoever the hell this man was, didn't give a damn about me and could only think of himself. He had the audacity to walk away from me after telling me something like that.

I would have followed him, but I couldn't move. My entire body was numb. All I kept thinking about was the fact that there was this tiny dot in my stomach that half-belonged to him. A dot that may not have a father—or even a mother.

Harrison came back and sat down beside me, inhaling and

exhaling loudly. I was sobbing quietly, not understanding what to think, what to say, or what to do next.

"They live in the Bahamas," he said, exhaling. "I've been visiting them back and forth."

I gasped. These were the trips that he had claimed were a part of his training. My family flew to Haiti back and forth all the time. It was a normal thing that people who were from the islands would do. I never in my life considered that Harrison was doing this to be with his wife, whom he was betraying with me. Not to mention, he only went three times within a year—and for only weekends.

I stuttered over my own coming to realization. I slapped the shit out of him on the side of his face meeting his ear. I was certain he should have hearing loss.

"So you mean to say… I'm… I'm the side chick?" I said this with sheer shock. Thinking to myself for a second, how not only did Harrison make a fool out of me and our relationship while getting me pregnant, but he had also made me the person whom I would never have agreed to be. It was not in my nature to go after another woman's man. He had made me feel dishonorable, like I had done something wrong when I never had any idea. For this, I could never forgive him.

"Oh, please, Leila. Don't be dramatic about this," he muttered sharply, looking around to see what people thought of the crying woman that was sitting on the bench.

"Dramatic? Harrison, please. Please tell me you're not serious. Tell me this is a fucking joke," I pleaded with him. I held onto his shirt as I cried, and I begged him to give me another reality, any other reality. But he shook me off.

"I'm sorry, Leila. I do love you. I really do. But my wife is 36 weeks pregnant. She's coming home to raise the baby here." And then he sighed before continuing. "That's why I was looking at that house. Not for you and me, but for them."

Harrison was holding a knife at my heart and choosing to stab me continuously, even though I was already wounded. I could barely breathe. Suddenly, my breaths were shallow, and I could never inhale enough. I started to panic at the thought of the predicament that I was in. Here I was, on the boardwalk, pregnant and in a relationship with a sociopath who had completely used me for his sexual affair with his wife while they were in transit. I had heard about these pilots. These types of men had a woman for every country that they flew overseas to. His sorry ass wasn't even fully a pilot yet and was already playing the damn part. Harrison and I had even joked about some of his older colleagues, as if he was so far removed from that reality. Little did I know he was living proof of it.

9

THE TRUTH IS BOTH BRUTAL AND AMUSING

he clinic was cramped and hot, with the air conditioning blowing what seemed to be hot air. It was a small square room with plastic seats lining the walls and a medium-sized TV mounted in the far corner, displaying segments of daily news. Tania took a seat as I walked up to the queue, putting my decision on paper, making it all seem very final and deliberate.

But none of this had been deliberate. And I had utterly no closure from Harrison. I hadn't even been able to get my things from his side duplex. To think that we were playing house, meeting with his family and attending events together, doing all of the things that normal couples our age were doing. I imagined my forever with him while he was trying to escape from his.

The lady at the desk booked me in for this afternoon, and I went back alone, giving Tania an estimation as to when they'd be done with the procedure so that she could drive me home. It was as clinical and cold as you would expect. No woman on earth decides she wants to one day attend an abortion clinic. This is a point that so many people get wrong. This was the last place on earth I wanted to be. This was not where I saw my life going.

I could no longer trust in reality. I had to consider how I had so easily fallen for Harrison's delusion. Was there something wrong with me? Was everyone else in on it and watching as I smiled and looked on, without a clue? After all of the time and effort and love I had put into that relationship, here I was, having to go through this traumatizing experience alone. None of my efforts had seen any goodness in my current reality. I was somehow left with absolutely nothing.

Not for the first time that week, Nicholas popped into my head. I so wished that our closeness allowed for me to be able to share the heartache I was going through. He was the only person in the world who I could think of that I genuinely trusted to tell anything to. It didn't matter that it wasn't with him; it didn't matter that we may not see each other again, or at least not like we used to. The only thing that mattered was that we loved one another—and that love had transcended time and distance since we'd met.

But being in the thick of it, I couldn't think of uttering a word to anyone. This felt like a burden I would have to shoulder alone. I thought about what my mother would say, what her mother would say, what my ancestors would say if they could see me in this cold clinic, single and broken. I thought about the bible verses they would put upon me and whether their staunch views would change if they knew the trap that had been set for me by a man I willingly and earnestly loved.

I was brought into a ward that had around four beds, each with its curtains pulled over. Behind one curtain, I could hear quiet whimpering by a woman. In another, part of the curtain opened, and I looked at a couple. The man sat on a plastic chair, leaning over the bed of a woman who was lying and sleeping beside him. The nurse who had wheeled me into the room and given me my hospital gown was chirpy and heavy-set. She busied herself around the room and chirped away about this and that. I found it difficult to concentrate on what she was saying, but I got the gist of it. She took my heart rate and some blood tests and said we'd be ready to prepare for the procedure once they came back with normal results. They'd warned me that I was a little bit too early. I thought about the likelihood that this would not work and that I would have to bring a poor, innocent child into a world where they were not wanted by their father. I tried to calm myself and focus on letting the clinic staff do their jobs and take momentary control over what was going to happen to me.

When the nurse came back, the doctor entered, and they gave me an anesthetic that had a slow release. The nurse was flicking through a gossip magazine that had been left on the table by one of the staff members. She was showing me pictures of women in bikinis who the paparazzi were slating. "Can you believe it?" She asked, her voice becoming muffled as I began to lose consciousness.

"No," I responded drowsily. "No, I can't."

It was dark and cold, and I was alone. There must have been a way out. I felt my way around the floor with the palms of my hands and tried to look for a path. I was stuck. It was just a small square of space—a square hole that I was stuck inside of.

"Hello?" I called out to be heard by someone, by anyone. My voice echoed through the small space, and a drip of water dropped in the distance.

"Huh!" I gasped. That echoed too. I put my palms back down on the floor, and suddenly, a path was felt before me. The path was leading towards the sound of the dripping water. It was still and very discreet. The water dripped every two to three seconds. "Drip.... drip... drip." It was inconsistent and almost too quiet for me to follow, but I took my time and felt my way. There was a light; it was a small crack of light that could be seen way, way up, on the very top of this—well.

That's what it looked like. The crack of light was shining onto the bottom of a well. I was crawling towards the base of this well, seemingly trapped in the gutter. I found my way with the small beacon of light, and I cried out to no one.

"Please, please help me! Anyone!"

There was a noise above me, a rumbling that sounded like the moving of a stone. It rumbled and echoed and filled the space that I was trapped inside of. Suddenly, light poured into this dark hole that I was stuck in. I shielded my eyes with my arms, the intense brightness hurting my eyes as they slowly adjusted to the newfound surroundings, now that the stone top had been lifted. I opened my eyes again and saw that I was in a round hole in the ground, about thirty feet deep. The walls that surrounded me were stone and rose all the way up towards the light. The top. Someone had removed the top and known that I was here. Someone had come to save me.

"Help!" I cried. "Someone, please help me! I'm trapped down here!"

I heard muttering from above me. It sounded as if I were underwater, and I only heard the rippling movements of voices, but not the words themselves. There was a male and a female voice, and they were having some kind of an argument, as they decided together what to do about the voice inside the well.

"Help, please, I'm somebody. I'm somebody, and I'm here, trapped inside this well. Please help me!" I told them. I spoke whatever words came out of me in my panic. I couldn't remember any identifiable features about myself—what my name was, where I came from, what I was doing there—but there was something familiar about their voices, something both ominous and memorable.

A part of the light was shadowed, and I put my forearm down, squinting my eyes to see who had bent over the well and was looking inside.

Harrison stared back at me, unable to recognize me from all the way at the bottom of the well. A woman pushed him aside, and she peered in next, her belly expanding and bulging as she pressed her arm onto Harrison's shoulder and muttered something into his ear.

"Help, please! Somebody help me!" I cried. They stared at me, deadpan in the face, and said nothing. Slowly and without struggle, they dragged the stone top over the well and covered me back into complete darkness.

"No," I cried and then whimpered, knowing that they were already too far away to hear me. The stone blocked all light and sound from my possession. "No..." I curled into myself and cradled my legs as I cried, waiting for someone else to find me in this dark, pitless hole.

~

Tania was waiting outside of the clinic, just like she said she would be. I breathed a sigh of relief, feeling thankful for her and thankful to myself for packing a spare set of clothes to walk out with. The nurse had told me not to shower for twelve hours and to call them if there was an abnormal amount of bleeding, although some spotting and even heavy flow was normal and could be expected.

They gave me a pamphlet for after-care instructions and told me to go home and get my dinner given to me in bed. The nurse also insisted that I keep the gossip magazine while I recover. Gossip magazines weren't really my thing, but then again, none of this was my thing. I was just living it and waiting for it to be over.

Tania had given me a big hug when I got into the car, and I immediately felt comforted by her being there. Through all of the different stages in our friendship, she never judged me for what I went through. She was always there to support me and to remind me that even if the men in my life were useless, the friends that I had were incredible.

I followed the nurse's advice and set up the next few days to spend in bed, eating chocolate and reading trashy magazine content, watching Friends, and looking at talk show reruns of Rikki Lake and the Oprah Winfrey show. The countless and often absurd stories on the talk shows allowed me to cry and feel anger at scenarios that had nothing to do with me. It was a way of expressing my emotions when I was unsure of my own as I was healing from the traumatic end of my and Harrison's relationship.

A couple of times, I allowed myself to toss and turn, thinking about how beautiful some of my evenings had been with Harrison—how we laughed until there were tears streaming down both of our faces, how we dissected films after watching them over a big bowl of popcorn and some drinks, how we had taken trips away together and watched endless sunsets and danced in each other's arms. There was so much in the relationship that I had genuinely enjoyed. The idea that it had all been fictionalized and that I had literally gone through terminating any trace of it was an extremely painful thing to process.

There was only one person that I trusted with this information in my family: my sister. My sister was older than my brothers and me and hadn't lived at home with us while growing up. She'd also had a baby in her teens, and that changed things in the family. It made my mother aware that we could slip through her Christian veneers, despite her best intentions at imparting on us her morals and beliefs.

My sister understood what it felt like to be alone and to have to fend for herself. She knew how to land on her own two feet and how to count on herself when everyone else was gone. This is why I trusted that she would always understand what I was going through. The distance that we had had growing up meant that we felt extremely close to one another and like we could share intimate things. It didn't matter what our mother thought about abortion or whether my sister had thought that I'd done the right thing or not. The security was that my sister always had my best intentions at heart regardless of what she thought. She had my back, and she trusted me to make my own decisions.

I called her on and off as the hours and days had passed. I'd left Harrison a voicemail after the clinic, telling him that it had been done and that he didn't have to worry anymore. There was no response. In fact, it had been radio silence since that day at the pier when he had made his confessions known to me.

I didn't understand it. What had I done to deserve this? How had he been able to get away with his poor actions, scot-free, while I was bedridden and healing from the termination of his child? Our child? It was one of the darkest times in my life, and if it weren't for the support of my sister and Tania, I truly don't know what I would have done. My sister had had countless conversations with me as we went over Harrison's bizarre actions in our heads, trying to search for answers that simply weren't there.

"Don't paint yourself as the one who has lost, Leila. You were in an honest and loving relationship. His lies and manipulation have nothing to do with how you loved! Don't let his nastiness mean something about you because it doesn't."

But it was hard to view my experience with Harrison as anything other than traumatizing at this stage. So much of it still confused me. How had Harrison had time to impregnate both his wife and me while spending the majority of his waking hours with me? Did his wife know about me? What had he told his friends and distant family members when we had gone out dancing or to dinner? How could his sisters never utter a word about him being married when I'd been over their house a million times?

I searched my brain for signs, and there were few things that I could come up with. There had been occasions where he was uncontactable, but I had always assumed it was because of work, and he'd never left it long enough for me to worry about him. There were times when he had private conversations on the phone, but I trusted him enough not to think that anything suspicious or out of the ordinary was going on. He was a cop, after all. So much of his job was private and confidential. Harrison had been a master manipulator—that was for sure. It wasn't until my sister phoned me six weeks later that I truly understood the extent of his manipulation.

I was cleaning my small one-bedroom apartment when my sister rang me.

"You've gotta turn on the news, Leila! Tell me you've seen it."

I had considered for a moment whether a hurricane was on the way. That was the level of panic coming through from her voice, and I couldn't think of any other reason for it. But then, just as quickly as she'd spoken, my sister burst out laughing hysterically.

Through her laughter, she said, "You're not gonna believe it, Leila, really. You're not gonna believe it."

I didn't say anything, only kept the phone pressed close to my ear and then looked around for the remote. It was on the floor, and I picked it up and turned on the news channel.

There was a report flashing up in front of the TV with the headlines: "Local Police Officer Arrested for Major Cocaine Deal with DEA agent." There in the middle of the screen was Harrison, attempting to shield his face from the camera by his suit jacket as the paparazzi hounded him all the way to the cops' car.

I couldn't believe it. My mouth gaped open as I watched it unfold right in front of me. It had been a total of three and a half months since I'd seen or even spoken to Harrison. My sister was filling in the gaps for me as I slowly recovered from the shock.

"He's a crooked druggie cop. And he's going to do some serious time in Federal prison if found guilty."

"What?" I gasped.

"Yeah…"

My sister and I paused for a moment, watching the same news channel in two different parts of the state.

I mused on this newfound information for a moment, looking at the man that I had very nearly started a family with. It was the ultimate sign that I had made the right decision and had gotten out of a situation that could have been a lot more detrimental. Considering all of the madness that had happened in my life with Harrison, I burst out laughing down the phone to my sister.

My laughter was infectious, and I heard my sister break out into a similar fit of laughter. We howled, and I jumped up and down, holding the phone cord and watching my own life as if it were someone else's.

"Well, he sure 'nough needed that money!" I said, and my sister laughed some more.

I thought about everything that had happened to me over the past couple of months. The clinical hands that held mine when no one else was around. The menial television that I filled my mind with to stop it from thinking about my broken heart. All of the time that I had lost with Harrison, yet all of the life I had gained back, now knowing the truth of deceit and ill intent.

It was in those quiet moments alone in bed that I vowed to myself I would never be fooled by a man again. I was no longer going to be fooled by words but was only going to consider actions. I was crying alone, praying to God and asking him why I had had to suffer by myself while Harrison got to be off with his loving wife and their two babies in the very house that I had put my own fingerprints on.

This was God's very humorous way of telling me that I had gotten out just in time. All of the pain and the difficult experiences that Harrison had caused me had come up to this one crescendo moment, and I considered my losses.

Suddenly, it felt like I had gotten out of the situation pretty unscathed. And besides, Harrison was given 11 years to consider his wrongdoings. I thought that was a fitting punishment—although I considered my punishment for aborting my baby.

NOSTALGIA AND COMING HOME

our years had passed since Nicholas first signed up to be in the military. Finally, his training had come to an end, and he was due to come home to pursue his next endeavors.

Nicholas had visited quite a few times while he was in Missouri, but certainly not enough for me to get a great idea as to who he really was, at least in the same intimate way as I had first known him. We had gotten into the on and off habit of phoning each other, but what we especially liked to do was write letters to one another.

Nicholas had always been talented at poetry and writing, and I shared the same interest. His letters were some of my most prized possessions, and I yearned to read more every time a new letter came to my door. I'd even joked about him sending two at a time so that I didn't have to wait as long for the next one to come. Sometimes, when I was feeling isolated and alone, I would read Nicholas's letters, and they would take me somewhere else, far away from my own reality. I imagined him sitting on his bunk bed in his uniform, writing in silence. I imagined the boys grabbing the pages off of him and then

Nicholas snatching them back as they quizzed him about who his sweetheart was.

In my own mind, Nicholas still called me his sweetheart. Despite the two of us having not been romantically involved since we were teenagers, there was a special spot that I reserved for Nicholas. This was a place in my heart that still allowed me to think of him in a romantic sense. To me, he was someone who I loved and who loved me, someone who had my heart and whom I trusted my heart with. After everything that I had been through with Harrison, it put the longevity of my bond with Nicholas into perspective.

Although the time away from each other was a little difficult, every time Nicholas came to visit, I was able to see how much good this distance did for us. We were fascinated by each other again; there were so many unknowns, a sense of mystery. I would see him hanging around the town with a group of guys, drinking beers and chatting, sometimes still in his uniform, having just got off the bus. It would feel almost like we were in a movie. There was my guy. My best friend, my main support. But in front of me, Nicholas was changing and maturing into a man that I no longer knew everything about. I would run up to him and tap his shoulder, and he usually lifted me up and twirled me around as our mutual friends laughed together. No one ever questioned the closeness that Nicholas and I had for one another. Time had surpassed any speculation.

Depending on who I had been dating at the time, I either planned on seeing Nicholas, or we would end up bumping into each other. We lived in a small urban community where the neighborhood hung out and was interactive together. There was a buzz about town when Nicholas came home, or at least, that was how it felt to me. Suddenly, I was aware of how my hair looked and whether to get it permed or not. I would hang around a bit more outside, wearing my professional attire and wanting Nicholas to be impressed by my newfound sophistication. When the girls wanted to meet up for some drinks, I was in. Usually, I would stay late at the firm and do the paperwork that no one else was bothered to do. But if Nicholas was home, I was active in my social life. The idea that I would very likely see him out in the town was exhilarating to me. Even if I were dating someone else, there was still this undeniable spark between Nicholas and me. We would see each other at the bar or the club, have a drink together, and loosen up before our group of friends would go separate ways, and we would look back at each other, both of us unwilling to address the elephant in the room.

Life was not like how it used to be when we were teenagers. We couldn't just go back to "hanging out" all the time. Nowadays, we had jobs, commitments, everyone was on a schedule, and most of us were working our asses off just to get a seat at the table. Everything came harder for communities like ours, and that was why so many of us were tied up in serious commitments with work and education at such young ages. The only choices we had were to work hard and put ourselves through school or take out student loans and live off of that.

About six months after Harrison's sentencing, I got a letter from the Missouri Military Base sent from Nicholas. I opened the letter as soon as I saw it in my mailbox, tearing the paper off there and then in the lobby, then picking up the envelope and reading the letter as I walked back to my apartment.

It read:

Dear Leila,

And just like that—I have completed four years in military training. Forgive me for a moment as I become reflective.

Mostly, I am grateful for the time that I have spent here. The discipline in training, along with the camaraderie and friendship I found in my brothers, was what ultimately got me through. I have a newfound respect for leadership, for being affirmative in your choices and promises to people, and I wish to someday protect people and keep them from harm's way. That is ultimately what I saw this training program as. I thought, if I could train to serve for the United States, then perhaps I could influence an entire community, an urban community like ours. There is so much that works in our town. But then again, what about those streetlights that were never replaced and the women having to walk home alone with darkness giving their predators an advantage? What about all those kids we grew up next to, who didn't have mothers and fathers who were active in their lives and who the state was too disorganized to care for? What about even the menial things, like making sure that the local grocery store was protected from robberies and had back up when he needed it? Remember the way we used to joke as kids about how the police never came round to the rougher neighborhoods? Well, what if someone was brave enough to try and make a difference?

These are the sort of things that have been going through my mind as I become close to the end of my enlistment. Perhaps that is why I have decided to come straight home afterward.

My heart skipped a beat. I read the sentence again.

Perhaps that is why I have decided to come straight home afterward. I wanted to give myself enough time to take a vacation and ease into my next career path.

Vacation. What did that mean? Was Nicholas planning on getting a job in town, or was he just stopping by? I was so eager to see my love and my dear friend, and the thought of him coming home was the pick me up that I needed right now.

Things had felt stale with me for a long time. Even though karma had caught up with Harrison a lot sooner than I had expected, there were still a lot of unhealed wounds within me about that entire situation. In fact, I hadn't dated anyone else since.

It also felt like enough time had passed to maybe share what had happened with me to Nicholas. At this stage of our lives, I knew we were close enough that he wouldn't judge me or make it about us. Nicholas had matured greatly in the years he'd spent away. I noticed little intricate changes every time he came to visit. For example, Nicholas no longer hung around doing nothing, watching T.V and smoking weed. His military diet was strict, and he had gotten himself into expert shape. He enjoyed a couple of drinks every now and then, but any drugs were out of the question.

His attention span had improved. The regiment of the army had trained him into repeating a predictable sleep pattern, he ate his meals the same time every day, and if something were to happen that would knock him out of his schedule, Nicholas would simply excuse himself and make no attempt at apologizing. He would say something exact and matter-of-fact like, "I'm sorry. I have to get to bed in an hour. It was so nice seeing you!" Usually, this was in a group setting with shared friends that we had, and my eyes would linger over to him, watching as he walked out of the door and hoping that he would look back. Sometimes, I walked him out, and we would have a small and quiet chat. On rare occasions, he would say something meaningful, and we would embrace. He would affirm something within me, leaving me feeling more confident and sure about myself than before he'd visited. He would say something like: "You look incredible, and I'm so proud of what you're doing with yourself." or "I know you're going to do great things in life." Something that would encourage me to keep going, despite all the life drama, until the next time he visited.

I wanted to do well for Nicholas. I saw the positive changes that he was making in his own life, and I wanted to do the same with myself.

His letter went on to read:

I wanted to give myself enough time to take a vacation and ease into my next career path—whatever that career path may be. All I know is that I have wanted to see you for quite some time, and the only person that I want to celebrate my accomplishment with is you. So, I hope you'll be there with me, and we can raise a toast to the brutal training of the military.

I can't wait to look into your eyes and have a real, genuine conversation. I want to know all about your life and what you've been up to. Save all of the details until I get there. Which—well, by the time you get this, it should only be a couple of days.

I booked a bus for Tuesday the 12th of September. If you can, meet me at the bus station—my bus gets in at 16:45pm, but then again, you know how those buses can be. Let me take you out to dinner, and we can take a walk on the beach afterward. Until then, I'll be thinking of you, Leila. Like I always do.

— NICHOLAS

I held the papers close to my chest, now standing in my sitting room. It was Friday the 8th of September. Nicholas was coming home in just five days. I couldn't wait to see him, and there wasn't much else I thought about that weekend.

I prepared as best I knew how. I got my hair done, and I

booked a reservation at an Italian restaurant that I knew he loved. I painted my nails and went shopping with Tania to look for a dress. I did all of this without actually considering how it would feel to see Nicholas again. The last time he had visited, I was all wrapped up in Harrison and expecting to be engaged any month, which I thankfully didn't tell Nicholas. After everything I had been through with Harrison, I was craving familiarity. I was craving nostalgia and the feeling of certainty that came with Nicholas.

We had met up casually on occasions when he was visiting home, but this was the first time that he had specifically asked me to meet him as soon as he got off the bus. There was a natural romantic element involved. It did feel like my sweetheart was returning from the war—without having to deal with the effects war had since Nicholas had only been stationed.

I stood at the bus stop at exactly four-thirty, wearing my new black, white, and red floral summer dress that I had picked out with Tania. I put my hair up into a bundle of curls that lay on my head and crowned the outfit perfectly. The dress showed off my slim figure. I had lost quite a bit of weight since the whole ordeal with Harrison, but I was enjoying how my body now looked in this dress.

Nicholas's bus pulled up, and after four or five stocky men piled out, there he was. He smiled and waved over at me. I could barely recognize him. Standing in front of me was a buff man who had swapped the shaggy teenage curls for a buzz cut. He still wore his dark khaki military uniform that had his name imprinted on it. Underneath his overalls, I could see the shifting shape of muscles and broad shoulders. Nicholas gleamed at me, smiling with his whole face. It was the only thing that I still recognized about him. He was fine as hell!

"Oh, my God!" I laughed as he came over to me, and we embraced in an intense and meaningful hug. I took in his familiar scent and remembered how it felt to be held by him. The teenage angst that we had gone through all those years ago seemed quite far away—and so did the teenage boy I used to know. The person in front of me was masculine and exact, measured and dignified.

"It's so good to see you. You look beautiful as ever." Nicholas said in this deep and affirmative voice. I gushed a little, not expecting to care so much about whether he called me pretty or not. One thing was sure about Nicholas, though. It never mattered whether we were together romantically or not. He always complimented me. When I was with him, I swear I felt like I walked ten feet taller. It was amazing, knowing that someone had seen me for me and still found me beautiful.

We walked to the restaurant, and the conversation was a little formal and awkward. I asked him how his journey was, and he told me that it had been pleasant. He had his earphones on the entire time, and his cassette tape's battery lasted all six hours. I teased him and said that the chicken parmesan special from his favorite Italian restaurant had been taken off the menu and that there had been protests by the regulars about it. He didn't believe me, of course, and asked for proof. I kept teasing until we got into the restaurant, and he saw it on the menu board.

"Hey!" He pointed at it and looked back at me, flashing one of his incredible smiles again. To me, he looked perfect.

This newfound attraction to Nicholas was a little bit troubling for me. For more years than we were together, we had maintained a close friendship where we stayed out of each other's business and knew that the other would be there if we needed them. Was I really about to put all of that into question again?

Nicholas's family was dying to see him, so we parted after dinner, and despite having a delicious meal, I left feeling empty and dissatisfied. It had felt like Nicholas was coming home with all of this life experience, and meanwhile, I had been conned by a guy who claimed he was in love with me when in fact, he was not. There was now this gap in my life that I would have to put down to Harrison stealing from me. I wondered what Nicholas would think about the abortion and what he would have said to me had I asked him to come with me and not Tania. I didn't know why I needed this sort of support from Nicholas now, nearly two years after the abortion. But not being able to share this with him was hurting me, as was not falling back into a romantic relationship upon his return.

That night, I couldn't get Nicholas out of my mind. I thought back to how it felt when I clung to his arm, the bulk of muscle that was now there after his time away training. I thought about his eyes and how he spoke about the lonelier days, the days where he felt isolated and far from everyone who had once known him. My heart had skipped a beat when he opened up his wallet, and there, I saw a polaroid picture of him and me from our Graduation, beaming at the flashing camera, excited and anticipating a bright future. I wondered what this meant: for Nicholas to have kept a photo of me in his wallet. It wasn't just me, of course. It was the two of us. And at the time, we weren't dating. We were more than that. We'd always been more than that.

When I broke up with Nicholas all those years ago, he was a teenage boy. But since then, I had watched as he slowly progressed into a man, a man who was sophisticated and hard working and handsome. A man who was gentle and kind and who had valued me as a friend even when we were no longer romantically involved. This part of our story was what meant the most. I couldn't help but compare Harrison and Nicholas to one another. How stupid I had been. I had thought that someone like Harrison—just because he was a couple of years older, more measured, and seemingly stable—would be right for me instead of seeing what was right in front of my eyes.

I decided to approach these feelings with Nicholas, who was irritatingly busy since he'd gotten home. I didn't realize how many people wanted to reconnect with him now that he was back. I knew that he still had some tests and exams to complete, but I didn't know what his plan was after that. Was he going to reenlist and be sent to another completely random country? Was there any possibility that he would be coming home for good? Was there anything that may influence his decision?

∿

I phoned his house a couple of days later, deciding that I would have to take things into my own hands and ask him to hang out with me. The way he'd been talking when he was away, I expected him to be all over me!

His sister answered, and I mumbled a little, feeling like a school teenager again, calling her high school boyfriend. Felicia yelled out for her brother, and he came down, grabbing the receiver slightly out of breath.

"Leila? Hey, I was just going to come by."

This stunted me. Currently, I was in my pajamas that had a hole in the armpit, and my hair was undone and tied up with bobby pins. I tried to act calm.

"Oh, really? What for?"

"Just thought we could grab a coffee, go to the beach for a walk, you know, nothing crazy."

These were both reasonable suggestions—but I wanted to elevate our connection with one another to the next level, so I thought it better to plan something a little more formal.

"How about dinner? I would love the chance to go on a date with a military soldier."

Nicholas laughed, and I could tell he was embarrassed with the flattery.

"A date, huh?" He said. I let my fingers twirl the phone cord and left my words up to interpretation.

"Alright then." He answered himself. "If it's a date you want, then a date, it is."

That night, I was nervous to see Nicholas for the first time for an actual date since high school. I spoke on the phone with

Tania, and we walked through the different outfit choices and what lip color I would wear. I settled on a black sleek cut short fitted dress with a pearl necklace that my mother had given me on my 18th birthday as a family heirloom. Tania came over to give my hair a kink and insisted that I wear her white linen perfume that made her fiance fall in love with her.

Nicholas had borrowed his brother's car to come and pick me up. He had only been back for a couple of days, and there were so many normalities that he hadn't gotten set up yet. Part of me wanted to know what his plans were and whether he was looking to plant roots in our town again. I was not necessarily married to our area. But I loved Miami and always saw myself living there. It was where I grew up, and it was part of my identity. Besides, we were close to the islands, and I had relatives in both Florida and Haiti, so it was an ideal location for me.

Nicholas was in the same situation as I was. His Dominican family was both in America and DR. He traveled back and forth, and we had similar family structures. In both Haitian and Dominican culture, there was no such thing as distant relatives. You were close to your first cousins and second cousins, and third cousins. Family was everything and essential to reminding ourselves and our children where we came from and who we were. Nicholas has just spent four years of his life away from his home, so I also suspected that this would encourage his decision. But then again, I didn't know what his career prospects were. I knew that he was trying to express his thoughts about his next path in his letter, and maybe the letter was a good place to start. His words were where his affection had always been.

Nicholas had gotten out of his seat and parked the car so that he could open the door for me and escort me into the passenger seat. I laughed out loud, feeling a fondness for his playful nature. We got into the car together and closed the doors, looking at one another for a moment.

"Hi," he said.

"Hi," I beamed.

We took each other in some more before Nicholas whistled. "You look amazing tonight, Leila." He said, grinning as he took the turn out of my driveway and onto the roadway.

We shared small talk in the car, not getting into any of the serious stuff before either of us had had a drink.

We sat down in the restaurant and were given a killer view of the ocean. There were mostly fish restaurants on the board-walk, but this was a Mexican restaurant that had recently opened. It was Nicholas who had suggested it. I loved all of the efforts he had gone through to make me feel like I was on a date with someone for the first time, as opposed to it being my high school sweetheart. But the fact that this was Nicholas from high school made the night even more special to me. Time had passed between us, and I was ready to connect and feel close to him again.

The waiter poured our wine, and Nicholas held my hands and smiled at me with his big, bright smile. He was wearing a pinstriped shirt with the buttons half done and some jeans. It was the most formal I'd ever seen him. He still had his buzzcut and was sporting some stubble on his face, giving him a rugged, masculine look.

"You look really good, Nic," I said, and I couldn't help but gleam smiling back at him.

"Look who's talking!" Nicholas exclaimed and fell back into his seat, fainting being out of breath. "I mean, come on, I told you that you'd develop to be an even more beautiful woman, and you have."

I was taken aback by this compliment, and sure enough, remembered when he told me that I had the type of beauty that only grew as each year went on. Now here he was, claiming truth to his word. This was the confidence-building that I needed after going through so much.

"You're making me blush, and I haven't even tried the wine," I said and took a delicate sip out of my glass, feeling the power of Nicholas's eyes on me, how he was taking in my slim figure with every swift movement I made in my skin-tight dress. The sexual tension between us was palpable, and I couldn't help but feel giddy with excitement.

I looked outside at the not-so-distant waves and felt an overwhelming sense of calm. There was such a familiarity with Nicholas—even though he was nearly unrecognizable, both physically and mentally, from high school.

We ordered entrees, and I knew that we would be here for a while, and I could relax a little. We decided to switch to a bottle of wine once we ordered our main course, and we knew that we would have the companionship of alcohol to get us through the date. We got onto the more meaningful and serious conversation.

"So come on, I'm dying to know. Have you been seeing anyone?" Nicholas took a dignified sip of his glass as he tackled some of the tempura prawns, attempting to look nonchalant, but I could tell that it was a question that had been burning inside him since we sat down.

I smiled, considered his question, and said, "Is there any reason you've been dying to know?" I'd made my voice sound sultry, and he had laughed, a little taken aback at my indirect answer. But Nicholas was always up for a challenge.

"I've been dying to know because I've been dying to take you out on this date," he said swiftly. We made eye contact with one another, and a knowing look passed between us. It was as if he was saying, 'Of course I want to know. I love you.' But I wasn't going to let myself jump to conclusions just yet.

Our main course meal came, and we were briefly interrupted by being handed our Ropa Vieja that we had both ordered. I wasn't going to make him suffer any longer. I picked up my cutlery and began eating this shredded beef meal.

"There was someone. We were dating, and it turned out that he was a total scam. Everything he'd said had been a lie."

Nicholas's eyebrows raised up, but not in a judgemental way, more in a concerned way.

"Oh, really?" He asked. "That sounds pretty horrible."

I nodded my head, reaching for the salt and pepper and making a conscious effort not to get emotional over dinner. It wasn't so much that I was still hung up over Harrison, but rather that I had gone through so much and hadn't been able to have Nicholas around. Now, here he was, eating dinner with me. I realized how much I had been craving his presence without even knowing it at the time.

"Yeah, well, I chose to forget about it," I said, taking my first mouthful and reacting at the incredible flavors. "Oh, my God, this was a great choice."

When I thought about it, there really wasn't much of a difference between the fictional lifestyle Harrison had offered me and the lifestyle that Nicholas was trying to give me. I'd been afraid that he wouldn't be up for being a real adult, but it seemed like he was mature and sophisticated now and knew what he wanted. I wanted to pry more about his plans. There was no point in me getting invested in something when he had no intentions of staying around.

"So come on then, how about you? Are you reenlisting? What's next for the soldier?" He laughed and wiped his mouth with his cloth napkin before answering.

"I thought you would have guessed from my letter."

I looked back at him, confused. What had he said in his letter that I had missed? I read it two or three times. It read more like he was pontificating about life than telling me any direct plans. When I didn't answer him, he cleared his throat and took a sip of wine before continuing.

"I've been offered a job in the local police department. It's going to be shift work, and to be honest, it might be that way for a while. $10 an hour for now, but I just need to do a month's training, and then I'm good to go. My military training is coming in handy, and I don't have to go out and live in the middle of nowhere."

I could barely contain my excitement. "Oh my God, Nicholas. That's brilliant! So... does that mean you're staying?"

He laughed. "Of course it does."

We cheered together, and I poured up our wine glasses. Now that I knew Nicholas was going to be around, it felt like there was more meaning to us meeting up. He had clearly wanted to tell me the good news on the day that he arrived, but there were probably a million other things on his mind that day, and he hadn't gotten the chance to.

We finished our dinner with a walk along the pier, and we even stopped for some ice cream. We made a point of going down onto the sand and walking on the beach, listening to the gentle crashing of the waves and watching the sunset, the sky ablaze with oranges and reds and pinks. I thought about all of the seasons that were coming up where I could be with Nicholas. The fall and Christmas and the different celebrations that would be going on with each of our families. He took my hand as we got up to a rock pool, and when we got back down onto the sand, he didn't let go. Our palms stayed touching, and he gradually put his arm around my waist. We walked like this for a good thirty seconds, neither of us knowing what else to do in this embrace and perhaps feeling a little shy at being the one to make the first move.

Nicholas turned me to face him, and I looked up at his tall and stocky physique, seeing the powder blue sky melt into the waves as his backdrop.

"Leila, I took this job—hell, I applied for this job—all in the hope that you were still… curious."

He'd said the word "curious" lightly, as he seemed to get lost in my eyes, and I let myself become lost in his, repeating what he had said with soft lips.

"Curious?" I asked, still pretending not to understand what he meant. He whispered back at me, our lips very nearly touching.

"Yeah, you know. About us."

Just as we were so close that the tips of our lips were touching one another, I said, "Oh, I'm not just curious; I'm certain."

He kissed me, pushing my lips closer to his as he put his

hand on the back of my neck, and I dove deeper into his embrace, feeling his warm arms wrap around my body in both a familiar and unfamiliar way. We stayed like that until the sky had become completely dark. Even the sun setting and the moon rising wasn't enough to interrupt our embrace at that moment.

LOVE AND MARRIAGE

*N*icholas and I spent practically all of our time in bed for a couple of weeks, once the dinner had finalized our feelings for each other. It was so exciting, making love to him as a completely new man. Now, we had both experienced other partners, and there had been changes to our bodies. We were adults continually growing into ourselves. I wore expensive perfumes and nice earrings. My entire wardrobe had changed now that I worked for the law firm.

We would meet at my place after a long evening of work and end up making love. Nicholas was still looking for a place of his own, and my tiny studio apartment got really humid in the summertime. I had a plug-in fan, but it wasn't enough to keep the place cool. So the subject came up of us renting together, but it felt a little strange discussing this.

Both Nicholas and I had come from religious families where God, marriage, and honor were extremely important. We didn't think our families would let us get away with casually moving in with one another. I could already hear my mother nagging me, asking if I cared at all what the people in the church thought. To this, she was referring to her Haitian friends.

Nicholas's parents were the same. This made our getting back together a lot more serious than if we'd met again in a different state. But I wanted to be serious. I was looking to settle down and start a family. I just had to make sure that no secrets or surprises were waiting around the corner before I said, "I do."

I was never a spontaneous person, but one evening, I suggested we pull up to the jogging park close to 7:00pm. Nicholas let down the driver and passenger side windows simultaneously. For whatever reason, I was aroused. It was such a beautiful evening. We'd spent every single second of that day together. As the day began to lose its battle to the night, I could not focus on a single sentence as he spoke in the car. I watched his mouth with such intensity, it wrinkled his forehead with confusion. Despite that, Nicholas continued talking. All I could hear was, "I went over the listings last night...."

Just like that, I was deaf again. With every "l" word, I imagined his long tongue wrestling my clit into submission. In the middle of what seemed to be the most important part of the conversation to him, I grabbed his crotch—not worrying about if anyone walked up to the car or anything. He asked me in the most seductive way, "What are you doing?"

He proceeded to grow in my hand. I didn't need to reply. I grabbed him by the back of his neck, and our tongues began to dance. Then, I climbed on top of him. Between breaths, I exhaled, "The gear stick is in the way." With a smile on his face, he seductively replied, "That's not the gear shift." I had an unfamiliar excitement take over my entire body as I noticed Nicholas had unzipped his pants. I lifted my sundress, and a smile formed across my face while pulling my panties to the side. As I sat on what I had created, I came all over him immediately, leaving behind evidence of a full day of harbored arousal.

Nicholas turned me onto my back, placing me gently on the leathered seat. Over his muscular shoulder, I witnessed the beauty of a setting sun. His silence through our lovemaking revealed three things. Not only did Nicholas understand my body, but he understood me, and I felt loved. With this, I knew I had to have sex with only this man for the rest of my life.

~

One night, we were sitting on the rooftop of Nicholas's brother's apartment. It had an incredible view of Miami, and you could see the lights all light up in the distance like fireflies. We brought blankets up there and some snacks and cuddled inside one another. In the distance, there was a jazz bar that was on late at night. A drowsy saxophone sang out to the couples and families who were out for dinner, and his sweet notes were reaching our rooftop.

Nicholas closed his eyes and moved to the music. I could tell that he was playing an instrument in his mind, the same way I did when I heard a beautiful horn solo. It took me right back to listening to him play when we were younger and knowing that there was something different about him, something unique that not many people did. He was destined for great things, and I had always felt like he understood me on a complex level. He understood the things that were important to me, such as music and family. He knew that it didn't take me much to be happy, just love and commitment. I smiled as the sweet notes came over us, and we snuggled closer into the blankets.

We ended up falling asleep on the rooftop, and Nicholas nudged me awake when it was already bright outside. I squinted my eyes wearily and could hear the distant seagulls in the sky, looking out for the first bit of food from the sea.

The sun was peeking up over the horizon, and soon the sky would be lit up with its brilliant morning colors, the colors that most people missed by being asleep. Nicholas took my hand as we stepped into the upstairs window that led into the living room. We would stay on the sofa bed when we were at his brother's house since he lived in a one-bedroom apartment in the city. It was sort of like our own little apartment, but with a much better location than mine. Nicholas made some coffee, and I wrapped the blanket around me again, yawning and looking out the window to watch and see the sun light the sky on fire.

He came back with a pot and poured me a cup. I took it and brought it close to my lips, letting the steam warm up my face. Nicholas was fumbling around on the sofa bed, looking for something. Then he knelt in front of me with a box in his hands.

A ring box.

A black ring box.

He opened it up.

"Leila…" he began.

"Oh, my god!" I put my hand to my face and immediately sat down my cup, fearing that I would spill hot coffee all over myself, over-excited.

"I have loved you for a very long time."

I started to cry. I couldn't believe it. Finally, it was the moment I was waiting for, and this time, it was with the right man.

"And I want you to be my wife. Will you marry me?"

Nicholas opened the box and displayed a sparkling oval cut diamond with a gold band. It was elegant and simple and perfect. I couldn't believe he got me so right.

"Yes!" I cried, and we kissed, lying back on the sofa bed as the sun shone in our victory, the sky ablaze with pinks and oranges, the witnesses of our celebration.

～

Planning for the wedding started almost immediately. We rang both of our parents after breakfast, and they were overjoyed, instantly talking about wedding sizes and a proposal party and trying to get everyone over to Florida in time for the wedding, considering how many families would have to be staying in the houses here, headcount for the reception, and when did I want to start looking for my dress?

It hadn't even hit noon.

But if it weren't for my and Nicholas's families, we would never have been able to have arranged such a magnificent wedding. We had been in each other's lives for a very long time, so it was a genuine celebration for everyone that knew of our love.

The first thing to consider was the engagement party, and my mother and Nicholas's mother had gone ahead and arranged everything. We decided to host it in Nicholas's mother's house since her house was bigger, as she'd like to point out.

There were cousins that I hadn't seen in years and a house full of fancy people dressed in their best, Haitians and Dominicans together, almost everyone bringing a gift or a large container of food. At first, I was afraid that the party could go on for days. Knowing our families, it was very likely.

I was both overwhelmed and excited about being the center of attention for the day. On the one hand, it was so nice seeing all of these cousins and family members that I hadn't seen in years. On the other hand, it was pretty exhausting being the guest of honor.

Just as I was pouring myself a glass of water, taking a break from the crowds, someone caught my eye. It was a young woman, around the same age as me. But there was something so familiar about her; perhaps she was a cousin I forgot the name of or a family friend I didn't recall.

Oh, well, may as well keep doing the rounds, I thought to myself, and I went up and introduced myself.

She turned around and looked at me, a little perplexed.

"Hi," I said, trying to jog her memory.

"Hi," she said, still confused as to who I was. "I'm so sorry," she continued. "Are you Nicholas's bride? I don't even know your name! I'm Fernanda."

"Wait—Fernanda?" As soon as she introduced herself, I

recognized her. Fernanda. It must have been. "Fernanda, it's Leila. From middle school! In sixth grade?"

"Oh, my god!" Her face lit up with joy, and we hugged each other instantly. It was my old school friend, the first friend I had made in sixth grade when I first moved from my childhood home. And now here she was, decades later, at my engagement party.

"Wait—you're engaged to my cousin? That's so incredible!"

"You're kidding me!" I said and laughed.

We hugged each other some more and gushed, talking to one another, trying to catch up on all the years that had passed. I couldn't believe it. Fernanda had made a real impact on my childhood, and she served as my first real loss, but seeing her here and knowing that she was Nicholas's cousin felt so serendipitous. It was surely a sign that Nicholas and I were meant to be. It was proof that no matter how much it felt like I had lost people, both Fernanda and Nicholas had come back into my life. It was fate, and I was so glad that they found their way back to me.

As I laughed with Fernanda and caught her up on the romantic love story between her cousin and me, Nicholas caught my gaze and smiled at me, lifting up a wine glass as we got ready to toast to the rest of our future together.

THE IRONY OF SELF-DEFENSE

I do, I do, I do.

In a thousand years, in a thousand lifetimes, I do.

I want to be the person who guides you through life. I want to be the face that you see every morning. You are the reason why I am, and I know we are going to make our own kingdom. We are going to leave a mark on the world with our children and with our love. Our love will be what people remember. I want to dedicate not only this day to you but all of my days. I want to be the person whose shoulder you lean on. I want to watch the sunsets with you. I want to share benches with you and birthday picnics and holiday vacations. I want to show my love for you every day. I know that with you, all things are possible. This is my promise to you, my love, my bride, Leila. On our wedding day.

— NICHOLAS

~

*W*ith the wedding over and families returned to their homes, I breathed an audible sigh of relief. It was finally time to enjoy the calm and to settle into our lives as newlyweds. Nicholas and I were renting a small one-bedroom apartment closer to the port and just ten minutes' walk from the National Guard. Our newlywed life was coupled with Nicholas starting his new low-wage job. For me, everything was the same, except I now had wife duties to consider. Nicholas and I weren't an old-fashioned couple, but I did like making dinners for him, having a place for us to eat and drink and catch up about our days. I was still working and attending college classes.

It was difficult, having so little money and trying to make ends meet. Even with the money that our parents and family members had given us at the wedding, we would still be paying it off for the next year. That was not including the student debt that I had to pay and continued to incur. This meant that a lot of our dinnertime conversations were centered around money and making ends meet. There was no doubt that Nicholas and I were taking strides in the right direction. But our families didn't come with a trust fund. There was no one willing to pay us out and into a cushy lifestyle. I considered my own mother, how difficult it must have been, working in hotels from the moment she arrived in America, as an immigrant who spoke little English when she first arrived.

At one such dinnertime conversation, Nicholas had convinced himself that if we just managed to make $13 an hour, we could start a family and maybe even look to purchase our own home. I laughed at him.

"Thirteen dollars?! You think that's gonna get us a house?"

But considering the fact that we were currently working for $7 and $10 an hour, it would certainly be an improvement. So I agreed that it would be great to get there.

I would work during the day and take evening classes.

Many days I wouldn't get back home until 10 to 11 o'clock at night. I had an old used car that I was afraid to drive on the expressway. On the evenings that I did not have class, I'd spend a great deal of time working late at the law firm. I liked working at the firm, and I knew that my bosses appreciated me and everything I did. A lot of the work was incredibly tedious, but it was also necessary for cases, so I tried as best as I could to compartmentalize my crappy wage and tell myself that I would move on up soon. But it was clear as day: I needed an education if I ever wanted more leverage on what kind of wage I was making.

I decided that even though there was always a reason to worry about how little money we made or that we hadn't bought a house yet, it was equally as important to take some time for me and do things that I genuinely enjoyed doing. When I saw a posted course listing in my college about self-defense classes, I thought, "Why not? At least it's something purely for me."

It had nothing to do with being a wife, college student, or administrative assistant in an office. I always enjoyed taking classes and learning something valuable. Besides, if my neighborhood was anything to go by, you always had to be prepared for anything.

The classes were a nice way of breaking up my college, work, and married lives. They were taken in the evenings, and I enjoyed the exercise aspect of it too. The teacher was a stocky older Asian gentleman who used to be a black belt and now taught self-defense classes all around Miami.

The thing about these sorts of classes, though, is that quite often, people will have a story. Perhaps they were taken off guard and attacked, or perhaps someone tried to rob their car or their store. Either way, some people hold a grudge when they walk into these classes. They think they have something to prove. They don't realize that the whole purpose of the class is to *counteract* violence.

Jack was one of those people. I had complained about Jack

on my third day of class. He had slammed someone down on the mat and really hurt his shoulder. We had to perform for the class all the time, and practice moves on each other. I didn't want this lunatic drop kicking me on the mat to prove some kind of a point to himself. But the teacher virtually ignored me.

Thursdays were my longest days. They were the evenings that I would stay late at the firm, trying to get as much paperwork done as possible so that we could all leave on Friday at 5pm and go to happy hour. No one wanted to be stuck in the office after 5pm on a Friday. But it was intense, trying to fit the majority of my work into one evening, so I always made sure to do a self-defense class early Thursday morning before I reached the office. It helped me get some tension out of my body before going into the office and sitting at my desk for 6-8 hours.

That day, Jack was my partner, and I already felt a wedge of anxiety knot inside my stomach.

The teacher was imitating the move that we were supposed to be making, and my heart started to race. I didn't want Jack to try this move on me. But I was too afraid to say anything—after all, what was I going to do? Make a scene in the middle of the class?

"Alright, left side first."

That was Jack's side; he immediately kicked me right in the stomach, and I fell to the floor, cracking my hip and missing the mat. "ARGH!" I yelled from the pain.

"Step aside! Step aside, class."

I couldn't get up. I didn't know if it was the shock or whether I was genuinely injured, but it felt like something in my hip had moved—and there was a shooting pain going up my hip where I had fallen.

"He drop-kicked me to the fucking ground!" I screamed, and the teacher came around, moving the other students out of the way and gesturing to them to back up.

"Leila, don't worry. You're going to be fine. Tell me what the pain level is, from one to ten."

I was finding it difficult to breathe. I couldn't believe that

Jack did this to me and stood over me, like a puppy in trouble for pissing on the floor. I held onto my hip and winced. "Ten... it's a ten!"

"We're going to need to call an ambulance. Somebody, please call the paramedics!"

～

The fact that I was more worried about telling my office that I couldn't come into work that evening than I was about my stomach and hip might give you a clear indication as to how hard I was working.

This was the last thing that I needed. I was so upset with myself, with my teacher, and with that absolute nutcase, Jack, who had kicked me on the floor and damn near broke my hip in such a way that I now was having difficulty walking. I was on a stretcher in the back of an ambulance as they asked me whether I had any family that they could phone to meet me at the hospital.

"My husband," I panted as I felt the pain relief start to reach my body and bloodstream. "Call my husband. You can phone the Miami National Guard's station. He works there. His name is Nicholas."

Finally, I had someone that I could call on and who I could trust would be there for me. Despite there being psychos in my self-defense class, I knew that Nicholas would be able to make me feel better.

I tried not to think about what was going on and whether I needed surgery or not. This would be my first time in a hospital, and I was fretting about the bill that this very ambulance ride was going to cost.

～

By the time I was moved into a hospital room on the stretcher and Nicholas arrived, a nurse was taking my vitals and doing blood work. Everything was happening at lightning speed. The doctor explained what was going on, but I only took in half of it. My hip joint had been moved out of place and fractured, likely due to the kick and fall that I experienced thanks to Jack.

I couldn't believe it, but the doctor promised me that the surgery was not as serious as normal hip surgery—they needed to make some internal repairs with screws and metal plates and push my joint back into place, and I'd be able to leave the very next day. He said I needed to fast and that I wouldn't be heading to the operating room until some time in the early hours of the following morning. It was all so traumatizing. I couldn't believe the irony that taking a self-defense class had landed me in the hospital.

Nicholas was livid. "I'm gonna fucking sue that teacher. Who the fuck does he think he is? I'm gonna figure this out. I don't fucking care what it takes."

"Nick! You need to calm down. We don't have the money to sue anyone. It was... a freak accident."

In truth, I felt the same way as Nicholas, but there was one thing that was for sure: I was not about to consider suing anyone or getting into the legality of things before I had my surgery. Besides, I was already pretty confident that one of the guys in the law firm could help me get compensation or expunge the hospital bills, considering what had gone down. None of the lawyers worked pro bono, but I figured for me, they would.

Nicholas sat down beside me and held my hand. His face was pale, and I could tell that he was traumatized. I held onto his hand tightly, trying to reassure him that I was fine. We were waiting for a while, and around forty-five minutes later, the nurse who'd taken my blood came in to give me my results. They wanted to confirm that I was OK to have surgery, that I wasn't pregnant or had diabetes or anything like that, but her face was showing me something that had gone wrong. I always had a sixth sense for this sort of thing, and there was something she wasn't telling me. Had I really gone and injured myself?

Was I going to have to walk in a wheelchair for a period of time? Whatever it was, I needed to know right now so that I could begin to process it.

"What? What is it? Tell me," I said, and Nicholas held my hand, waiting for the nurse to announce her news.

"No, it's—I'm sorry. Is this your husband?"

"Hi, ma'am / I'm her husband, yes. Please tell me that everything is OK with my wife."

"No, of course, she is fine! You're fine, Leila. Only… were you aware that you're pregnant?"

Pregnant.

Pregnant? Me?

How?

"Pregnant?" I echoed my thoughts out loud and Nicholas looked at me in shock. As our eyes met, we burst into smiles— but my heart was racing, thinking about the baby and the injury and the surgery that I was about to go and have performed.

"No… No, we didn't know before. I mean, are you sure?"

The nurse nodded, smiling. She showed us a print-out piece of paper that had my blood results, including a checkmark beside "pregnant," and told us I was about four or five weeks along.

The nurse came over to my bedside, getting ready to check my vitals, which was probably a little out of control right about now, especially with my blood work.

"I'm gonna need you to stay calm, OK? Look, we still need to do the surgery, especially if you are going to be giving birth! But… it's very early…"

I looked at the nurse in despair. Every word she said was imprinted on my mind as I tried to consider being told that I was pregnant, only to wake up after surgery with the baby lost. The level of anxiety was real.

I thought back to my abortion and the feeling of waking up and knowing what I had done to the baby inside of my stomach. In this reality, with this man, now that I was wed and looking towards a brighter future, I wanted this baby more than anything. I tried not to let my mind think that God was punishing me, that all of this was happening to teach me some sort of a lesson—but this time, I wasn't in the hospital alone. Nicholas was right beside me, and he was able to hold the faith for the both of us. Tears streamed down my face as I felt my right arm tighten with the heart rate monitor.

"Listen to me, Leila. You're going to get through this. That baby is going to be fine, and so will you. This is meant to be, and I promise you that you are safe."

He kissed my hand, and I looked over at him. He was still in his uniform, and he gave me a kind smile as if to say that he was sorry I was the one who had to be brave here and not him for once.

But Nicholas had been brave. He had been brave enough to come home, all with the hope of marrying me, which had been done. We were now an item, and just as I had always wanted, a little baby was on its way to us. It was so difficult not to let myself get excited, to run away with the thought of having a child in my lap in as little as nine months.

'It's *very early*,' the nurse had said. Too early to hope? Too early to believe?

I was brought into surgery at four in the morning, and just before my anesthetic, I flashed back to the nurse who had seen me through my abortion with Harrison. I remember her talking about the celebrities in the magazines, how vacant my mind was in that moment, not allowing myself to become emotional about something painful that had to be done.

But this time was different. This time I needed to wake up with the baby still inside me. I needed this baby to grow and to become one of my own. I needed this baby to make it, and I needed my body to keep it safe and to heal. I prayed to God before I got into the operating room; this is what I remembered as I once again drifted off to sleep to be operated on while a baby was in my stomach.

Please, God,

> If you give us this child, I promise you that I will look after it with all of my heart, with my very being. With every dollar that I make and with every mouthful of food I take, I will make sure that this baby is cared for before me. I will make sure to be a loving and considerate mother. Please, God, give me this gift of life. Give me this chance to be a mother and to get it right. Please don't let this be it, God. Stay with me as I go into this surgery. Stay with me....

I drifted off to sleep, and Nicholas's face was the last thing I saw before going into a deep sleep.

~

'How much more can I tell you that I love you, except to say I do, I do, I do. A thousand times, over and over, in any lifetime, in any reality. I want to be with you.'

I could hear Nicholas speaking his vows—or an alternative version of his vows, but they were definitely the gist of them. It was as if his voice was narrating over me, from the sky or from the clouds; I wasn't so sure of where.

Here I was, sitting in the middle of a flower field. There were all types of flowers. There were daisies and roses, and there were even some wild rabbits in the field, further away from me. I thought to myself, "How delicate. I better not go up to them in case they get hurt."

Then, I started to worry about the rabbits in the field. What if a fox or other animal was going to come and eat them? They didn't have a cage or any type of hut to get into. But all the while I was feeling this physical sense of anxiety at the thought of the rabbits being in danger, I could still hear Nicholas's vows being recited over me. It was as if his words were blessing me and making me feel secure and safe about everything. The more I listened to them, the more comforted I was.

'In all that I do, I want to do it for you. I want to be with you until we are old and grey and we have nothing else to worry about except loving each other. Loving each other in the same way that we did when we were just two innocent teenagers. I want us to share the same love and then to pass that love onto our children.'

Our children.

Our children.

Who would be our children?

I started to look around for something, something that I was missing. Perhaps my house was supposed to be near this field, or Nicholas. Was Nicholas supposed to be here? Where was his voice coming from?

"Nicholas?" I called out to him. But then his vows stopped being recited. So I wondered if I had scared him away or if he had had to go back somewhere, go back to Missouri and not return. What if I was lost and I was taking too long to get back? How did I know that Nicholas would wait for me?

"Nicholas!" I called out again. The only thing that answered me was a break of thunder. It was a guttural rumble, and it was followed by an equally loud rumble straight after. A storm was coming. Somewhere in the distance, towards a dark green pinewood forest, I could hear murmured voices, mutterings that sounded like Nicholas.

"Nicholas, I'm coming!" I cried. I tried to run towards the forest, but my legs were walking in slow motion. It was as if I was stuck in tar, and it was so difficult to move them. Everything was going in slow motion for me except for my beating heart. My heart was beating so loud that I could hear it thumping in my ears.

Thump, thump, thump, thump. It was beating to the sound of the thunder, which kept breaking every five or so seconds.

"Nicholas, wait—the storm! Don't leave without me!"

I tried to move faster, but my legs would not allow it. So I just kept my focus on the pinewood trees. The pinewood trees. As soon as I could feel their bristled branches, it would mean that I was closer to Nicholas. I kept running in slow motion, refusing to give up, even though my legs did not want me to move. It was as if they were stiff and needed some oil to work properly.

"Please, wait! Can you hear me?"

Suddenly, I heard an echoed whisper: "Leila?"

That was Nicholas! I knew it was him. So I called back to him. "Nic, I'm here, I'm here! Can you see me?"

"Leila, it's OK. You can wake up now." The voice was soft and quiet and peaceful. And I knew then that it was time for me to open my eyes.

I was awake.

Everything was blurry as I got back in touch with reality. There was the beeping of my heart monitor and a couple of tubes placed on my wrist, putting me on a drip and keeping me hydrated. My mind was foggy, and I felt like my head was filled with concrete. It was a darkly familiar feeling. The last time I remembered feeling it was waking up after my abortion. And I recalled the empty feeling of knowing what once was never would be again. But would this be true for a second time?

"The baby," I murmured. "How's the baby?"

"Perfectly fine." Nicholas smiled at me and pet my hair back.

I dug underneath the covers for my stomach and put my hand across my belly, feeling the slight pain of my hip but also the sheer relief at knowing that I wouldn't have to say goodbye to this unformed thing.

I couldn't believe it. I had survived. And now I had something inside of me that I would fight for every day of my life. I closed my eyes and thanked God for taking care of me. It was finally time to celebrate the gift that Nicholas and I were given. We were going to be parents together.

"Oh man, you scared me, sweetheart." Nicholas breathed a sigh of relief as he leaned back into his chair. It looked like he hadn't slept a wink since he was at my bedside earlier that afternoon. And now the ticking clock on the wall was reading 6:25am.

"I never knew you were scared. You were so brave." My voice was hoarse after surgery, and my body felt weak, but knowing that my husband was here and that I was in the very early stages of recovery gave me hope.

"I knew you would be fine, Leila. You have that survival instinct inside of you. Now, we've gotta be brave for that little baby of ours."

I smiled weakly. After all of the excitement, all I could think about was going to sleep. Knowing that there was a precious baby in my stomach that needed rest as much as I did, I slept soundly and in peace.

HUSH LITTLE BABY, DON'T YOU CRY

The accident was the first hurdle of my pregnancy with my beautiful little girl, but it was by no means my last. In many ways, I think what happened to me that day in the self-defense class was a sort of sign that there were going to be significant challenges to come, and I would need to be prepared for all of them.

My job offered no paid maternity leave, which meant that I had to quit when I was six and a half months pregnant. It was devastating for me, but I was determined to find another law firm to work with. When your own job does not consider you as a valuable asset and a mother, you start to think of yourself in the same disregard.

It never occurred to me that I would go through struggles while pregnant and breastfeeding and looking after a newborn. All around me, so many women were having babies and taking to motherhood like a duck to water. I never for a second thought that I would be someone who was suffering and feeling completely lost.

I gave birth to a perfect little girl whom I named Nicole. I still remember the surreal moment when they first handed her to me. I was delirious from 20 hours of labor, but then I saw this tuft of black hair and a tiny little head, and the doctor pulled her out of me before setting her on the table and cleaning her up. I cried with the weak strength I had left, hearing my little girl's voice for the first time through her tiny tears. It was like music to my ears, hearing this perfect being that Nicholas and I had created, calling out to tell us that she had life and she was here. I will never forget that moment.

But Nicole's cries were more frequent than other babies'. I think I first noticed this when we were in the maternity ward, and the nurse was trying to help me get her to latch on for the first time. Nicole was squirming inside her blankets, screaming, crying with her eyes tightly shut and her little face red and scrunched up in her own pain and torment. It was breaking my heart. I was still so emotional from my post-birth hormones and from having had very little sleep since giving birth.

Here I was, alone in the hospital at two in the morning. My husband had gone home to get some sleep, but I wasn't able to sleep. I was left here in the hospital room, unsure as to how to feed my own baby. Seeing her in pain like that was breaking my heart, and I started to cry too. My cries were softer, they were whimpers, and there were a lot of tears. All I could do was watch as they dripped down to my neck and onto my nightdress, tiny little splashes as they landed on the cotton fabric. My tears were so close to Nicole that they were practically landing on her little skin. And I thought about how connected her pain was now to my pain. Her skin on my skin. How could I ever bear to see her upset or hurt? How was I going to do this?

"Don't worry, honey, plenty of mothers take some time to get their babies to latch on. Don't you go making it mean something. You're plenty able." My maternity nurse was a large Barbados woman who had shuffled and busied herself around my room when all the while, I tried to get Nicole's tiny lips onto my nipple to drink my milk. But she refused; even when I put my nipple into her mouth, she didn't recognize it as a source of food, and I had no idea why. Besides this, my nipples were extremely tender and in pain. This was making me so afraid of the idea of breastfeeding. But my entire life, my mother and grandmother and all of their mothers had said how crucial breastfeeding was. It was a real scene, watching American women use baby formula, having come from Haiti. It just wasn't a thing that was practiced there, and I remember how my Haitian aunties and mother would judge the American women they worked with who fed their babies formula. Not considering we live in different worlds as far as how busy American women are with careers and everything around us.

The formula vs. breastfeeding debate is the first judgemental challenge you face as a mother. Of course, any mother will know that this is a debated topic and that many women feel different types of way about it. But a lot of women don't consider how the mother feels who struggles with postpartum depression. I never imagined that I would have a difficult time latching my baby onto my breast milk. This went on for days so that the maternity nurse had to part-feed her formula from the hospital, as I tried and tried for hours to get Nicole to drink my milk. During those first couple of weeks, I barely slept. It was a nightmare, feeling like I couldn't properly feed my baby. I didn't understand what I was doing wrong. It felt like my body was failing me, failing my baby. Everything I needed to look after her was supposed to be within me, and yet, my baby was not drinking from my milk.

When Nicole put on enough weight, we were finally released from the hospital, and I had my maternity nurse visit us twice. The sensitivity of my nipples did not improve, but thankfully, Nicole's latching had. The nurse was delighted to see it.

"I told you, girl. She knows what's best: her mama's milk. She just needed some time."

I smiled at her, whimpering quietly as Nicole guzzled from my breastmilk, her hungry little mouth causing pain to my nipples. I winced in silence. I didn't want to put her off from feeding now that she was getting the hang of it. But the idea that I would have to go through this pain for the foreseeable future was a terrifying thing to consider.

The maternity center stopped visiting after that, and she said that she would call and check from time to time until Nicole was six months old. I missed her desperately, the same way that a grieving daughter misses their mother. I had my own mother and a stepmother who were very hands-on. But there was something about my Barbados maternity nurse. She didn't know me as a daughter or as a wife. She knew me as a patient. She trusted that I had what I needed within me to make this little girl of mine happy and feel cared for. I didn't have to impress her or hide my pain, although I did hide quite a lot of both my physical and mental pain. Most of all, I was feeling guilty for struggling when I had a perfect bundle of joy in my arms. I had seen the other mothers who weren't going home as quickly as me. I had met mothers who had only held their babies once before they were placed into an incubator. I'd met mothers who had irregular heartbeats and light bleeding and were bedridden for most of their pregnancy and bedridden. So why was I crying, hurting alone when I had a perfectly healthy baby right in front of me?

I don't know if Nicole was picking up on my struggles, but she soon started to suffer from colic. It was as if I had cursed myself with the worries and fears I was having from her not taking to breastfeeding as quickly as others. That first little cry would always be the happiest day in my life, but her cry began to change as she got a little older. At around two months, Nicole developed colic practically overnight. Suddenly, she got into the habit of crying every evening at 7pm at night. There was nothing that could settle her. I ran her temperature and gave her a little teaspoon of gripe water. I cut out dairy and wheat in my own diet. I already was abstaining from alcohol and coffee since pregnancy and hadn't gone back on either. But now, it seemed like I would have to sacrifice more of my life simply to stop my daughter from crying for hours on end.

It was torturous. On any occasion, hearing your baby cry—hearing any baby cry—instills a desire in people to make it stop, to have the mother comfort the baby and settle them back into bliss. The bliss that they deserve for being such innocent, perfect little beings. But my baby was crying, and I had no idea why. Every evening like clockwork, she would start to roar. Her little face would go red, and I would do everything in my power to make her stop.

I spent hours rocking her back and forth or burping her on my back. I burped her after every feed. She was a hungry little girl, and although my nipples winced at the sucking and guzzling for milk, I fed her regularly and on routine. I wasn't feeding her any formula and hadn't since she started feeding properly, so I couldn't understand what was wrong with her.

"Have you tried taking probiotics? Maybe it's a gut thing that you're passing on."

That's what one of the mothers at the breastfeeding class said to me. "What does my gut have to do with my breast milk?" I responded. She huffed a little since she could sense the irritation in my voice. "Well, it doesn't hurt to try."

Just like breastfeeding, people were full of suggestions for colic, as if I hadn't already tried everything in my power to stop my baby from crying.

"You've gotta get the nighttime bear. Oh my gosh, he's adorable. Works a dream!"

"Try getting her down for a nap at one, then not again till her bedtime."

"Look, it might be time to switch over to formula. You've had trouble from the beginning, huh?"

All of the constant opinions and suggestions were making things worse. I was so exhausted from waking up at night for feeds and then from the crying that I knew was to come every day, like clockwork, no matter how much I did. It made me feel like a failure of a mother. I couldn't understand what I was doing wrong that was making my baby feel unsettled.

It was at this time that Nicholas truly came through for me.

He was such an attentive father, and while I lay in bed, trying to get caught up with some hours of sleep I had missed, he would coo and play with his little girl. He brought me my food in bed if I wasn't up to going downstairs, and he never commented on how I wasn't wearing makeup or that I hadn't felt like showering. The unpredictabilities that came with motherhood, as well as the guilt that was coming with my feeling depressed, allowed me to keep my postpartum depression a secret from everyone except for Nicholas. He held me in his arms as I would cry at night, listening to the wails of our little girl as we tried to settle her in her Moses basket, in her cot that swung, in the rocking chair, in our bed.

I had bought the damn bear that sang and was supposed to be wondrous. I remember going into my breastfeeding class and the women gathering around me, dying to know the update on whether the bear worked or not. My eyes were tired, and there were dark bags underneath them. I hadn't been to the class in a couple of weeks. I was avoiding their questions, no matter how much good intent was there. I had joined the breastfeeding class on the advice of my maternity nurse, who said that it was important I found a community of women to lean on. These women all had their own struggles; I do not doubt any mother's struggle in comparison to my own. But this was at a time when it was seen as acceptable to let someone go for having a baby and not offering them maternity leave. So, if a woman could hide some struggles that she was having as a new mother, she would. Keeping up appearances was more important than expressing your feelings.

"How was the baby bear?"

"She loves it, doesn't she?"

"I used it to sleep train my first."

They came over to me and Nicole, who was bundled up in a blankie as I walked over to join the circle. I thought about admitting the truth and telling them that the bear had done nothing but cost me $30 that I couldn't afford right about now. I thought about telling them how I hadn't showered because I was so afraid Nicole would start crying if I left her, and I couldn't take any more excessive amounts of crying during the day, because I knew that at 7pm every night, she would start again for one hour, maybe two.

There was no rhyme nor reason for it. She wasn't unwell, I had gotten her checked, and she was still too young to be showing any allergies—she was only drinking my breast milk.

The group and my mother kept telling me to wait it out, wait it out. It was just a phase; I would get through it, and so would she. In the meantime, I had the women's support. But how could I admit to this group of mothers that their advice had failed me? How could I tell them that, in fact, they were wrong and nothing was helping? How could I tell them that on some days, I wanted to scream so loudly, blood-curdling screams, if only to feel something other than complete exhaustion? The way I saw it, I had to hold myself together. If one mother lost it, then there was the potential of every mother losing it.

So I swallowed my tears and smiled at the ladies.

"Works like a dream." They squealed and *ahh*-ed in response.

That night, when I got home and Nicole's crying commenced, I accidentally stepped on the musical bear. I brought him up to her face, and she went redder and redder, squeezing her little fists and refusing to be comforted by anyone or anything. I laid her down on her bassinet, and I cried myself, hugging the bear as I listened to his melodic tune, which played twice every time he was pushed to.

I can't do this, I thought. I started to think of some very dark thoughts. I considered walking out of my house door and never looking back. But these thoughts never gained any roots. Instead, I tried to focus on fixing something other than my daughter. This was a difficult phase she was going through, and I had to believe that it wouldn't last forever.

~

I put all of my attention and focus on trying to find work again, just three months after giving birth. I used Nicole's fifty-minute afternoon nap time to search on a very old computer that we were given as a wedding present. I also looked at the news-paper ads and highlighted anything that looked like it would suit me. I still had no idea how I was going to manage, but Nicholas's parents had been over in the apartment quite a lot. They were very hands-on, and I was grateful to have them there, helping with the cooking and the cleaning and taking Nicole off of my hands. Still, I dreaded to think what both Nicholas and they would have to say about my going back to work so soon.

Nicholas was still only making $10 an hour, and money was an issue. So from that perspective, work was something I didn't have much choice in considering. I needed to start making money if we were going to pay for this baby's education and food and clothes, and all of the things that it needed to survive in this world. There was immense pressure on me. Not only did I have to be her sole physical provider as she was a newborn, but I also needed to consider being her financial provider. Both Nicholas and I were not making enough for one of us to stop working. That was the reality we had faced when getting pregnant.

I applied for a firm that was hiring an administrative assistant for $9 an hour, which was a two-dollar increase compared with what I was getting at my last place. It wasn't much, especially since I would have to be working part-time at first, with Nicole being so young. But it was hope. It was some-thing separate from my current reality that I knew for a fact I was good at.

~

A couple of days after applying, I received a phone call at the house. Nicole had just woken up from her nap, and she was fussy, with some trapped wind. Sometimes her colic came on earlier than other days, or sometimes she was fussier. On this day, in particular, she was screaming and crying in my arms so loudly. I half-expected the person on the other end of the line to be Nicholas, letting me know that he was doing overtime again.

"He-hello. I'm sorry. Is this Leila Nelson?"

"Speaking!" I said, suddenly trying to sound different and not panicked and exhausted. It was a formal voice on the other end of the line.

"Yes, I'm calling... "The voice spoke louder over the cries of my baby. "I'm calling about the admin position! Are you—are you still available?"

I tried to shush Nicole and soothe her without making any obvious baby noises.

"Oh, yes, I'm available," I chirped. It disturbed me a little how easily I could change my voice from sounding utterly desperate to chirpy.

"Great! Well, listen, Leila, I know you have your hands full!"

I laughed effortlessly, trying to hide all of the torment that Nicole's cries, especially those that were outside of her usual hour crying window, caused me.

"I'm going to email you over some interview times on the email attached to the resume. Does this work for you?"

"Perfect, thank you so much!"

I hung up and walked straight over to the computer, getting my emails on the screen. I shushed Nicole as she started to settle down as soon as I was off the phone. Typical, I mused.

But there was an electric feeling of adrenaline inside of me. That phone call had handed me hope. It gave me the prospect of getting more money for our family. It also handed me the opportunity to get away for a while and feel like myself again. I thanked God every day that I was a mother, even on the days when nothing could soothe Nicole's cries. But there was no doubt that I was seriously struggling. I needed a way out without putting myself or my family at risk. And this was something that was controlled, familiar, and professional.

The email invite for the interview came, and I jumped for joy in my seat while still keeping Nicole safely in my arms. I snuggled into her and inhaled her precious scent. She looked up at me with a blank expression, and I touched her button nose with my finger.

~

The interview was the following Friday at 9:45am. I had managed to get into one of my old power suits that I wore around the previous office. It had a sleek cut and a sharp, black blazer with a matching above the knee-length skirt. My hair was tied up in tight short curls, and I put some lipstick and mascara on, swapping baby spit-up for a spritz of perfume. Nicholas looked me up and down as he put on his uniform in the same room.

"Wow! Doesn't my baby look delicious?"

He came over and kissed me on the cheek. "Uh, professional too, I hope."

"Baby," he said to me, his voice low. "You're gonna get it."

I marched around after Nicholas's mother, who was taking care of Nicole for the longest span of time since I had given birth. This was so difficult for me to maneuver, even though I completely trusted Nicole in her care—but in my eyes, no one knew how to look after my baby as well as I did, and even I was finding it difficult.

"Now, you know to rock her gently after she feeds, I left some breast milk in the fridge, and there are about twelve ounces there—you won't need it all."

Marta barely paid attention to me. She was too enamored with her granddaughter and looked into her eyes as Nicole cooed back at her, acting like the little angel.

"Oh—and the picture book! The picture book she likes with

the monkeys and the mirror at the end, she likes to see herself. She smiles and moves her little arms up and down."

Marta never answered me but kept her gaze on Nicole as I ran around, trying to find every accessory and playtoy I could that would prevent Nicole from having one of her screaming matches, with which I had become all too familiar.

Marta looked up at me and gave me a knowing look. "You know, you're gonna be leaving her for a lot longer if you get this job."

I hadn't gotten as far as considering that yet. And even though it was completely true, it angered me that Marta was bringing it up now as I walked out the door.

"Stop fussing! Everything is OK. Sure didn't I raise five of my own? Don't worry now, girl. Go on."

She turned away from me with Nicole in her arms and continued cooing at her.

I made sure to catch the tears in my eyes before they fell onto my face for fear of smudging the newly applied makeup. I kissed Nicole's forehead and then grabbed my keys, making my way out of the house without my fifth limb.

The firm was larger than my last place, and it had a marble lobby that was pristinely clean. They practiced in property and family law, which both interested me. I sat in the lobby on a cream leather couch and was already offered a coffee by two separate people before my boss arrived to greet me.

"Leila! Such a pleasure to meet you." Tom was the man I had spoken to on the phone, and he was also the man hiring. I was happy to put a face to his voice, especially such a friendly face. He had a large stout mustache and thinning hair on top of his head. He wore a dark brown suit with a white shirt and yellow tie, and he introduced me to all of the offices and some of the people sitting inside before we reached the interview room.

We sat down in a room with a large oak desk, some family photos and degrees hung on the wall. Tom had my resume in front of him and was skimming over it. I noticed that he had written some notes in places, which gave me further hope. I wasn't some random person walking into his office that he had totally forgotten about.

"So," he beamed, looking up at me. "Tell me about yourself."

I didn't know what to say. It was the last question that I was expecting. Or maybe it was the way he asked it. It didn't feel like a professional question, more so a personal one. But I wasn't going to fall for that trap and start spilling my guts out, so I answered professionally anyway.

"Well, I worked with Henry J. Lyons for about three years. It was a great job, really! I left once I became heavily pregnant with my daughter—"

"Aah, great set of lungs she's got." Tom smiled, making the connection between who the screaming baby was on the phone the last time we spoke. I laughed awkwardly, not knowing whether to be embarrassed or not.

Then Tom pointed a framed portrait in front of me. It showed him smiling by a willow tree with three girls, each cuter than the next, and a beautiful wife.

"Now, imagine being the only guy in that house when they all reach their teens."

I smiled at him, realizing that this was a safe space to talk about families and motherhood and everything that came with that. "I don't envy you." I laughed.

Immediately I felt more relaxed. We went through some of the accounts I was filing for in Henry J. Lyons, and Tom asked me a number of basic questions. How many cases had I filed to date? Did I understand non-disclosure? What were my reading and assessment skills like? And then the final question: When can you start?

I stared back at him blankly for a moment.

"You mean… you want to hire me?" I asked.

Tom laughed at me. "Well, of course! Look, Leila, you clearly have the experience that we need for this role. I can tell that you're intelligent, you're studying in college, and your previous employer had only good things to say about you. Tell me, is this doable? Now, the hours are nine to five, but you have the option of taking a half-day on Fridays. But—Leila…"

And there it was. The but. The doubt. And why wouldn't he be doubtful? He was about to hire a woman who probably looked exhausted and had a three-month-old at home. Now that it was becoming more real, I didn't know if I was making the right decision. Would this even be possible? How was I supposed to leave my daughter every day for $9 an hour? But I had to go back to work eventually. And here was this lovely man who was considering hiring me and even trying to give me a more flexible work life. I had to take it.

"Look, I'm in. Truly, I need this, Tom. I have a beautiful little girl, and thankfully, I have support. I'm a great mother—but I am also a great worker, and I want to do both."

Tom smiled at me.

"OK then, you're in."

~

I went home in my suit and with my head held high. I couldn't believe that I managed to get a job just three months after giving birth. It gave my mood the lift that it needed on that day.

But at that point, I wasn't aware of the complexities of postpartum. I didn't know that just because I had found a job did not mean my postpartum was at bay. If anything, I had just signed a contract that promised the impossible. I was now supposed to have a newborn, be away from her the entire day, and come back home just around the time when she started crying for no apparent reason. Motherhood was my first true lesson of sacrifice, and those sacrifices were far from over.

14

THE BABY BOOM

For all the times that Nicholas had claimed we weren't having enough sex or lovemaking, I sure as hell had enough kids. By the time Nicole was just nine months old, I had become pregnant with my son. This, of course, was a joyous occasion, and we were both over the moon with the news. But the financial stresses that we were under as a family meant that I needed to return to the law firm that I was working in long before I was truly ready.

I had never considered what it was like for my mother, working and being our sole provider. She worked in jobs at hotels with minimum wage and needed to make up a lot of hours just for us to get by. Truthfully, I don't know how she did it. Here I was, a mother of two babies under three, working and feeling like my heart was being ripped out of my chest. This was when my children were being minded by their grandparents. It didn't matter to me. I yearned to be with my babies, but it wasn't financially possible for us at that time.

The law firm was busy, and I understood the work in the same way that I had understood it in my last job. It wasn't very intellectually stimulating, and I still yearned for something more. As a new mother of two very young children, I felt more connected than ever to my own mother.

I thought about the days where my mother would have to clean toilets for below minimum wage. I thought about how she was the only person there for us, truly there for us. My father was constantly coming and going, showing up whenever he felt like it, which wasn't often. I never understood the reason, and he never bothered to explain it. But I can tell you that it wasn't for his work. It wasn't because he needed to travel. It wasn't because he was a doctor or a scholar or someone else with a demanding job. He was simply an avoidant.

All throughout my childhood, I never anticipated him coming back. It's not like he made everything a whole lot better when he was there or anything. My mother was always the sole person to take care of us. But I saw the effects of what that stress did to her. I knew how strenuous her job was, how she had to deal with shitty guests, day in and day out. I knew how she stressed about what groceries we were able to buy and when bills were due. I knew that Dad wasn't giving her child support because we always had to share. It was a strange feeling of knowing that one parent would do anything for you and the other parent might not even show up. On the days in the firm when I was really struggling to be away from my kids, I thought of my mother.

I thought about her hard-working hands, making the dinner when we were toddlers and she had returned from a long shift. I thought about the anxiety she must have felt when she realized that there was another evening, another week, another month where my father wasn't showing up. I thought about how difficult it must have been for her to have to be the one to tell us the bad news. Those mornings, when we recognized that his car was gone and all we had for an answer was our mother's blank expression. She had no clue either. I thought about her never being able to have a choice as to where she worked; she always needed to consider us first. Sometimes, I liked to daydream about where my mother would have worked if she had had the opportunity. I always thought that she would be an excellent school teacher. The way she placed lessons onto us and her attention to detail, as well as the way she interacted with children. I imagined my mother in a big, bright classroom, with a chalk blackboard, telling the kids about Haiti, the beautiful country that she had come from. I thought about how it would have felt, having a teacher from the place that I was so connected to yet far away from.

These were the types of things that I thought about while working at the law firm, when I was running on empty sleep, trying not to cry over not being with my children, and keeping my head above water. I already knew that I had more opportunities than my mother had. I had a husband for one, a husband that was great with our children and who was earning a living. This was more support than my mother had ever been given, and yet, I was finding working and being a mother really difficult.

There was another reason why working at this law firm was difficult. I felt like I was stuck in a poverty trap. No matter how many hours I picked up, there was never going to be enough money to get my kids through college and all of the other things they needed, so long as I was stuck on a low-wage job. I worked so hard in the law firm and had a great attitude. But how was I ever going to feel valued as a worker while earning $9 an hour?

There were also times when I was asked to serve the clients as they came into the office. This invariably left me feeling strange. For one, I was not a waitress. I sure as hell wasn't getting tips for getting a client their tea or coffee. It reminded me that I was at the bottom of the company, despite being given more responsibilities and constantly being told by my boss how he thought I was intelligent and a great asset to the company. But then, why the hell was I being asked to serve clients coffee? To me, it degraded my position, and it made me feel less than.

One day, I had left my four-month-old son Avery and thirteen-month-old Nicole at home with their grandparents. It had been harder to leave for the office that day. Avery was beginning to communicate with others through his smiles and cooing sounds. It was such a joy, seeing his beautiful little face light up when he thought something was funny or when he saw his reflection in the mirror of his jungle gym. That night, he had been a little restless, and I was up late feeding. I didn't mind waking up with Avery. It hurt less to breastfeed him than Nicole, as my body somehow decided that this time, it wouldn't be excruciatingly painful. These feeding hours in the middle of the night, when everyone else was fast asleep, were some of my favorite hours. I used to stare at Avery's face as he nuzzled into my chest, softly snoring after being in a sleep coma. I rocked him back and forth and felt so thankful for these private hours where it was just my baby and me. No outside world, no one telling me how to hold him or how to prevent cradle cap, no boss telling me to get clients their coffee or to work overtime for the third time that week. This was just my baby and me. For me, I was grateful for our time together. Even if it meant that I had to do without sleep.

I yearned to be back in my rocking chair with my baby the next day when I would be stuck at work, going over piles of papers for a new client and being stuck in the yellow hospital lighting of the office, making lists in my head about things I had to do as soon as I got home. I made lists for everything. I would usually give these lists to my mother-in-law, although I am not sure how much she actually looked at it. I would plan the dinners for the week and the grocery shop that needed to happen for the dinners to be cooked, I'd pack the children's bags if they were going to be staying at my In-law's house, if one of them had a cold or a runny nose, I would stress about them for the entire day, calling every one or two hours to check up on them. In general, it was difficult to keep my mind in the present moment, so long as I was without my babies and not in a place of work that was meeting my requirements for pay and career progress.

It was on this day in particular when I was running off of minimal sleep and daydreaming about being back with Avery that I was asked by Sheila to serve one of the clients from the Dolphin football team.

I didn't much like Sheila. She was a Floridian native who had come from quite a lot of money, and I always felt like she looked down on me. She would glance up at my hairstyle and make a point of commenting when it looked less "done." She would cackle and laugh with the male staff but make little to no effort with me as one of the one women her age in the office. There was a general feeling of "us and them." And I was the "other" to her—just a typical administrative assistant who could be told at any moment to make coffee or to run down to the store to load up on soft drinks for the clients, even though the rest of the staff, clients, and management adored me. I think this was what really bothered Sheila. Essentially, she was reminding me of my inferiority. Everyone else was so incredibly busy; how could Sheila possibly have the time to serve the clients coffee and to be responsible for replenishing the creamer?

Sheila tapped on my desk, and I jumped, not expecting her to be beside me. I was scanning my computer for cradle cap remedies. I quickly ex'd out of my search engine and smiled up at her.

"Hi, what's going on?" I asked.

"Coffee. The Dolphin's football manager is inside with one of the players. Semi-skimmed milk, please." Then she just as quickly scooted off, unwilling to deal with my protests or the forlorn look on my face. I sighed slightly to myself, knowing that I wasn't in a position to say no to anyone. When you are at the bottom of the pay scale, you are usually the most vulnerable for a firing. Ironic, considering the fact that I was costing the company the least, and at times, it felt like I was doing more than the lawyers themselves, who enjoyed lengthy lunches that often involved one too many beers and a nap in their offices after.

I stepped into the office and saw my boss as well as the manager for the Dolphins football team and his player. Raymond, my boss, gave me the same friendly hello as he always did. He was a lovely guy to work with, which was probably the reason I had not yet asked for a pay raise. That and the fact that I had become pregnant shortly after being hired by him. These were not the days where maternity leave was readily available and respected.

"Well, look who it is, my favorite employee. Hi, Leila. How are you doing?" Raymond beamed as I sat the cup of coffee down next to the Dolphins manager and smiled at him.

"Hi. I'm doing well, thank you, and it's a pleasure to see you again, Mr. Jackson."

The Dolphins football team was one of the firm's favorite clients, and there was a great buzz in the office when one of the players came in accompanied by their managers. They also usually had some pretty colorful cases going on, but all I got to see was the information that I read from the cases when filing.

We exchanged small talk for a while, and I made a point of staying longer and using my charm to communicate with Mr. Jackson since I knew that Raymond appreciated that. I walked out of the room and smiled. It was a genuine smile. Despite the fact that I had some notions about serving clients, it was always a good feeling to be well received. It made me think about how much more of a credit I could be to a company if only I were given the opportunity.

I walked back into the kitchen to clean up the coffee containers, and Sheila walked in at the same time. She looked me up and down and smirked, staring at my blouse.

"I hope you didn't serve the client like *that*."

What could she possibly mean? It wasn't even lunchtime yet, and I didn't usually drink coffee at work. I glanced down at my blouse to see two large imprints of breast milk that had leaked from my bra. I gasped audibly, unable to hide my devastation at the discovery.

I couldn't bear to look at Sheila and her smirking face. It was all I could do to drop everything in my hands at the sink and run out of the kitchen directly to the bathroom.

Once alone, I walked into a stall and locked myself inside, unable to face myself in the mirror in my own humiliation. Here, I cried silent tears, grabbing a tissue from the toilet dispenser and attempting to dab the damp stains that had come through my nursing bra. I knew that it was utterly useless, it was a blue top, and the imprints of milk could not have been more obvious. Hoping that no one would come into the bathrooms, I unlocked my stall and tried tackling the stains at the sink. But I had no gusto to do so. All I could think about was how dumb I must have looked, serving the coffee to one of our biggest clients with breast milk leaking out of my top. I thought of Sheila's smirked face.

"I hope you didn't serve the client like *that*." Like what? Like a mother who had just given birth to her second child only months previous? Like a woman who was trying to keep her head above water as she navigated two babies and a full-time job that was paying her less than $10 an hour? For me, it was a simple sign. It was the sign that I had been looking for. I just couldn't help but feel as if I wasn't supposed to be there. My body was now telling me that I was supposed to be with my baby, feeding him. Meanwhile, my work employee was trying to embarrass me for the natural reaction my own body was having from being away from my son.

I looked at myself in the mirror, at my tear-stained and exhausted face, at the two large imprints of breast milk on my blouse that I couldn't help but feel deep shame for. But, shame for what, I asked myself? Shame for being a mother? Shame for being human? Shame for feeling any type of shame at all.

I crumpled up the piece of tissue paper in my hand and threw it in the trash can. I marched out of the bathroom and back to my desk, without considering looking up for a second, took my purse, and stepped out of the office. There was only one thing I was certain of, and that was that I was going home to feed my baby. As far as I was concerned, Sheila and her mom-shaming could go straight to hell.

15

UNDERAPPRECIATED

$\mathcal{B}$ eing a wife and a working mother who was going to school as well as taking hours at the law firm had its obvious challenges. But I think more than anything else, I was most worried about becoming "stuck." There was no doubt about it—I was managing this entire firm and getting no recognition for it. To me, I knew my value. I was just waiting for everyone else to catch up and see it.

After the breast milk incident, I took two days off from going into the office and instead stayed at home with the babies while still maintaining my work and school hours. It was a time of reflection and a time to consider what I truly wanted out of life. There were many positives to the law firm that I was working in. But as a working parent trying to buy a house for my children, I had bigger goals than what they were able to offer me. I felt far past serving clients' coffees and was hungry to get more into a leadership role, one where my pay could reflect the hard work that I was more than willing to commit to. But of course, leaving a job when we had four mouths to feed was not exactly on the agenda.

I didn't know whether Sheila had let the others in the office know about my faux pas, and I didn't know whether Raymond had even noticed the stain on my blouse when I had been with him and the client, but I still felt a sense of nerves as I walked into the office the next Monday morning. Something in the air had changed for me, and it was impossible to shake. I was definitely in a negative space with my work, and I didn't know how to resolve that.

It was a busy and bustling morning, much like any other morning on a Monday at the firm. Raymond was standing and leaning against one of the desks, making a schedule for the upcoming cases and leaving stacks of papers of the admin desks to sort through, as well as answering questions that had arisen from the lawyers going to court the previous Friday. I had made a real effort with my appearance this morning, and I tried not to blame myself for feeling obligated to do this. It was a difficult thing, trying to shift the feeling of embarrassment to one of complete understanding. Breast milk was breast milk. It wasn't some ominous thing that had to be hidden away from the workforce. It was simply the biology of my body. But my heart ached whenever I thought about the incident. It was a bare wound that made me feel vulnerable and hurting like I hadn't hurt before. To me, it was the crescendo of all that I had been through as a new mother since I had Nicole and struggled badly with postpartum depression. Now, my breasts were working with me and ready to feed my hungry child, and here I was, having to squeeze out excess breast milk in the bathrooms at my lunch break, or else I would have a spillage. The only thing that I knew how to do was tailor my appearance on that Monday morning so that if there was nothing else in my life that I felt I had control over, at least my sleek ponytail, perfectly painted lipstick, and neat black suit, teamed with a blazer to conceal my blouse, if needs be, at least I had control over how I looked. "Dress for the job you want, not the job you have," I said to myself that morning, laughing a little at my own conundrum.

I wanted to slip back into the office unnoticed, but as

Raymond was making his morning announcements, he made a huge deal of me.

"There she is, my favorite employee—and my, my, you are looking ravishing today, Leila."

The others said hello as I settled into the room, and I smiled, evidently a little more reserved than usual. I was certainly a character in the office, and being a social person, it was always in my nature to make friends and to be popular in school and workplaces. Today of all days, however, I still felt like slinking in my corner and just getting on with the work in silence. But Raymond wasn't having any of it.

"Leila, actually—quick one in my office. Let's go!"

His chirpy demeanor stopped me from thinking that there was anything ominous going on. Even still, it wasn't like him to take me into his office. I prayed to God that he wasn't going to bring up the breast milk incident and make me want to be swallowed by the ground any more than I already did.

When Raymond closed the door, he took a seat and gestured to me to do the same. He had this big beaming smile on his face like he had just won the lottery.

"How are you doing?" he asked, in his sincere way, like he genuinely expected and cared about an answer.

"I'm fine," I said, smiling.

Raymond hesitated, not used to me being more reserved. But he still held an excitement in his face that I knew wouldn't leave until he had a chance to tell me what he wanted to.

"Leila, what can I say? You go above and beyond the job role here, you know the filing system like the back of your hand, and you are incredibly knowledgeable in our cases, client files, and maintaining the office day to day. When I leave for vacation, I have no worries that the firm will continue to run smoothly, and clients will be answered as long as you're around. The clients and everyone else around here love you."

Raymond was no stranger to giving compliments and praising me for my work. That is part of the reason why I like working with him so much. But this seemed slightly more rehearsed as if he were making an announcement. For a brief second, I allowed myself to think that regardless of my unfinished college degree and my lack of official qualifications, perhaps Raymond was really going to take a chance on me and promote me to a higher position. I scanned my brain to consider for a moment what it would be like if he were to make that change and simply trust that I could do it from the work ethic that he was currently praising me for. Our Paralegal in the firm had been out due to an ongoing health problem. Raymond had some temps in and out, but no one knew the books like Rita. Since her absence, I had been doing more of the heavy lifting and helping out as and when I needed to. It was the sort of knowledge that could only be acquired through working in this particular office and from being in the industry for a number of years, which I had been.

Raymond continued.

"Throughout all my years here, there have been few people as competent and as valuable as I think you are to this firm. And it's time you get the recognition you deserve!"

By God, I thought. Perhaps he was actually doing it. If I were to replace Rita as the Legal Secretary, it would only be a temporary position, of course. Most people need to earn their Bachelor's degree to be considered. But the more I thought about it, the more Raymond's decision made sense. Having Rita's wage for even six to eight months would dramatically change my and my family's finances. I knew that the average salary of a Legal Secretary was around $50,000. That was more than double the amount of my annual salary. And even though it took me a minute to get the ropes, even though everyone in the office would be aware that I wasn't technically qualified, I think everyone could agree that I was up for the challenge and heck—if Raymond believed in me, then who else did I need?

"Raymond, I—I want to do anything I can for this company in order to prosper. I'm thankful for my job, of course! But I've felt like I am ready for a bigger challenge for quite some time now."

Raymond nodded his head and smiled as if he were waiting for me to finish.

"Uh-huh. Sure! And that is precisely why I'm here speaking with you today, Leila. I have some excellent news for you."

Here it was, the moment I had been waiting for. The change that I had seen coming, that I had felt underneath my skin. The itch that I needed to get onto my career ladder and finally get out of the poverty trap I was living in.

"I'm increasing your wage by $500 annually." Raymond beamed with the landing of the great big news that he had been so excited to tell me about—only I had completely misread him.

Silence. For a moment, I couldn't think of anything to say. Raymond's big beaming smile started to lesson as he wasn't getting the reaction he had seemingly been expecting. My heart sank into my stomach as I felt the weight of disappointment over what he had just told me.

"Are you... are you not happy?" he asked, and this annoyed me even further. How could Raymond be so far removed from my own reality? Did he care at all about the livelihood and the future I was trying to prepare for myself and my family? Calculations were swarming in my brain as I considered exactly how much more an hour Raymond was proposing to give to me and how on earth he could have thought that would be met with my overwhelming gratitude and thanks.

"No, I am I. Thank you, Raymond. Thank you! I just... I have some emails to get back to." I smiled and thanked him once more, trying my best to keep my composure, before excusing myself and going to my desk.

My mind was racing, and I felt hot underneath my skin. I divided $500 by the average 2,086 work hours in a year, excluding weekends and holidays. I looked back at the cents that were displayed on the calculator. Raymond was offering me a pay rise of just 24 cents per hour. I couldn't believe it. He had estimated my enormous value to the company at just 24 cents extra an hour.

The disappointment fluctuated throughout the day, as I kept my conversation with Raymond to myself, despite there being a couple of other admin temps that were in the same shoes as me. But none that had given what I had given. I was working a job that was way above the expectations of an administrative assistant temp. No wonder Raymond was so happy, I mused to myself. I was about the cheapest labor he had. The fact that I didn't have a Bachelor's degree was, if anything, a financial advantage to him. He could get me to fill in on the jobs that were above my pay grade without me ever actually being paid the usual amount those positions were paid. It was humiliating.

That evening, I spoke things over with Nicholas. Lately, it felt as if we barely got to see one another. The baby bubble had burst with the need for both of us to go out and keep earning. Sometimes, he had incredible momentum and encouragement for both of us. He was my shoulder to lean on, and he believed in me and in what we were capable of. But other days, he was just as exhausted and as exasperated as I was. I guess I wasn't much of a shoulder for him either. We were both going through it.

Avery was so close to being asleep in Nicholas's arms, and I loved the way he looked at our children. It was such an incredible gift, having children with someone whom I had known for such a long time and whom I was able to watch and witness become an incredible parent.

I sat in front of my computer, reiterating my conversation with Raymond for the umpteenth time and finding no solace in my frustration. Nicholas was stirring the rice in the pot as he held Avery close. He always insisted on holding the babies as soon as he got home, no matter what else he was doing. His physique was still strong and masculine as he was working in the police force, where they had a gym close by. Our conversation had been halted momentarily as he rocked Avery back and forth, and we kissed his bundle of curls before Nicholas crept into Avery's room and put him down into his crib. Nicole had miraculously gone down earlier than her brother and slept soundly in her crib next to them.

Nicholas came back into the room and handed me a glass of wine, which I was just about to protest since I was still breast-feeding Avery, but Nicholas got there first.

"It's low alcohol, only 5%. One glass for the working mommy won't hurt." Then he kissed me on the forehead and uncracked a beer, attending to our bean sauce that was bubbling in the pot. I looked around at our quaint little apartment. The kids' toys and jungle gyms were still out, Nicole had spilled some of her spinach on the carpet earlier in the day that I hadn't gotten around to scrubbing properly, and since we didn't have a dishwasher, I knew that either Nicholas or I would have to wash the utensils before we could even begin to eat. But I couldn't help but feel grateful for my little family. Regardless of what was going on in work and regardless of the continual financial and life stresses, I knew that my love for Nicholas was true, and I was so thankful to have him there with me and for me.

I sighed, taking a small sip of my sparkling wine and feeling a phantom relief from the stresses of the day with the very first taste of it.

"It's just... I just cannot believe the balls. I mean, the way he came in there as if he were going to make me partner!"

Nicholas took a sip out of his beer and laughed. "Five hundred dollars sounds a lot better than 24 cents. It's all a matter of perspective. I'm sure the old guy thinks he's doing you a favor. But you've gotta wonder, how would he feel if you explained to him how your pay rise wouldn't even cover one pack of diapers a week?

I thought about it. One thing was for sure of all the things that I had picked up through my time working at the firm. Words and an executed argument could get you very far. It was true. After all, Raymond debated things and negotiated for a living. If I was ever going to get to the position that I truly wanted to be, and if I was ever going to make something of myself, then I needed to stand up for myself and what I thought I was worth.

I thought about how Raymond had caught me off guard, how much I wanted to let him know how I was feeling without coming across as petty or ungrateful. I took another sip out of my wine and opened up my emails, getting an email ready for Raymond. It was now or never. I had to say how I felt before going back into the office the next day. After all, this wasn't personal. This was business.

Dear Raymond,

I want to thank you for meeting with me earlier and informing me of my hourly pay rise of 24 cents an hour. I regret to inform you that this has left me feeling undervalued, perplexed, and quite frankly, a little insulted.

I think that it is fair to say that I go above and beyond in my job to facilitate the law firm in whatever way I can.

As you know, I have taken on more responsibilities and duties than is to ever be expected by someone ranked at my position and on my pay grade. I am managing this entire firm and have dedicated so much of my time to seeing this law firm soar. We have seen an influx of clients, and as you know, it has been my job to essentially manage this entire firm, gathering information from all of the attorneys to ensure that everything runs smoothly.

With a paralegal or someone undergoing the same amount of tasks and responsibilities as I have, they are being paid at least $45,000 a year. To be offered a mere 24 cents on top of my $9 an hour is less than encouraging. To put things into perspective, the pay raise that you have offered me does not even cover one bag of diapers per week. This is why I cannot accept this as a meaningful pay raise and as recognition that my work is being valued at a regular rate as anyone else working my job. I hope that you can consider what I have written and that you understand where I am coming from.

Kind Regards,
    Leila Nelson

After reading over it a dozen times with Nicholas, I pressed send, feeling a jolt of excitement and exhilaration as I did so.

"You don't get anywhere in life without a bit of confrontation, baby." Nicholas cheered me with my low alcohol beverage, and we enjoyed the evening watching TV and eating the rice and beans he had prepared for us.

The next morning, Raymond was quick to ask me into his office. My heart was pounding. Despite knowing I was doing way above what he was paying me, I felt almost guilty for asking for more. I thought about all of the men that had walked into his office, fresh out of law school and with some student debt that would be paid off by their trust funds. I thought about the confidence and guffaw of some of the attorneys I directly managed and helped handle all of their clients and cases each day. I had to convince myself of my worth and the value that I was giving to this company, even if no one else was willing to do so.

Raymond sat across from me with a much more somber expression on his face than he had worn the previous day.

"Look, firstly, I want to apologize. These years of working at the firm have done you some. You sure as hell know how to argue your case."

Raymond laughed, and I laughed with him, timidly and a little unsure. This conversation could go either way, but I knew one thing, this was for sure. I was working in a managerial position and being paid at an entry-level wage, all the while my children were the ones who were taking the hit. This was not worth leaving my children for. But I was still eager to see if Raymond had considered what I said and thought about my actual value in the company some more.

"I agree with you, Leila. It's true. You completely manage this place, and your position is worth more than that of an admin assistant—far more. That's why I am willing to give you a two-dollars-an-hour wage increase. I have considered the company's finances, and I think we can just about make that happen."

Raymond started shuffling around the papers on his desk, the very papers that I kept organized for him. Everything in this office had practically been filed by me. If anything, I had enabled Raymond to take the back seat and enjoy client luncheons and complimentary seasonal tickets to the Dolphin football games, while I managed the attorneys and the cases that were coming in and out of this door, all for a measly $11 an hour? And this was supposed to be the *increase?*

My heart was no longer broken. I wasn't feeling emotional or as if life was unfair or like I couldn't do this. If anything, this was the first time where I truly began to recognize my value. I had only been working in this firm for a short of a year and a half, and I had already completely turned it around. We were handling more cases than ever. I knew how much revenue Raymond was getting into the firm because I was personally looking after some of the books! This was the final straw. He was not willing to see my value, and no matter how nice or kind he was as a boss, kindness does not pay the bills.

"I think my time here is done, Raymond," I announced, right out of my mouth.

He looked at me, perplexed. "I thought... I thought you would be pleased."

"I will be pleased to work in a managerial position when I am being paid a managerial wage. If you can't do that for me, then I'm going to find somewhere that will."

My words were measured, diplomatic, without a strong tone. But Raymond still looked injured. He resembled a young animal that was hiding from a predator in the distance. If anyone was making this emotional affair, it was him and not me.

"But you can't just... how could you just leave? I—listen, Leila, my hands are tied. We have some money in different accounts, and you know, we're still paying for Rita's sick leave, and we don't have a replacement, I mean... No one knows the system like you!"

He whimpered the same way my daughter Nicole did when I told her that it was time to get out of the bath and stop playing with her rubber ducky. If anything, Raymond's resistance to paying me what I thought I deserved gave me more strength to officially decide that I wouldn't overwork myself just so that I could be underpaid.

"Raymond, I'm so grateful for the chance you took on me as a new mother, for the experience you have given me, and also, for the friendship. Please understand—this isn't personal; it's just business."

I walked out of the office with my head held high. It was both exhilarating and terrifying. I was enrolled in college and getting closer and closer to obtaining my Bachelor's every day. Things were finally starting to balance out financially between Nicholas and me, and regardless of the fear I felt, I no longer wanted to work for a job that couldn't offer me what I was worth. No more late nights, no more filing systems, no more working overtime and not being paid for it. This was my path to a new life, one where I was independent and valued. It didn't matter to me that Raymond was reluctant to give me the pay increase that I felt I deserved. All I had to do was find one person who valued me the same way I valued myself. And until then, there was always plenty of housework to be done.

16

THREE'S A CROWD

*T*ime passed both slowly and in a heartbeat. Suddenly, my babies were growing, and Nicholas and I kept chipping away and attempting to find jobs that were willing to pay us a better wage. Before I married my husband, I wasn't aware of how his attention deficit issues affected his everyday life. But the intimacy that comes with living with someone, having children with them, knowing them for the majority of your life also reveals a person's deepest faults.

I had found a job that was willing to pay me more while aiming for an even better one as soon as my studies were complete. I was so close to completing my Bachelor's degree. Together, Nicholas and I had even bought a house. It was a new home and was more expensive than our humble wage would have allowed for. But as soon as I saw the kitchen, I imagined myself cooking for my children and tending to their needs as they grew up, not in any old house, but in this house that we had gone and searched for.

When discussing whether to buy the house with Nicholas, I'd simply said, "Call this my 'giving birth to two children in less than two years' present." Having a place to call our own was incredibly fulfilling. My schedule was so consistently busy with the goals that I was aiming for, the children and all of their needs, and the housework that I barely had time to think, let alone reflect on who did what around the house.

But it was evident. I was pulling far more of the weight than Nicholas was. The children were getting older now. They were in grade school, walking and talking—actually, they never stopped talking, as most young kids their age. I was so completely immersed in them, it was impossible to consider how anyone else would feel differently.

It's not that Nicholas didn't love his children. He so evidently adored them. But there was a comfortable distance when it came to the responsibilities of getting school books, driving them to their extra-curricular activities, making sure that forms for school trips were signed off, cleaning up, making sure they were fed, putting them to bed. Once the children had gotten out of diapers, there was a sort of indifference that fell over Nicholas. It was a similar feeling to the one I had when working in the law firm. I was capable, willing, and determined to get the things done that needed to be done and to the best of my ability. But all around me, there were these men that seemed to take advantage of that, including my own husband.

When Nicholas came home from work, he liked to crack a beer and sit in front of the television. He would play around with the kids, but only if it were for fun. He had no real interest in the responsibilities: in changing a light fixture, cutting the grass, putting up a broken frame, in putting them to bed, getting them ready for school. All of the actual parental and even husband tasks were falling on me, and this was while I was trying to keep up with the housework. I got into the habit of nagging Nicholas to do things. There was real resentment growing inside me with every day that went by that I didn't see a change in him. Most of the time, I kept this resentment deep inside of myself, buried for no one to discover. The result of this, of course, was continual nagging and pestering for him to do things. Nicholas's ADD meant that he couldn't focus on one thing for long—unless, it seemed, watching television or playing video games. I wanted to be understanding, to discuss with him how we could better share the house chores, but anytime I went to do so, anger would take over, and I would just get irritated, leaving him upset with his confidence knocked. I'm pretty sure he was frustrated with me as well.

Resentment is silent. It is often discreet. And for the most part, it is left buried somewhere underneath indifference and the desire to live in harmony. But it festers. It stays in the silent mind, and it can be deafening when you don't do something about it. It wasn't until I became pregnant with my third child unexpectedly, with just two semesters away from graduating, that I truly felt the full effect of it.

~

Nicholas was kissing my neck as I was reading college notes for class. I was around twelve weeks pregnant at this stage, and I still hadn't gotten over how this pregnancy would delay me from getting my degree. But Nicholas was overjoyed with the news and didn't seem to understand the problem. He tried to take the notes out of my hand and kissed my collar bone, back up to my neck, nibbling a bit of my shoulder, which he knew always got me in the mood. But I was a hard sell that evening.

"I just don't know how we're going to do this. Just as I start to get my freedom back." I sighed, thinking about the impossibles running around inside my head. Every baby was a blessing, and I, of course, knew that. But truly, it was the dread of knowing that everything was going to fall on me that was making me feel so unsteady about having a third baby.

"Come on, Leila. We can do this. You know we can." Nicholas continued to kiss my neck, and I pushed him off of me, suddenly enraged.

"I can. I do! Who takes Nicole to her gymnastics class? Who has the debate with Avery every single night about why he has to do his homework? Who cooks the dinners, puts them to bed, wakes up with them every Saturday morning? So, who is more likely to look after this baby? Me or you?"

My voice had a harsh tone to it. I spat the words out faster than I could even think. This was the resentment that had been spewing up inside of me for years now. As much as I denied it, even inside my own mind, it was exhausting taking on everything. Sure, I wasn't in the same position as my mother was. And I think the fact that my mother had never had any support made me feel so grateful for even having a present father in the kids' life. But I needed more from Nicholas. He must have known that.

We were silent with one another for a minute. I tidied away my papers, just for something to do. When I got back onto the bed, Nicholas held my hand, looking at me in the eyes.

"I get it. It's... it's true. But this baby, Leila... we can make a change. I can be the primary caregiver. I'll do everything for this baby, just you wait. Let me prove myself to you. Come on, I love you, baby."

I considered what he had to say. I thought back to my postpartum days with Nicole and how Nicholas was there for me, getting up with her for the night feeds and letting me rest while he took her out in her stroller and staring at her as she cooed in his arms. That was the thing. I knew Nicholas was capable; it just depended on whether he felt like it or not.

"Easier said than done." I huffed, grabbing some moisturizer and putting it on my hands and then on my neck. But Nicholas was determined to convince me.

"Come on, baby. Believe in me, and I promise you will get through college and graduate without having to take months off. I'm here for you. I love you, and I love this baby too."

He lifted up the top of my silk pajamas and kissed my stomach. I laughed, telling him to stop but enjoying the tickling sensation that his kisses were giving me. He didn't stop. He came up to my neck again and started nibbling. I sighed, closed my eyes, and let myself feel the sensations of his touch. His tongue pointed out and licked the trace of my collar bone, and I winced the way he liked me to.

"You're so sexy," he said, in his gruff voice, that was anticipating pleasure. I smiled, feeling his groin expand and grow against my thigh underneath his boxers. Love-making was always a good escape—for both of us. And more than anything, at that moment, I wanted to escape.

I let his groin go in between my thighs as he lay on top of me and kissed me, unbuttoning my silk top and exposing my breasts. He kissed my nipples and licked them with his tongue. The pleasure was immense. My nipples were sensitive enough to almost bring me to a climax when Nicholas licked them like that, and I winced with pleasure, feeling his mouth take over. He sucked on them, and my nipples became hard. I felt myself becoming wet in between my thighs and yearned to feel him inside of me.

Nicholas slid down to my crotch and delicately took off my panties, smiling eagerly at what he saw. He brought his head back up to my crotch and took his tongue in between my legs. I winced with instant pleasure. His tongue was pressed against the pulse inside of my legs, and I moaned as he ate me with passion and greed.

"Oh baby, you're going to make me cum." I winced as I felt the vibration rise from inside my thighs and then ripple all the way up to my nipples, my neck, everywhere around me. I felt this incredible release of tension as I orgasmed for at least fifteen seconds, all the while feeling his tongue lick everywhere around my second lips. I tried to escape his tongue, thinking that I couldn't take the intensity anymore, but he just kept going, licking me like I was the last living woman on earth and his life depended on making me cum as much as possible. He didn't stop there. Just when I felt like I couldn't take it any longer, I felt the familiar build-up, the pulsation from my clit, the wetness in between my legs soaking the bedsheets. He was taking all that he could get, moving me around the bed as his tongue pressed, licked, and sucked.

"Oh, FUCK!" I yelled as I came a second time.

Instantly, he stood at the bed, and I saw his rock-hard erection facing me. I spread my legs open wide, ready to take him. I loved the way he was so hungry for sex and for me—and I was hungry too. All I wanted was to feel the pressure of him inside of me.

He slid inside me gently, and we moved slowly at first, his face coming up to me again. I kissed his mouth, and he groaned like an animal, loving how dirty I was being. He groaned like this for another couple of moments as I felt him grow rock hard. Having him inside of me like that, after I had just orgasmed twice, made me gruff and moan like never before. I took my nails to his back and put my fingers deep into his skin, then grabbed him and flipped him on his back, wanting to take control. I held onto the headboards and ground on top of him, feeling our wetness soak the bed, looking at his face wide-eyed and wholly immersed in the control that I had over him at that moment. I saw his face crease, and I felt the pulse of him inside me as he was about to climax. He almost looked confused, deranged at how much pleasure was erupting inside of his body. I kept riding him as I felt him explode inside of me, wincing and moaning before we slowly stopped grinding, and I got off of him, then we both collapsed next to each other, panting at the energy of our lovemaking. Whatever else was going on in our relationship, there was one thing that Nicholas was extremely good at, and that was hot, passionate lovemaking. It was something that I felt would never truly be lost.

We lay there, sweating, and he traced his fingers over my naked body, then kissed my forehead.

"I promise you. This baby is my responsibility. OK? You have my word."

His word hadn't always meant much, but that night, in the bed that we had just made love in, with this tiny little being slowly growing inside my stomach, I chose to believe him.

THE UNWANTED TOUCH

*B*aby Carter was born, as if completely by fate, on Nicholas's birthday. The baby boy that Nicholas was so determined to prove himself with showed up on the same day that Nicholas was born, his own little twin flame. I had an easy pregnancy and was able to work and study throughout. For the first year of baby Carter's life, Nicholas was completely amazing. Anywhere that Nicholas went, baby Carter was with him. He was his sole provider and was waking up for the night feeds, changing his diapers, running out to the store late at night to get him a pacifier after Carter had lost his, wailing until Nicholas popped a brand new one back into his mouth.

It was beautiful to see, and I finally felt closer than ever to obtaining my bachelor's. I even made a point of switching from part-time college to full-time for my final two semesters. I knew it was going to be difficult, becoming a full-time student with three babies at home, but with Nicholas taking care of Carter, it certainly made things a whole lot easier.

But habits are habits, and they take a lot longer than one baby to eradicate. I hated that I was picking up on Nicholas's unkept promises, but the truth was that once Carter reached a year old, Nicholas was already becoming distant. He was no longer attending to his needs. As soon as Carter was showing a small bit of independence, in being able to crawl around and try walking, it was as if something in Nicholas's brain had shut off, and he was ready to hand the baby back to me. Maybe he was simply tired of my going to school.

As with everything in a marriage, this was gradual and discreet—but it was also a very obvious change. Not to mention that both Nicole and Avery were very much my responsibility. All of a sudden, the three children were under my care when they were not being minded by Nicholas's grandparents.

I couldn't help but feel resentment towards Nicholas. When I saw that he was lacking in his duties as a parent, as a man of the house, it turned me off him as a husband. For me, the two were inexplicably connected. I was also trying to keep my head above water and focus on my final year in college. On evenings when Nicholas got home from the police station, which, to be quite honest, he would walk straight towards the TV. I cooked the dinners, being the better cook anyway. But I was also studying and prepping for final exams with three children running around. The house was chaotic, and it felt as if I was the only one who was in charge or who had any authority. Nicholas could just as well be lumped in with another respon-sibility of mine. After all, I made his dinner every night, got things ready at night for the next day for everyone, focused on homework, and managed everything else the majority of the time. I was rearing his children so that he could sit at home after he got home from sitting around the police station or in a cop car. It's not that his work wasn't valuable; he was still a beat cop. Not having much seniority, he wasn't on the best wage, and he was given the jobs that the other cops were too busy to manage, like managing parades or marches, asking homeless people if they had anywhere else to go when sleeping outside of storefronts, parking tickets, perhaps helping out on a case every now and then, but by helping out, it probably meant that he had to file a great deal of paperwork. I was afraid he was becoming complacent.

Studying for finals felt like Mount Everest. The children would be running around, always getting hyper just before bedtime. There would be pots and pans in the sink that were catching my eye and irritating me, but the domestic chores would have to wait. It was essential for me to spend the evenings studying when I wasn't in class. I had never been so good at taking exams, it's not like they are an enjoyable experience, and if I wasn't hyper prepared, then I would run the risk of freaking out and going blank. That was my worst fear—after all of the years I had sacrificed, after all of the evenings, I drove to and from college, not getting back to the house before 11pm, after all of the time with the kids that I had missed out on.

Just before Carter was born, Nicole was having an event at school. She was only seven at the time, and there was no way that I could have run it by my boss since we were preparing for trial and everyone was working overtime. Nicholas rarely took time off work for these school events. That was my job. I'd asked Nicholas's father to attend, not realizing that the whole purpose of the event was to celebrate Mother's Day. When Nicholas's father attended, Nicole had presented him with a Mother's Day craft illustration book, one that was intended for me, had I only known to show up. Nicole had looked around at all of the other mommies, gushing over their handmade little booklets and having tea with their daughters, and she burst out crying. "Why isn't my mommy here?"

When Nicholas's father had relayed what happened to me, after an exhausting day of work, I ran into Nicole's room, only to find her sleeping softly, the handmade Mother's Day booklet left on her bedside table for me to discover. I flipped through it, saw a drawing of me, with a briefcase in my hand, and some sentences she had been practicing.

"Mommy goes to work." "Mommy cooks great food." "I love my Mommy, but she works too much."

It broke my heart to imagine Nicole gazing around at all the other mommies who had shown up for their children. It ached in my chest like an infected wound. Because with children, you don't really get a second chance.

Of course, the next morning, I sat Nicole on my lap and tried to explain to her what had happened, attempting to have the booklet moment with her there and then. But it wasn't the explanation that Nicole would remember. I hadn't been there. That was what she would be left with. And it hurt so much to think about this.

So, this is why, when I saw the pots and pans in the sink after coming home from the library for an entire evening, or seeing the children run around with dirty clothes, having not had their evening baths, jacked up on sugar and too much TV and video games, I went hard on Nicholas. I yelled. I probably made him feel useless. In fact, that's what he told me.

"You make me feel like a piece of shit sometimes, do you know that?"

But I didn't care. That was the truth. To me, he was *being an ass*, so as far as I was concerned, I was just calling it as I saw it.

Perhaps his issue prevented him from maintaining a schedule with the children, or perhaps my nagging and constant criticism was just serving to make matters worse. But it was the only way I knew how to get anything out of him. If I didn't nag him, remind him countless times of the things that needed to be done, micro-manage the domestic duties as I was also getting ready to sit my finals, the place would have been complete and utter chaos—more so than it already was.

I hated how the humdrum of domestic duties was getting in the way of our romantic relationship.

But for the last few weeks of studying, everything else had to be put on the backburner. The house cleaning, the laundry, the usual standard that I tried to keep at home, even my relationship with Nicholas. Everything else had to wait. I was so close to the finish line that I could almost taste it.

Nothing could have prepared me for the actual feeling that I got when at last, after a marriage, three children, a few jobs, countless nights looking over textbooks, and hundreds of cups of drip coffee, it was finally time for me to graduate.

Everyone was there: the children, Nicholas, my mother, my brothers, my sister, my in-laws, some friends, and even old colleagues. I remember seeing my crowd of family and friends, my mother and sister waving the Haitian flag and whistling before the ceremony had even begun. The cap and gown felt like I was playing dress-up, even though this was all very much a real graduation, one that I had been waiting on for years. As my name was called out, and I walked towards the Dean of the college who held a rolled-up flimsy piece of paper that I had been waiting to receive as soon as I had enrolled, I couldn't help but be so thankful to myself for getting me through it all. I remember thinking, *If you can do this, Leila, you can do anything.* And that was the thought that ran through my mind as I looked out onto the crowd, tears in my eyes at the sheer relief and excitement for the life that was waiting for me as I accepted my BS in Marketing.

Things did change. It finally felt like a huge accomplishment. At last, I can relax and enjoy my life a little bit more, without obsessing about the next hurdle or the countless hours of work that I would have to try and fit in in one day.

I got a job in a top marketing firm in South Florida. The buzz in the office was electrifying. Everyone wore suits and carried briefcases. And as I strutted in with my briefcase and low heels, nodding at my colleagues as I passed by, perhaps stopping to grab one of the complimentary fruits or muffins, I felt really good about things. It was worlds apart from the environment that I had been in before getting my degree. It was wild, the sheer difference.

My boss was intelligent, down-to-earth, and incredibly charming, someone who could sell a used piece of gum to just about anyone and who didn't possess the usual type of ego that came with the other top executives on the fifth floor. I was down on the fourth floor, but I had a boss who always ensured she included me in some of the more important client projects because she knew that I was willing to put in the hours and the actual work that was required.

Marketing, I soon learned, was an absolute chancer's game. Another thing that I learned was that there are not too many people in this world who are willing to work hard, consistently, and with sincerity. But it didn't bother me, the way other employees would take "emergency days off!" or how lazy they would become with a certain campaign when it wasn't generating any commission. As far as I could tell, this only left more room for someone like me to come along and climb up the invisible corporate ladder.

And that is exactly what I did. It wasn't long before my potential was recognized. Our CEO, Mr. Richardson, took on a sort of fatherly mentor role with me. He was one of the most brilliant people I had ever met. It was incredible, being in a room full of these effervescent people, and then being asked my opinion on projects, constantly being given projects that were above my experience, and being given the respect I had worked so hard to gain.

Suddenly, I was being invited out to have lunch with the execs. We'd go out to restaurants nearby, all paid for by the company. Looking around at some of my new lunch buddies, I couldn't believe how easy it seemed for them. Half of the people on the table didn't have any real clue what was going on in the company.

I was with the company for about eight months when the executive group, my boss Mr. Richardson, and I were walking back from the restaurant after lunch. Mr. Richardson was in my ear, talking about a client that he thought would be perfect for me and whose accounts he wanted to hand over to me.

"He's gonna love you, Leila—you know, your charm. The way you can make clients feel—feel special! That's it. That's how I want him to feel. And hell, how could anyone not feel special when talking to you?"

I laughed with ease, then gave Mr. Richardson a knowing smile. He was always trying to sell something—an idea, his opinion on a piece of art or on a missed business opportunity, the dish to order at the restaurant, anything.

"Well, you know, I don't want to step on anyone's toes." By anyone, I meant Clive Hamilton, who currently owned the client. Mr. Richardson glanced over at Clive now. He had half of his shirt unbuttoned and was smoking a cigarette out of the side of his mouth, his eyes red and watering from the five beers he'd managed to fit in at lunch.

"Some toes are meant to be stepped on." Mr. Richardson spoke low into my ear before putting his hand on my ass, giving it a pat and then a tight squeeze. He winked at me and walked towards the office doors.

I *froze*. Stayed right where I had landed when he had touched me. I just stood there, my mouth gaping open, unable to comprehend what the fuck had just happened.

Mr. Richardson turned around and looked back at me with glee. "Well, come on! You don't think I'm just gonna give a pretty face the afternoon off, do you?" Then he walked back into the office without looking back.

My body was still frozen. My mind was racing as if there were a million needles pricking my brain with hyperactive thoughts all at once. What had just happened? Had Mr. Richardson just given me one of the most lucrative clients in the company before he sexually groped me? The two just didn't match up.

I looked around, tears stinging my eyes as I tried to silence the deafening thud of my beating heart. My heart was drumming loudly in my eyes, and my body felt cold. The rest of the guys from lunch were completely unaware. How had Mr. Richardson managed to be so discreet and yet so blatant at the same time?

But then, seeing the sway and the laughter, the ruffled hair and the cigarettes of the rest of the group, I knew they wouldn't have noticed anyway. Or even worse, perhaps they wouldn't have even cared.

As the rest of them waltzed into the office, I stared up at the windows with pain. My eyes were stinging as tears dropped one by one onto my cheeks and then onto my blouse, as I looked up at the place that had once been my dream environment, and in one swift moment, had become a place that I no longer felt safe.

The only thing that I could think of doing was running to my car, locking the door, and sitting there with my purse in my lap.

"Just breathe, Leila, don't be so sensitive," I muttered to myself, the tears now erupting into crying. I was sweating profusely. *What the fuck? Shit like this don't happen to me!* I yelled in my head. My mind was racing between whether I thought I was overreacting to the horrible realization that I would have to quit the first real job that had valued me—or so I thought.

I thought about the sleepless nights of nursing while I read over textbooks. I thought about the neglect of my relationship. I thought about my mother's face on the day of my graduation. I thought about the changing rooms in the expensive clothing store, how proudly I had looked at myself with my grey knee-length skirt and matching blazer, the day that the job offer came through. And now, in a moment, in the quickest instant, it had all been taken away from me.

His imprint was left on my body. I felt him all around me. The tight squeeze, his sweaty palm, the scent of the booze on his breath from lunch.

'You don't think I'm going to let a pretty face get away with the afternoon off, do you?' That was all I was to him. Sure, I could climb up to the top, I could be given the best client in the company, so long as I endured an ass grab or two.

No way in hell. I put the keys in the ignition and drove out of the place so fast that my wheels made skidding noises. This was something that I would bury, deep down inside of me, too ashamed to tell anyone about. But one thing was for sure, there was no way in hell I was going back to that building. I cried to myself quietly on the way home before surprising my kids to come pick them up on time from school.

When I got home, I took off my suit and hung it up in the closet, showered, and replaced my suit with sweats and an off-white t-shirt. Today would not end with me being a business-woman who had gotten groped. Today would end with me being a mom—and that was the greatest therapy that I could have asked for.

18

ISLAND OF DECEIT

I decided to take some short time off after my untimely ending with the company that had hired me technically straight out of college. After so many years of grinding and running off of five hours' sleep, as well as my unfortunate introduction to post-graduation work life, it became clear to me that all I really wanted to do was be with my children and Nicholas.

My children were everything to me. They were my security, my main purpose for waking up in the morning. No matter what else was going on in my life, as long as they were ok, nothing else mattered.

Nicholas often suggested throughout our marriage that we go away on a couple's weekend or to a romantic getaway. While I appreciated his efforts in keeping the spark alive, I couldn't bring myself to leave the kids. My mind would be racing with intrusive thoughts about accidents that could happen. Even the idea of them crying before bedtime and missing me was enough to stop me from ever wanting to leave. It was clear that Nicholas was frustrated at this. As much as he tried to convince me that everything would be fine, the imagined risk in my head just didn't make it seem worth it. This limited us as to where we could go for vacations. Mostly, we traveled around different states in the US and flew back and forth to both the DR and Haiti.

As any Haitian woman might know, there's an unmistakable sense of conflict within when traveling over to the Dominican Republic. My children were both Dominican and Haitian, and while I could accept that, it was difficult for me to sit back and relax at a resort, knowing how my own Haitian people were suffering just a simple border away. Regardless of how well I knew Nicholas's family, I couldn't help but feel this sense of "other."

I still had family in Haiti, my grandmother, my uncle, many cousins and aunties, and second and third cousins. They spoke to me when I visited about their mistreatment by the Dominican people. Many Haitians spoke of being hit, kicked, and spat on by the Dominican guards and others. Meanwhile, the DR was thriving in comparison to Haiti. They had an affluent tourism industry and a lot of the usual amenities that could be found in the United States. The Regularization program, along with countless other predatory and racist policies, succeeded in keeping Haiti in a state of poverty while the DR thrived.

More than that, I was afraid when traveling to the DR. I knew how black people were treated and racially profiled there. I knew actual family members who were pulled over by guards, as they spoke perfect Spanish and tried to justify their Dominican citizenship. So it was difficult, to say the least, to sit back and enjoy all of the things that the DR had to offer, knowing that my people were a stone's throw away, directly suffering and struggling.

Haiti was the first Black republic to ever exist in the world —and the world reacted by ensuring that it would never thrive as a nation.

But like many integrated families, I tried to put it behind me as best as I could. We did all of the tourist activities, went to nice restaurants, and swam in the turquoise blue of the island water. Spending intimate time with my family-in-law also helped me understand how as a people, we are more alike than different.

During our stay in the DR, I found myself debating the fact that they loved to take advantage of every bit of their stay at these resorts, even if it meant the discomfort of the burning sun. Debating this with my in-laws was just another way that I felt totally different. I tried to bear it as best I could, but even with that, we were a lot alike as far as loving the time spent with family.

The resorts we stayed in were usually all-inclusive, with entertainment in the evenings, food and drink at our disposal. We usually got a family-sized room, with the children's beds close enough that I knew they were OK.

Around this time, I started to realize how Nicholas and I differed in the sense of what we wanted our lives to look like. To me, family was the most important thing. Spending time with my children was the only time that my anxious mind stopped itself from running away with itself. I could relax and feel the love and warmth that came with being around my children.

But Nicholas seemed restless like he wanted to get away. I knew that it irked him, my needing to be close to the kids. But I couldn't understand why that same urge was not within him. How could he not want to be with them the same way I did? Why was he so comfortable with being half-there? Where did his mind go, when we were sitting at a dinner table in a family restaurant, and I was telling Nicole and Avery to stop messing, or fixing Carter's bib, or cutting up some of their food, while Nicholas just stared out the window, daydreaming about being somewhere else?

Nicholas's distant nature became apparent during one of our trips to the DR, shortly after I had left my marketing job. It was as if he wasn't present when it was just us, the five of us hanging out as a family. He seemed restless or bored, totally disengaged.

The resort that we were staying at put on shows during the nighttime, and because we were on vacation, I let the children stay up and watch them as they played games and ran around with their cousins or were at the playground that was a couple of meters away from where the parents sat. The performances differed; sometimes they had flamenco dancers, or a singer with a band, or perhaps a magician. There were activities for all age groups. There were also a group of dancers that got on stage and performed with the main act. The dancers wore glittering costumes with revealing corsets, sparkling ruffles, and colorful feathers. They looked incredible, and it added to their overall performance.

Female dancers were being flipped around by their male partners, their limbs bending and stretching to places that most had never gone. I began to notice how enamored Nicholas seemed to be with one of the dancers on stage. Of course, it's not like I saw anything wrong with him checking someone out or discreetly finding someone attractive, but it was like his entire body was on fire. He could not sit still in his seat. He stared at her with his intense chocolate brown eyes.

Perhaps he thought that the more he stared at her, the more of a possibility he could have at connecting with her. I don't know. But Nicholas was more alert and more present in those moments that this dancer was on stage than he ever was for the rest of the vacation.

As the nights went on, Nicholas would make a point of sitting ridiculously close to the stage. When the children complained about how the speakers were hurting their ears, Nicholas went up and sat there anyway, making sure to be on the side of where his beloved dancer would be. I tried teasing him about this when we would go back up to the hotel room, but Nicholas would get all hot under his collar and explain that he was just enjoying the talent show, and weren't we supposed to be having a good time?

It was our final night, and Nicholas's family tried to convince me to come back with them for drinks, leaving the kids in bed in our hotel room. I was feeling outnumbered.

"You're not *leaving* them, Leila! Come on, you can practically see your room from where the stage is!" Henrietta, Nicholas's cousin, told me as we all sat together at dinner. I didn't like being singled out and being made to feel like I was insane, but there was no way in hell I was going to leave my children up in the hotel room alone.

"Are you crazy? Don't you read the reports about kids going missing while their parents are eating down in the common areas?"

Nicholas sighed, taking a large gulp out of his drink. "Well, I hope you don't expect me to stay in with you."

I didn't. Just like I didn't expect him to do *anything* without being persistently nagged by me! But I wasn't going to say this at the dinner table in front of his whole family. So instead, I smiled at the table, knowing that it was partly my anxiety that was preventing me from really letting go of the vacation and having fun. But I didn't care so much about having fun. Nothing was worth the idea of something happening to my kids. This fear, for some reason, was just not shared between Nicholas and me. And he wasn't so bothered with trying to make me feel better. He was like a child who wanted to be allowed out to play. I knew when to surrender.

"Of course not." I smiled. "Go and have fun."

It was 12:30 at night, and there was still no sign of Nicholas returning. It was a family resort, and I knew that nothing really happened after the show ended at 12:00pm. Families and overly tired kids would float back to their rooms as the wait staff started to stack up their chairs and get the sunbeds out for the morning.

The bar closed at midnight, so there wasn't much chance of

a nightcap. I considered whether Nicholas and his family went out for some drinks in the town, but then again, where would it be open? Everything was closed around 1am. It was off-season, and we were in the quieter part of the town.

At 1:30, I started to panic a little. I thought about the possibility of Nicholas having too much to drink, stumbling home and hitting his head, or trying to have a late-night swim and being swept out by one of the stronger waves. But neither of those scenarios seemed very likely. Nic wasn't a huge drinker, and he knew better than to put his life at risk.

At 2:30, I thought about calling the hotel reception. But I had nothing to tell them. What could I say? *'Hi there, my husband hasn't returned to his bedroom, and I was wondering if you can see him out on one of the verandas, chatting up a dancer.'*

"Don't be jealous," I said to myself. It was the same line that Nicholas had said to me when, the night before, he made a point of going up to his favorite dancer and chatting to her for twenty minutes. "Don't be jealous, Leila."

At 3:15, Carter woke up and crept into my bed from his own one. He was half asleep, but when he asked me, "Where's Daddy, momma?" my mind started to race again. Nothing could have happened to him.... Could it have?

I put Carter back into his own bed at 3:45, and at this point, the lamp in our room was on, and I was fully awake. "This is insane." I thought. At this point, I was alternating between a state of delirium, fear, and anger. I was angry at Nicholas for keeping me up like this and worrying me. But I was also afraid, and so my fears outweighed any sense of anger—that was until 4:30am when he finally showed up.

I had tried to get some sleep at around four, and just as I was dozing off, I heard the hotel card slit through the door. Nicholas crept in inconspicuously and tried to get into the shower before coming to bed. I met him in the bathroom and spoke to him in harsh whispers.

"Where the hell were you? What were you doing?" I asked,

looking into his eyes and trying to take in any signs of where he might have been.

"With my family, for the last time until who knows when! You should understand that!"

Nicholas had responded overly defensively. He also had a hoarse, slurred voice. I grabbed his face and inspected it, and found little sparkles of glitter on it.

"What the hell are you doing?" he said, backing away and walking to the other end of the bathroom, signifying that he wanted to get into the shower—but he didn't take any of his clothes off. Why was that, I thought? Was he hiding the scent of another woman on him?

It was nearly five o'clock in the morning, and we were due to fly at noon the next day. I had spent the entire evening and then much of the early morning worrying about him, all the while he was quite clearly out, either with the dancer or with some other wilful young woman. It was like a switch for me. It was almost physical, the feeling of my blood turning cold for him.

"I want you on the couch. Do not come near me." I pointed my finger and snarled at him, like an animal ready to bite. The venom and the rage that I felt, exhausted and seemingly alone in my concern for the kids, had me seeing red.

Nicholas just shook his head. "I'm not sure why you're so jealous all of a sudden."

I walked out of the bathroom and let him take his shower, the shower that he so clearly needed. Well, it would take more than a shower to get him clean. I went back to bed, biting the insides of my cheeks with sheer rage. The resentment that I was already feeling around him was crescendoing to enragement. But I took a deep breath, put on an eye mask, and lay my weary head on the pillow at long last. He would not take another minute of my sleep away from me.

By morning, I vowed to myself, my anger would turn into indifference. I didn't care anymore. And I would be damned if I let that man take any more of me than he already had.

19

DELUSIONS AND REALITY TV VORTEX

*I*ndifference towards Nicholas was working out relatively well for me. I had gotten an excellent job and was hired as an Ops Manager. My boss was a female entrepreneur who had come to America from Bangladesh when she was just four years old. Her success story, as well as her goals for the company, were inspiring. I was finally starting to feel like I belonged to a company that respected me and saw both my financial and human worth.

Nicholas had moved up in the ranks at the police force, and he was earning a pretty decent wage plus overtime. He had friends there, and we went to cookouts and all sorts of family functions. But it wasn't his passion; I could have told him that. Anyone could have.

Nicholas was a brilliant and intellectual man and had always had a talent for a number of things. His entire time spent in the military, he remembered negatively and as a terrible experience. The police and military force was never something that he had been passionate about.

I think because of his attention issues, he was hardly motivated. He used to come up with brilliant ideas but could never follow through. It was as if his own personality, the one that I had known for years, and his bright, kind habits that he used to perform to make me happy were a complete distant memory. I was starting to realize that I may have contributed to this.

Lately, Nicholas had found the perfect distraction from his own reality by binging on someone else's reality. At Forty years old, Nicholas became hopelessly obsessed with *Keeping Up With The Kardashians*. At first, it was something that we would make a joke about at dinner parties or at one of the police cook-outs—but it was anything but humorous when you were actually witnessing it. It was creepy and weird.

Nicholas had an obsession with Kim Kardashian, and he never missed a second of that show. He watched it with his mouth gaping open, waiting for a scene when Kim would be in a bikini or getting changed for a fitting. It was the same way that he had watched the dancer in the DR. Like a dog who was watching a deer being skinned, and was keeping his mouth open to take a bite out of the flesh. Nicholas was hungry, and for whatever reason, he was satiating that hunger with low-grade and mind-numbing reality TV.

Besides the fact that Nicholas's obsession with the Kardashian shows was obviously embarrassing and weird, it was also incredibly annoying. There I was, having come home from work, the kids floating around, needing help with their schoolwork, submission forms signed, the usual life admin. And there was Nicholas, fresh from work on the couch listening to the vocal fry of the Kardashians talk about whether "hippo" was spelled with one or two p's. I would even ask him, "Nicholas, why do you always wanna watch this show? It's so boring and ridiculous. These people are so fake!"

"Because it's hilarious!" he'd say, turning the sound up even louder.

I thought about giving Nicholas and me some ideas to go out for the evening, especially now that the children were growing up and we lived close enough to the city that they wouldn't be alone for longer than what would make me comfortable.

I thought about his laugh, the laugh that I used to hear often. When Nicholas found something funny, really truly hilarious, he laughed from his belly right into his entire inner being. His laughter would take over his whole body, and I loved seeing him laugh like that. I booked a couple of comedy shows for us to go to, which we did, and they were enjoyable. But we'd only really manage to go two or threes times a year, with everything else going on.

I thought that it couldn't get worse than *Keeping up with the Kardashians*, but then Nicholas found another show to become addicted to. He started watching a reality show called *90 Day Fiance*, where a couple, one of them being an immigrant from a different country, would have 90 days to decide whether they would get married and live in the US or not. The whole comedic aspect of the show was that many people from the US were being scammed by young and beautiful people from poorer countries who were using them as personal banks or means of acquiring a visa.

Again, this wasn't normal television watching. This show essentially took up the majority of the time that Nicholas and I would spend together. There was only a short window in the evening that we had when the kids were in their rooms, and we'd done our work and tasks for the day. By then, I was tired and still engulfed in my work, and we would both be doing our own thing. The only thing that Nicholas was interested in doing was watching this damn show. On that same note, I guess he may also say all I did was work.

And not just watching—commenting, laughing maniacally at the scenarios, and repeating endlessly: "How can these guys be so stupid? Of course that girl isn't into him. How can they be so idiotic? Really, though, how?"

He would be laughing on the couch, enjoying the show as I sat, skimming through a magazine or, at times, trying to understand and find the same sort of love for the show as he did.

"Pretty crazy, alright. They're stupid," I would mutter—but Nicholas wasn't listening. He was trying to consider a reality where he was so crazy, or so damn bored, that he tried to do the same thing. He was shunning these men for falling for a beautiful woman from one of the islands or from somewhere in Asia. But really, he was excited. He was excited to see these unattractive men with these knockout women who were younger and smarter than them. All they had to do was see-through 90 days with a man, and they would get a visa to come and live in America—or at least that was how it was supposed to go. And who could blame them? These men were putting their entire life savings on the line, and women were doing it too. Both genders were involved in the cross-country scams.

Of course, the show had some authentic relationships featured too, but the ones being scammed always fit the same category: older, usually overweight or not typically attractive, and lonely. Unlike Nicholas, a lot of the people that were being scammed by these beautiful exotic visa grabbers were clearly miserable and lonely, looking for a distraction from their otherwise very isolating life. But what was Nicholas's excuse?

Nicholas's reality was what most people spent their whole life dreaming about. He had a wife who cooked and cleaned for him and reared their children; he had a good-paying job and a badge that he got to flash around, getting into venues for free. I wasn't bad looking. I stayed in shape.

I guess sometimes it takes more than being present and taking care of the house and kids to make someone happy. I was probably not doing my part, but at the same time, he wasn't doing his either.

No, it wasn't his family and wife that Nicholas was escaping from, although I am sure that's who he thought was the problem. Nicholas was trying to escape from himself. He was trying to escape from the fact that in all his years of living, he had never truly gone out and gotten what he wanted in life. In fact, I don't even think he knew what that was. He thought that it had been me. He told me, time and time again when he was in military training, that his entire life was turning out differently all because we weren't together anymore. And that he hated it. Well, now he had me, and he was looking to escape.

Things probably would have come to a halt a lot sooner if it hadn't been for what was to come next. In exactly four months' time, my entire world would come crashing down around me.

2 0

A HEART'S GREATEST TREASURE

*O*f all the things that I remember about that day, I remember the rain the most. There was a weather warning of possible flooding in the city. My company allowed us to take the afternoon off so that we'd get home safely.

So that we'd get home safely. I hadn't given it a second's thought. I was distracted, I know that much. I was supposed to call my sister back, and I hadn't had a chance that week. She'd left a voicemail, asking me over for some Haitian Corossol Ice Cream, and I hadn't seen it in time to even respond to her.

"Aww, man," I said to myself in the car, listening to her message on loudspeaker. My windshield wipers were going 90 on the window, trying to keep up with the rain. It was pouring down, and there was a traffic jam since everyone's company had clearly had the same idea. But storms are quick. And as I would learn so brutally, storms can decimate everything in their path, leaving little survivors.

But this was just a rainstorm. There wasn't any thunder and lightning just yet, the power hadn't cut out, restaurants were running as usual, albeit desperately trying to move tables and chairs indoors—it was just a heavy rainstorm. There was nothing to worry about. We just had to get home safely.

Something flipped over in my mind as I was stuck at the traffic lights, watching as buckets and buckets of rain thudded down onto my windshield. *Go get the kids,* I thought. *Go get them.*

It was a thought so discreet, but it was a feeling that I would learn to recognize as anxiety. Anxiety over something terrible happening to the people I loved. Anxiety about getting something wrong or doing the incorrect thing when it came to my children. It was an anxiety that had consumed me, in the same way it did when I didn't feel up to going on dates with Nicholas one on one or to romantic getaways. If I just took precautionary measures that prevented bad things from happening, then bad things wouldn't happen.

I arrived at the school and piled in the kids, as they used their books and book bags to shield them from the pouring rain. As it so happened, other moms had gotten the exact same idea, and I felt less dramatic in my quiet and constant fears. It was normal to worry like this, I thought. That's just what mothers did.

I hated driving in the rain, and there was a large traffic jam coming out of the school. Carter was bawling and crying because he wanted to go play with his new best friend, a little girl named Jasmine. Nicole was huffing because the bad weather meant that her soccer game wouldn't be on, and she had been talking about this particular soccer game all week. Avery was good-natured Avery, sitting in the middle of the madness and smiling back at me. I figured that he was just delighted to have gotten an afternoon off of school. Ever the optimist.

We got home, and I told the kids to go and change into their cozy clothes. We were going to have a movie marathon on the couch as we waited for the rain to calm down. Avery and Carter yelled "Yay!" at this, and Nicole shrugged, slinking into her bedroom away from her brothers.

I put on a packet of microwave popcorn, determined to turn Nicole's frown upside down and make the most out of the rainy day that had sent all of us home to our houses earlier than planned. Where else did we need to be than with our family? I had my children at home and safe. Nicholas was out on duty and would probably be helping with the mayhem that was bound to erupt in the city. Florida was no stranger to extreme weather conditions. There was no real way of knowing how this rainstorm was going to go.

Now that I was back inside with the kids, I began to think about what could be ahead of us. Would we have to evacuate? Would the sea levels rise to the point that was dangerous? But there was no real point in worrying where we were, out in the suburbs. We were far from the coast and the lakes; we lived more inland. The rain wasn't so bad at the moment.

I picked up the phone and dialed my sister's number while I was waiting for the popcorn to pop. I got her voicemail and then rang again, getting her voicemail again.

"Hey, Sandra, it's me. Call me back. It's bad out there! Look, if you can, try to come over. The kids and I are watching a movie. I don't know; I'm kind of in the mood for some wine." I chuckled, tapping on the desk. "Anyways, be careful. Those roads are a hot mess! Ok, later."

I hung up the phone just as Carter and Avery were coming out. They jumped up on the couch, and I cuddled them, then got back up to make the popcorn. Nicole slinked out of her room, still unsure whether she was too cool to join her mom and brothers for a movie or not. She folded her arms, looking at the microwave suspiciously. I smiled and grabbed a popcorn bowl from the kitchen cabinet, then opened the microwave door, pinching the corners of the bag so as not to burn myself, before ripping it open and letting the hot steam escape.

"Ooh, that's right, lady, you've got yourself some good snacks for this occasion," I said, and Nicole laughed.

"Mom, stop being so extra." But she went and grabbed some sodas and the butter to melt over the popcorn anyway.

We soon sat down, all four of us, and the rain became less of a threat, as we lost ourselves in Despicable Me. Nicole had said that it was too childish, but then she was the one who was laughing the hardest. The phone rang, and I assumed it was Sandra coming over, now that the skies had cleared up.

"Hello?"

"Leila, it's—I'm coming home, baby, just—are you and the kids alright?" It was Nicholas.

"What? Yes. Of course, are you alright?"

"Yes, but—"Nicholas whimpered on the phone. I felt my heart inside my ears. He was not one to cry at random.

"Nick, what is it?" I asked.

He continued to whimper. The kids were laughing inside, and the movie was deafening inside my ears. Something was coming over me. I couldn't understand it. But it was dark. It was a feeling, a dark cloud that was enveloping my entire body as I started to understand that something very terrible was about to happen. I felt it. I felt it coming inside my blood. Some people may disagree with me, but I knew. I knew as soon as I heard my husband whimper that something had happened.

He continued, and I held the phone up to my ear, my arm feeling numb as it began to shake. How can anyone prepare themselves for news that is bad?

"It's Sandra," he whispered. "I'm at the scene. Her car, it's… it's in the lake. They couldn't get her out in time." Nicholas's voice was now panicking as he tried to grab breaths in between the words that he was saying.

White noise. Darkness. Blood.

I woke up with only half of my hearing returned. There were the children, above me. Carter was crying while Nicole was instructing Avery to do something. My head had been cut from the fall. I tried to get up but couldn't. That piercing white noise was inside of my head. I couldn't hear anything. I couldn't make sense of my surroundings. 'It's Sandra,' he'd whispered.

"No," I mouthed. "No." Then a cry. A guttural cry and

scream as I started to wake up in a world where my sister no longer existed. *"No!"*

～

There was no hospital bed. There was no resuscitation. There was nothing they could have done.

That is what Sergeant Mike told me when I made it to the hospital, driven by an ambulance after the children had phoned them.

"There was nothing we could have done," the sergeant said to me with Nicholas beside him, his eyes stained with redness.

I looked at him coldly because the entire world was now cold. This was not a world that I wanted to be in. The rain was washing away any existence of her. I needed to see her. I needed to know that she had existed, and that our love had existed, and that it was still here—right here in this cold and dark hospital. I didn't know who I was without my sister. I didn't understand what it meant to live without her.

"Where is she?" I yelled. Nicholas held me and tried to restrain me. *"Where is she!"*

"Leila, please, this won't bring her back." Nicholas cried. He held me in his arms tighter, and I collapsed, my sobbing coming from the core of my being, from the pit of my stomach. I couldn't breathe. I was trying to gasp for air, but nothing was coming. I looked around to find her somewhere, but she was nowhere. And in her absence, I disappeared.

"Room temperature or cold?" Mike asked.

"Huh?" Nothing was entering my head. There were no opinions that existed. I couldn't form a sentence.

"The water. Room temperature or cold?"

"Oh," I uttered. "Room."

Nicholas sat beside me, holding my hand. In reality, I just needed her. My big sister. I hated how all I could think about was how Sandra and Nicholas never really got along, the way guys sometimes felt about their wife's closest companion. I tried to silence my anger and bring myself back to a state of numbness. Numbness was safe. Numbness was cold. Numbness was terrifying.

They asked whether I wanted to go to the morgue, and it shocked me how normal she looked, how the same. The doctor peeled back the sheet, and there she was, my sister, the same way as she had always been. Her sleek face and eyes painted in light makeup, her favorite turquoise necklace around her neck, her skin a little plump and bloated, her fingers cold. I held them even still, and I sobbed as I saw the bruises from the collision that had happened in the accident.

"It was the freeway. The roads were skidding. She isn't the only driver who has come in today. The toll count would be up later. There were bound to be more numbers." The doctor tried to make me feel better by telling me that the flooding body count was bound to go up. I began to cry, which turned into wails and gasps for breath as I panicked, my mind in total delirium.

They took me out of the room by force. I screamed. I called out her name because I needed her name to be heard at that moment. I needed to take a part of her with me. "Sandra!"

They closed the door, and she was left there in that cold dark room, in a damn box. "She must be terrified," I kept saying. "Please, she must be terrified! I have to be there with her."

But they dragged me away, and I closed my eyes, yelling her name and trying to picture her beautiful face—the face of my sister who was alive and living, and not the bloodied face of my sister who was in that cold, dark, empty room. It took Nicholas, Mike, and the doctor to man-handle me out of the morgue and leave my sister there.

MI CORAZÓN

Grief is both silent and deafening. Grief is a strange loneliness. It is a loneliness that I craved. The only way I knew how to be close to my sister was to be alone, shutting the rest of the world out, having made-up conversations with her in my head.

I searched for her everywhere. I looked in the skies, in the clouds, but there was nothing. No trace left. I went into her apartment with the task of clearing it and throwing out some of her things, but I couldn't bring myself to throw out anything. I brought every last scrap of what was left of her home with me to be stored and kept in a place that only I knew so that I could be alone with her whenever I wanted to.

My grief separated me from everyone. My kids were worried about me, about my complacency and lack of nagging. They could see the sadness in my eyes, and they didn't know how to react. Nicole and Avery both held my hand and cried with me at the funeral. I felt so hurt for her, that she had to know pain like this at such a young age, that she had to witness it at all.

But my dealings with grief were far from over. Once you

lose one person in your life, the next time you meet with grief, it becomes this all-too-familiar blanket of melancholy, the painful side of loving too much, and aloneness. Just six months after my sister died in the car accident, the Haitian Earthquake devastated Haiti, killing over 250,000 of my people. One of those people was my beautiful, insightful, and hard-working grandmother.

The devastation that followed the earthquake was unbearable for me to watch. The idea that I had escaped this devastation simply by being brought up in Florida and not Haiti left me with feelings of aching pain. I couldn't reach my family in Haiti for weeks.

My grandmother's own death was confirmed immediately because she was not located in the hardest-hit areas. It was devastating to lose the matriarch of a family. The mother who birthed my mother, who birthed me, who birthed my daughter and two sons. The family chain was breaking—that is how it felt.

All around me, my identity was threatened by these random bouts of devastation. Next would be my uncle, the uncle who had warned me all those years ago about falling too hard for Nicholas at a young age. Uncle Daniel had been battling cancer for quite some time, but I think it was the senseless tragedy of the earthquake that left him unable to fight anymore. And I got it. I couldn't blame him. I was losing the will to do anything.

What got me through was the undying love and devotion I felt for my family, as well as my children. Seeing grief in the eyes of an innocent being is incredibly healing. As my youngest child, Carter had the most innocence and lack of awareness as to what was going on, and yet, he had the ability to heal my wounds like no other adult could. When he saw me crying on my bed or leafing through old pictures of my sister and me, he would ask me sincerely, "Momma, why are you crying?" His brow furrowed in worry.

"Auntie Sandy went away," I would tell him, not yet ready

to wipe the innocence from his face. If I could protect him from loss for as long as possible, then that was what I was going to do.

Carter looked at the photographs that I had sprawled out on the bed, some of him and the children and Nicholas and family vacations, Christmas time—all perfectly stored memories, captured in still photographs. The people smiling in the pictures did not know about such tragedies as the ones I was now living with.

"But you have me, and you have Papi, and you have Nicole and Avery and even Uncle Michael," he said, looking at me with his big brown, earnest eyes.

I smiled in spite of myself. It was so healing. Out of all of the words that people had tried to comfort me with, my four-year-old had gotten it the most right. There in front of me were not pictures of all the people that I had lost, but instead, all the people that I had loved. It was the love that got me through.

Everything came into perspective for me, as it felt like my family was being ripped away from me. I couldn't handle any more bad news. I couldn't say goodbye to anyone else. And in this time, even though I didn't feel like Nicholas could really support me in my grief for my sister in the way I needed him to, it still gave me different feelings for what we needed to do in our relationship. One thing that hadn't been devastated and ripped away from me was our own family. My babies were healthy, happy, and well. Nicholas had not been hurt from the flooding that day, and despite the obvious problems in our marriage, I just didn't know if I had divorce in me right about now.

My continued absence in grief only gave Nicholas more time to stay in his reality TV vortex. He continued to watch *90 Day Fiance* whenever he had a free minute, and he continued to be enamored with the whole concept.

I got used to not expecting happiness and fulfillment from Nicholas. On one of my grief-stricken days, I told him that we should get a divorce, which he did not take kindly to. But he also had no solution to the obvious gap that was between us. When he suggested therapy, I wasn't too keen on the idea. It was probably the Haitian in me—the Haitian survival mode, so used to being in struggle and depending on no one to get you through.

But when I had some time to reflect on it, my opinion of it changed. I considered how therapy could help me through my own grief, and our relationship wasn't getting any better. Was I supposed to just be unhappy and accept that this was all there was?

When I brought divorce up to Nicholas again, even though he had been the one to originally suggest counseling, he was cynical and not bothered. His answer left me cold when he said: "A divorce for what? Do you think there's anything better out there? There's nothing better out there than assholes and trashy women. What are you going to do? Date and have sex with different men and call it a day?"

Of course that was not what I was thinking of doing. Something in his answer had made me fear going out and looking for happiness from someone else. After all, I was a mother with three children. I couldn't have the freedom of dating whomever, whenever I wanted. And so, indifference settled in again, and I just continued to live like I always had.

Regardless of what Nicholas was doing with his life, I was making sure to achieve the goals that I wanted to and to reach as far as I could, in honor of everyone I had lost that hadn't gotten the opportunity to do that.

This was why I decided, after my sister, uncle, and grandmother's deaths, to go back to college and obtain a postgraduate in law. I had been given this second chance. I had been spared from the horrific devastation that was impacting my people. I could not take my life here for granted, and so I wouldn't. I vowed to get my postgraduate degree in law in honor of my sister. I knew that I could do it, and I knew that I was studious enough to commit to getting it done.

Also, I was no longer having pregnancies and dealing with

toddlers running around. For the first time since I had gotten pregnant with Nicole, I was finally about to see some new freedom. And that is what I wanted to do. It was the only thing that could make sense out of the senseless tragedies that were all around me. Or it may have been my way of not dealing with my own reality.

I tried so hard to convince myself that Nicholas and my relationship was enough. I tried to silence the negative thoughts in my head, but the feeling of loneliness at not having a real connection with the person that was supposed to be my life partner was difficult to ignore.

Nicholas gave me a gift a few years back, a fancy camera. It was probably the nicest gift he had ever gotten me. I was able to take many pictures of our family with this camera. One night, Nicholas was working late at the police station, and I found myself picking up the camera and slotting the SD card into Nicholas's laptop. Once again, I was looking for traces, any trace, of my sister so that I could hold on to them as tightly as possible.

One of the photos came up with a website that I hadn't seen before and couldn't understand why a photocopy was made of it. As the photos continued to load, something inside me thought to check the browser history. Nicholas and I were so disconnected as of late, I think I was trying to find traces of him too—anything to hold onto that felt real.

I started typing the website that caught my attention. My heart flipped in my chest as I read the full URL address: Columbianmami.com. The first thought that came to my mind was, "Ok, this fool has gone and looked up one of these scammy *90 Day Fiance* websites out of curiosity." But when I clicked into the URL, I could see that his own email and password were saved into the login details. The slogan on the website said, 'Find your Columbian Beauty Today.'

I couldn't believe it. I laughed, right there in front of the laptop screen, as I was about to witness my husband's blatant virtual infidelity, the infidelity that was on our shared laptop screen, as he became a couch potato, watching this bizarre show about men like him being conned by girls like the one on this website. But it got worse.

It took a total of three clicks to get into the website, where I found a woman who he was chatting to. Their transcripts and conversations were right in front of me, scrolling back from a month ago. My husband was speaking to a Colombian woman who, in the very first message, had referred to him as "mi corazón"—my heart.

"You have got to be kidding me," I muttered to myself. Surprisingly, I was remaining calm. It was all so obscene that it was as if I was watching this play out in someone else's life. And besides, the man whom I had been married to the past year or two was not the man that I had fallen in love with. The indifference that I had subconsciously built between Nicholas and I was allowing me to be diplomatic, measured in my research. I walked to the kitchen and poured myself a large glass of wine, imagining what my sister would say if she had been there with me, discovering Nicholas's idiocy together. She probably wouldn't have believed it.

I went back to the laptop and took a large gulp of my wine and a deep breath. This was probably the only chance I would get to look through the chat, so I had to take the opportunity while it was there. The more I looked, the less and less funny this became and the more scarily real it felt.

Nicholas was speaking to this woman as if she were God's gift to Earth. But much more concerning than this, she was so clearly getting ready to manipulate him and use him for money. They spoke in Spanish, and I understood enough to get the gist of their conversation. She made sure that the conversation was mainly about him to show her level of interest in him and how amazing he sounded as a person—adding in how she wanted to be an actress in the US, and how she didn't have any means of getting there.

But she spoke more about the intense feelings she was having for Nicholas, whose profile picture was less than becoming. Meanwhile, this woman, his "corazon," resembled a Colombian version of Kim Kardashian. I skimmed through more and more of the conversation until the emotion of it all caught up with me, and I put the laptop down, picking up my wine and trying to figure out what the hell I was going to do. Mostly, I just could not believe how stupid this was.

But then it dawned on me. Nicholas didn't care about the truth. He didn't have any concept of reality. Nicholas only cared about being wanted and feeding his ego, about not having to show up for the actual responsibilities of life. This woman was the perfect escape for him. This obsession, this sickness that he was having with the entire *90 Day Fiance* concept, had finally leaked into his own life.

I shut down the site and put the laptop back where it was, going to pour myself a second glass of wine because Lord knows I needed it. I had to be measured when I approached Nicholas about this. But I also had to be fast.

It was clear that day that this woman was looking for money and a visa, and our accounts were joint. There was no way I was going to pay for the idiocy of his own mistakes and wrongdoings. Not after everything I had been through. If anything, our struggles as a couple deserved better than this mess. If Nicholas thought that he was going to screw over his own family and use our hard-earned money for his corazón, then he had another thing coming.

DIVORCE AND DANGEROUS HEARTS

The very next day, Nicholas was rooting around the drawers in the house, opening up cupboards that were used to store odd wires and spare TV remotes, and in a total panic, looking for his passport.

I sat at the kitchen island, pretending to read the newspaper with a cup of coffee, as he rummaged around the house. "What are you looking for, Nicholas?" I said.

He mumbled something underneath his breath, clearly not able to think of an excuse in time. And so I asked him again.

"Nicholas, what are you looking for?"

"My passport," he snapped back. The rage I felt had to be quietened. I couldn't show all my cards and tell him what I knew just yet. But for reference, Nicholas had never needed nor looked for his passport in all the years I had known him. Traveling to DR, Haiti, or around the United States meant that we had never needed to use our passports unless we went outside of the country—and all of a sudden, he was running around like a headless chicken, looking for it.

"What in the world would you need your passport for?" I asked.

He wouldn't look me in the eyes; he just kept rummaging around, taking everything out of the cupboard, then stuffing it back in again.

"Am I not entitled to know where my identification is? Are you that controlling?"

"Controlling!" I yelled. It had been harder to manage my reactions since the loss of the three members of my family, and the absolute chaos of this entire situation was crashing down on me. I couldn't believe the audacity he had of looking for his passport the very day after I had discovered his Columbian princess.

"Oh, I'm sorry, Nicholas. My bad. I should just sit back and let you take a foreign trip to see your *girlfriend* when you are married to me, is that it?"

Nicholas stopped what he was doing and looked up at me. We stared at each other for a moment as he considered his next move. Then, just as brazenly as he had messaged this woman, he looked me dead in the eyes and said: "Yes. I need my passport to go and see my girlfriend."

His words would have hurt a lot worse if I had any shred of hope left in him as a person. That day, our fight got ugly. We both totally lost it with each other—I was throwing his clothes out of the bedroom window, and he was threatening to call the police. In all of our years of marriage—hell, in all of our years of knowing each other—we had never had a fight like that.

There was no need for Nicholas to phone the police because a neighbor had done it for us after hearing the yelling and screaming. As if I wasn't mortified enough, now the police were at my door, separating my husband and me and possibly charging one of us with a domestic offense.

The days and weeks that followed were quick. My situation was becoming more and more severe by the day, and Nicholas went on the trip with his Latin lover. He had absolutely no consideration or care for anyone else. He had tunnel vision, and the rate at which he was utterly losing it was terrifying.

The connections and experience with lawyers that I had gained over the years of working in law firms came as an advantage for me, but there really was nothing that could stop Nicholas from decimating everything in his path on his way to the most predictable mid-life crisis ever. He was losing the run of himself.

As soon as Nicholas got on that plane to see his girlfriend, I filed for divorce. In a matter of months, Nicholas was spending all of his time and an excessive amount of money traveling throughout South and Central America and the Hispaniolas— the only places that his Latin lover was allowed to travel without a visa.

During the weeks that he was gone, I even tried reasoning with him, but we had little to no communication. He soon obtained a lawyer, who became the only source of contact I had from Nicholas.

Having Nicholas out of the house gave me time to investigate his sorry state of affairs in more detail because his actions were directly affecting my own life. He was spending money at an alarming rate, and there was nothing I could do about it since our assets were joined. It felt like the most ridiculous practical joke that the world could play on me.

As he was posting pictures of him and his girlfriend on social media, old friends that I hadn't heard from in ages were contacting me asking why was he on social media kissing his own daughter as they were confused about who this young girl was. People were sending me all sorts of photos of him and her in Mexico, Columbia, DR, and more, at different tourist attractions, taking boats across rivers and fancy dinners, going surfing and swimming with dolphins, all of these extravagant activities that were costing him thousands of dollars.

Her name was Gabriella, and her "job" was to con men. From further investigation, Nicholas was not the first man to be tricked into bringing her away on an all-expenses paid trip.

She had clearly done this time and time again. One quick search, and everyone was able to find this. How could Nicholas have been so blind? He wasn't in the right state of mind; that was clear from the moment he had been rooting for his passport.

His spending was getting totally out of control. So much so that his own attorney had phoned my attorney, stating that she had never seen Nicholas act like this before as she knew him previous to the divorce filings. She warned that he was money hungry and desperate to take everything he could, and we should try ending this quickly. My attorney and I frequently met as the bills were racking up, going through Nicholas's expenses that were increasing by the day.

I had met Mike a couple of years back, and I trusted him to get me out of this situation. One day in his office, we were once again going through Nicholas's rapid spending.

"Leila, I... I've never seen someone spend like this before. Take a look at these statements your bank sent me. It looks like he must have taken her entire family away shortly after the first few trips."

I glanced down at the thousands of dollars Nicholas was spending, taking it from our family funds to fuel his Columbian corazón. It was too insulting to bear. After the years and years we had spent busting our asses—and doing everything in my power to ensure that my children's futures were secure—this absolutely crazed lunatic who used to be my love and entire heart was destroying everything.

"But he can't just... Can't I put a hold on the account? On his credit cards? Can't I move all of the money to a single account?"

Mike gave a hefty sigh and raised his eyebrows, the way he always did when he had to deliver bad news, which lately, was often.

"Well, you can put a freeze on all of your accounts and assets, but that would mean a freeze for you as well and would involve everything being controlled and approved." He closed the papers to prevent me from seeing more accounts of Nicholas's reckless spending and looked me in the eyes.

"Leila, I have to warn you. This divorce needs to be quick. There's no stopping him. He's completely irrational."

For the first time in my life, I was afraid of my husband and what he was capable of doing to me, to our family, to our entire future. All the while, Nicholas was having the time of his life with a random woman who he was willing to risk everything for.

~

Nicholas

She was more beautiful than I could have ever imagined. When I saw her standing there, waiting for me at the El Dorado airport, it was all I could do not to faint right in front of her. She stood in figure-hugging jeans and a string top that showed off her large breasts. Her sleek, dark hair reached her waist, and she flipped it to the side when she saw me, beaming with happiness.

How could it be? I thought to myself. *How could someone so utterly beautiful want me?* But she ran over to me as soon as she saw me, wrapping her slender arms around my neck. I inhaled her perfect scent, not wanting to let go.

"Mi amor, so happy to see you," she said, and I could barely utter a single word. After all of the struggle I had gone through with getting over, here she was in front of me. Hugging me. Wanting me in a way that I had always desired. I had to show her that I was worth it.

"You look sensational," I said in Spanish. I managed to breathe, taking all of her in. Her olive skin, the dimples in her smile, her small waist that supported her large chest and child-bearing hips.

I was timid at first in my touch, keeping my hands on her perfect little waist. I had to be patient. I wanted to devour her.

Sweat had already gathered from underneath my shirt, and I tried to take all of her in, feeling like a rabid animal in heat. I had never wanted someone so violently. I was willing to do anything to get her.

We went straight to the hotel and settled down. It was a bit awkward at first, but we talked and talked. She was very interested in everything I had to say. For a few days, we shared stories about each other. At first, it felt as if she was shy and was hesitant to do anything.

But just as I had hoped, one evening after dinner, she wasted no time in showing me everything she had to offer. My Spanish wasn't as good as it should have been, despite being a DR native, and the dialect was a little different. But there was a universal language that I knew I was fluent in. I had to make her scream. I had to hear her groan. I had waited so long for this, another minute would have felt like a lifetime.

She sat on the bed timidly, patting the sheets beside her for me to sit down. The room was beautiful, fit for a princess. I made sure I got the best of the best for her. The scene was set, and nothing could have been more perfect.

"I think you're so beautiful," I said in Spanish, unable to think of anything else to say. She smiled, the way a sexy woman does when they're being told something they have probably been told their entire lives.

"I so happy to see you," she said, in her cute Latin accent. I touched her face, at which she grimaced at first but then relaxed more into my touch, like a delicate bird.

"I'm going to look after you," I said, wanting to let her know that I was serious, that her days of struggle were over. I didn't care what it took. The love of my life just happened to be living in Columbia. She was waiting for someone like me to come along, to be able to show her a better life and to look after her in the way that she deserved. "Anything you want, baby. It's yours."

She smiled coyly. "Anything?" she asked, then slowly started to put her hands on my chest and unbutton the first three buttons. I felt like I was going to choke on my own arousal. Every touch she gave sent shooting feelings of electricity throughout my body.

"Yes, baby, anything. I want to treat you like a princess."

She laughed at this. She loved when I called her princess. I had already sent her money to go shopping, to buy new clothes and to go to the salon for our trip. She liked to look good, and she spent money on her appearance. The way I saw it, she was putting in the effort to see me, to be with me, she was calling me the love of her life. Why would I not want to finance those things? After all, she was doing it for my own pleasure.

She had these plump, beautiful lips. As she approached me, she licked her lips, causing me to lick mine contagiously.

She pressed her mouth onto mine, and we kissed for the first time. It was like seeing a new color. It felt like my life was just beginning. It was beyond what I could have ever imagined.

I was hungry. "Oh, baby," I whispered.

She wanted to take full control of me. She straddled me and got on top, unbuttoning the rest of my shirt and looking at me square in the eye, pressing down on the erection that was hard and pulsating underneath my pants.

"I feel you, mi bello," she said and giggled, revealing these sharp little teeth. I groaned by just looking at her, taking all of her in. Her large chest was right in my face, and I put my hands around the form of her breasts, feeling their completely perfect shape over her top and bra.

She lifted her string top up and over her head, letting her hair fall down onto her chest, revealing a red lace bra and a toned stomach with perfectly olive skin. I thought that I had surely died and gone to heaven.

There was no time to question it. I would never let her go. The ecstasy that I felt in her presence was like nothing I had ever experienced before.

"Oh, baby, I need you. I need you." I whimpered like a dog, ready to be put on a leash and have her do whatever she pleased with me.

"You want it, cariño?" She asked, putting her hands all over her toned stomach and reaching the button on her jeans, which she undid slowly. I saw the top of some matching red lace panties along her midriff, and I wanted to rip them off her with my teeth.

"Yes, baby," I wheezed. "I want you, baby, please. I want you so bad."

She grinned, loving the power that she had over me. I would have been her slave and have her lock me up in her own sex dungeon if that is what she asked.

She flipped off of me and I jumped on top of her, sliding off her jeans and kissing her legs, her inner thighs, getting to her panties and kissing her hip bone, praying that she would let me kiss her second set of lips. Every kiss was rushed without certainty. I felt so clumsy.

I was a little afraid of taking my shirt off. Here was this complete supermodel in front of me, with the most perfect body. And here I was, having put on a little bit of weight due to the unhappiness I felt in my marriage. But she didn't seem to mind. She took off my shirt, and I kissed her perfect neck, caressing her ear and hearing her laughter. I couldn't tell if she laughed because it felt so good, or was it my awkwardness that made her giggle at my newfound inexperience. I grabbed a hold of her panties and shoved them to the side, putting two fingers inside of her and watching as her crotch rose and fell with the added pressure.

"Ayy, Papi, si." She groaned and I felt my erection grow even harder. I kissed her all over, shoving my fingers inside of her and then rubbing her pleasure spot, feeling her soak my hands completely. Surely if there was a heaven, then this was it.

She took off my boxers and pointed to a box of condoms on the table. I didn't usually like wearing condoms—being married for fifteen years, I hadn't considered it. But I didn't want to make a big deal out of it. Besides, it would probably help me to last longer—as I knew it wasn't going to be long, with all of the built-up pleasure inside of me.

I slipped on the condom, and she spread her legs out wide, grinning at me, ready to take all of me in. I pushed myself inside of her and she groaned, loud and animalistic, like she couldn't take the size of my package.

"Ayy, Papi! Oh, mi corazón. Fuck me," she said.

I stared at her rippling body, moving in reaction to the pleasure that I was giving her. I panted, thrusting myself deep inside of her and aching to hear her moan, to hear her scream my name. I held her legs up and she spread them wider to take more of me in.

"Say my name," I grunted. "Say my name, baby."

She moaned, hiding her face in the pillows as I thrust into her, deep and hard.

"Ohh, Papi. Oh, Papi, damelo bebe."

I was afraid that I would finish too quickly. Seeing her face wince in pleasure was driving me over the edge, so I flipped her to be on top of me. She thrust slowly, putting her hand against my neck and looking at me with these devilish, mystifying eyes.

"You want to protect me, Papi?" she asked.

"Yes," I gagged, barely able to breathe from her choke. The pleasure was intensifying with my breath being cut off.

"You can keep me happy, Papi? You take care of me and buy me nice things?" She looked down at me, thrusting her perfect groin on top of mine. I could feel her fluids soaking my thighs. I put my hand underneath us to feel it myself. I wanted to lick it all up and drink her for the rest of my life.

"Baby, I will give you a life that you couldn't even dream of," I said so sincerely, more sincere than I had ever said anything before. "Anything you desire, it's yours," I wheezed.

She let go of my neck and gripped the headboard of the bed, suddenly thrusting harder and harder, flinging her head back and screaming like a cat in heat.

"Oh, baby, you're gonna make me explode!" I watched her demonic body take over as she thrust herself deeper and deeper inside of me, her breasts bouncing on top, her eyes closed and head back, screaming out of pleasure.

"Oh, God, I'm gonna cum inside you!" I yelled, feeling the intense build-up as I burst and exploded inside of her, both of us yelling from pleasure and then collapsing on top of each other.

She looked at me with a coy smile, then looked at the condom, whipping it off and twisting a knot into it, her bare ass walking away as she popped it into the waste bin.

She turned around and looked at me. "I go for a shower now. You, rest."

Then she shut and locked the door.

I lay there, in a heap of our sweat, the sheets soaked from our lovemaking. Rest? Now? I would not rest again until that woman was mine, for eternity.

THE PERFECT DISTRACTION

I first met Terrance at the grocery store. My head had been completely fried from spending the afternoon at my lawyer's office—again. I was picking up some things for dinner, and the lines were the usual at rush hour.

This tall, dark, and handsome gentleman stood in front of me then looked behind, giving me one of the brightest smiles I had ever seen.

"Please," he said, gesturing to me to skip him in line. He had an entire trolly of groceries, and I just had the essentials: frozen pizzas for the kids and a bottle of wine for me.

"Thank you," I said earnestly. It was a kind and selfless gesture, and I was taking all the kindness that I could get.

We got talking in the parking lot, and he told me that he, too, was a divorcee who had separated amicably from his wife about a year ago. I laughed and said I wished that was possible for me. He didn't judge me as I began to tell him my story, right there in the parking lot, spilling my personal life to this perfect stranger. It felt good to talk to someone other than my lawyer, and it felt even better when Terrance had answered,

"So you mean to tell me that there is a man out there,

claiming that any woman could begin to be as beautiful as you?"

He grinned, almost as if he was aware of how cheesy and corny the pickup line was. But it was what I needed at the time. We exchanged numbers, and he asked me out to dinner the following evening.

Conversation flowed, and we found that we had so much in common. He had two children whom he adored and had full custody of, while his ex-wife traveled a lot overseas for work. He had a Technology background and was impressed to hear that I was currently getting my postgraduate law degree. We bonded over shared values and the desire to have a simple life that was family-centered. He paid for the dinner and insisted that he take me out for ice cream afterward before dropping me at my door with a kiss that made me melt.

We repeated this for a number of weeks, going out to the movies, grabbing dinner, going to the theatre. We also traveled quite a bit. He treated me like a queen. We literally did every-thing together. It was fresh and exciting. We had so much in common. He made me feel like I was the only woman on earth. It was giving me a totally new lease on life.

I couldn't help but think back to what Nicholas had said: *'You think something better is out there?'* Terrance was proving my soon-to-be ex-husband wrong, and I loved him for it.

I told him it was important that I waited to have sex until I was completely ready, after the craziness I had gone through with Nicholas. Terrance was a complete and utter gentleman about it, and the fact that he was so understanding made me want him even more.

~

After three months of dating, I knew I was ready to take the next step. We had had a perfect dinner at a five-star restaurant downtown, and this time, when he asked me to come back to his place for a nightcap, we both knew what he really meant.

I sat on his white leather couch as soft jazz music played in the background, and Terrance handed me a glass of red wine. He introduced me to new music, and I introduced him to music from my culture. He was a beautiful chocolate-skinned man with these unique, dark hazel-brown eyes. When I was talking about school or the divorce or something to do with the kids, he would look at me so intently, like there was nothing that would take away his attention from me, and at times, I would look back at him, and I would completely forget what I was talking about.

This evening, I had been talking about a paper that I was writing for school, and as usual, Terrance was leaning over me and listening with intent. I gazed into his eyes for a moment and considered the man in front of me. I considered all of the possibilities that were about to open up for me as I started to move on with my life and find someone that actually ticked all of my boxes. I stopped talking for a moment and gave him a seductive look.

"You know," I said, "I haven't seen the master bedroom yet."

Terrance smiled with his perfect teeth. "How rude of me. Please, follow my lead."

He held my hand, and I walked into the bedroom that had a four-poster bed with crisp white sheets and soft lighting. Terrance had put some art on the walls. The main picture facing the bed was a Lion, obscured from large brown and tan brush strokes. It was dark and moody and sophisticated. He took my wine glass from me and set our drinks on the dresser, then put his arms around my waist, looking deep into my eyes.

"Leila, I know you've been hurt. But I want you to know I'm all in. I am completely committed to you," he said, not a hint of humor or lightness in his voice. It really was his intention to make me feel as safe and as secure as possible. The way he treated me and made me feel was such a turn-on. I wanted to show him exactly how much it meant to me.

I put my fingers on his perfectly ironed shirt. Then I traced my fingers along his neck and up towards his face, pressing his lips against mine and feeling the light wetness of his tongue lick my lips and fill my body with the anticipation of desire.

"You're so beautiful," he hummed while his lips were tracing my neck. Gently, he started unbuttoning my silk shirt. His gaze was so intense yet comforting. I felt safe. I nodded slowly, letting him know that permission was granted, and I was ready to see all he had to offer.

He stood there, taken aback by what was beneath my clothes. I had picked a black satin corset that was giving my body incredible curves. He looked me up and down, shaking his head, and I laughed, putting my shirt back on teasing him.

"No, no, no," he said softly, taking my shirt off and letting it drop to the floor. "You were made to be admired, Leila."

We took off the rest of each other's clothes hungrily as the kissing intensified. He was kissing my neck and sending light chills all over my body, discovering my body with excitement. He took my physique in, his eyes widening at the shape of me.

I traced the ripples of his muscles, feeling the effervescent excitement of having sensual, sexual experiences again with a man I was deeply attracted to. Terrance was muscular, he was strong, and *damn*, he was fine. He was six feet tall, and I couldn't wait to see what he was packing. It had been such a long time since I felt this sort of sexual tension.

Suddenly, without warning, Terrance lifted me up by my waist. Instinctively, my legs wrapped me around him, and I groaned as he pushed me up against the wall. He kissed me deep and passionately, his hands feeling everywhere around my satin corset, feeling underneath my breasts to discover my nipples, the bulge in his boxers pressing up against my crotch, only the satin of my underwear and the cotton of his boxers separating us from being together.

"I want you so bad," I whispered, looking at him in his eyes and seeing the fire of passion build up inside of him. He whipped off his boxers faster than I could take a second breath and slid my panties out of the way, touching me with delicate and soft hands. I moaned in response as he held me up with one arm, still pressing me against the wall, touching me, and sending spasms all over my body.

Then he pushed himself inside of me, and I felt all of him. Every last morsel. It was euphoric. He thrust himself into me with hard and measured movements, and we never broke our gaze from each other.

He put his hands through my hair, his muscular frame still holding me up against the wall, my legs sliding down and then wrapping them around him again. He picked me up, still inside of me, and he carried us over to the bed, where he dropped me onto the sheets and continued to thrust, slow and deep and hard. Then he took my hands and pinned them against the sheets so that all I could feel was the throbbing thrust of him inside me. I came, and he stared at my face, kissing my neck as he watched me orgasm while he stayed inside.

It was electrifying. I couldn't believe the pleasure that I had been missing out on. It was like the birthing of my new life, a life with fire and sensual pleasure and deep erotic intimacy.

We made love for the entire night, finally dropping as the sun came up, only for me to feel his erection against my thighs a couple of hours later when we were slowly waking up. I turned around to kiss his mouth, and he slid himself inside of me again. We started to make love again, and I became instantly wet, my body remembering the type of pleasure that was about to fall over me.

He slid his hands down the curve of my back, sending cold shivers down my spine. Then he took his fingers and started to rub my pleasure spot, still thrusting into me from behind.

I felt like I had died and gone to heaven. The more we made love, the more I wanted it. His hands, his lips, his pulsing thrusts. I dug my hands into the pillow, and he turned me onto my stomach. I arched my back like a prowling tigress, showing him the slender curves of my body. He slapped my ass with his hand, and I groaned in reaction, telling him to do it again, only harder.

Terrance brought out a totally different side to me. We were amazing together; we had waited an entire three months to even touch each other, but now that we finally got the opportunity, we couldn't get enough. I stood on my knees and reached up towards him. He cupped my breasts in his hands as the thrusting became faster and faster, and he winced and let out a long, elusive moan. I turned to face him as he took himself out of me, and he kissed me on the lips and smiled.

"I think we're gonna need a lot of coffee this morning," he said, and I laughed.

∼

It had taken a lot for me to trust someone again, and after I saw how passionately Terrance could make love and how we connected, I was certain that he was the one. The sex was so good that it almost was enough for me to ignore the red flags. But soon, more and more flags were popping up.

There was no doubt that Terrance was a little controlling— or perhaps he had just been brought up with the notion that women were supposed to be obedient, that they were supposed to act in the way that he deemed appropriate. But Terrance's standards were unpredictable and not always based on logic.

One night, we were attending the opera, and I sat down beside him, with a gentleman to my right. He had said that he had seen the opera twice since it was on in town and that it would be a brilliant show. Terrance was huffy for the entire first act, and I couldn't understand why until the interval. He stormed outside the theater, and I practically had to run after him.

"You think it's OK to sit beside other men and flirt like that, right in front of me?" he asked, taking a packet of cigarettes out of his pocket and lighting it up, taking a puff. I had never seen him smoke in my life, and seeing so was certainly not attractive.

"What are you... wait, excuse me?" I said, wanting to grab the cigarette out of his hand and crush it on his forehead. Was he serious? The gentleman that I had sat beside and uttered a mere few words to?

This was not the first time that Terrance had displayed jealousy. In the beginning, he tried to play off his jealousy as being "intimidated by my beauty," sort of like a backhanded compliment. He would say things like, 'Well, it's your fault for being so beautiful,' giving me a smile and a squeeze. But I knew better than to put up with those sorts of toxic traits.

"What do you expect me to do then, Terrance? Are you seriously suggesting that I am not allowed to sit beside another man at the theatre? Do you know how crazy that sounds?"

Terrance looked at me in the eyes sharply, with his beautiful speckles of green. But on this night, they looked cruel. He was lost in his own insecurities.

"I expect you to act like a lady when I bring you to the opera," he hissed, and I took a step back, completely dumbfounded by what he had just said. Thankfully, I had taken my purse out with me during the intermission.

"Well, I expect you to act like a real man and not a jealous little boy. Goodbye, Terrance. Enjoy the second act. Alone."

My rage was so strong that I walked out and ordered an Uber. I had the driver drop me off on the way and treated myself to a crepe, taking a large bite and walking slowly across the boardwalk, wondering what on earth was wrong with all of the men in my life that were so unhinged. I was less than a mile away from home, so I walked the rest of the way. I started to wonder if I attracted jealous men. What was I doing wrong?

I got home to an empty house since the kids were staying with their grandparents. I double-locked the doors, feeling paranoid at the unstable men that were surrounding me as of late. It was disappointing, having to end things with Terrance so quickly, but it was in no way worth the risk. I had had my fair share of crazy. I was not going to entertain that again. I changed out of my dress and got into my comfortable clothes, wiping my face clean of make-up and putting on my night cream. Then I sat in front of the TV, getting ready to disassociate the old-fashioned way: not by toxic men but with a thriller movie.

Just as intro music began to play, I heard a set of keys rustle in the door, and I jolted up, a shock of cold sweat going through my body. Turns out I didn't have to watch a thriller movie. I was just about to entertain one of my own.

TILL DEATH DO US PART

$\mathcal{N}$icholas opened the front door and walked into the house. I stood up immediately. He looked unhinged. I had no idea where he was staying when he wasn't taking his corazón on vacation. I had assumed his mother's, but then she had told me she could barely get a hold of him.

He looked like a completely different person. His eyes were bloodshot, distant, and red; he wore a creased shirt, and he had a bottle of opened Hennessy in his hand.

"What in the world...!" I barked, my fear coming out in anger. He looked at me with a stony expression on his face and took three to four steps towards me. I backed away and then yelled at him again. "Nicholas," I said, "What the hell are you doing here!"

But he just stared at me silently, continuing to walk towards me with slow and measured steps until he was so close that our noses were practically touching. I could smell alcohol and ciga-rettes on his breath. He must have been drinking at a nearby bar. He took another sip of his drink and finished the last of it, flinging the bottle onto the carpet.

I stepped away from him and picked up the bottle. "Just get

out," I muttered, walking towards the kitchen to put it in the trash. He reached out and grabbed hold of my arm tightly. I whipped it away from him just as fast.

"Are you fucking crazy? How dare you!" I yelled, arching my eyebrows at him in disgust. But in truth, I was petrified. I had never seen Nicholas like this before. He seemed so full of anger, so full of hate. I didn't know this man. There wasn't a trace of the person that I had married in the man that stood in front of me.

When he finally spoke, his voice was low and barely audible. "How dare... *I*?" he asked while slowly taking steps towards me again. I backed away, bumping my back into one of the corners of the island and pretending not to feel the pain.

His voice was so low that it was almost like a rasp. He was speaking in a voice that I had never heard before. "How dare *you*," he said with such venom in his eyes that I was sure he was going to do something. Something irreversible.

I didn't want to show my fear, so I busied myself by getting a cup from the cupboard and placing it underneath the coffee machine, putting a capsule in, and hearing the all-too-familiar buzz of water and steam and coffee and milk. The very sound that both Nicholas and I had woken up to for fifteen years of our marriage.

"Get a grip, Nicholas," I muttered, pretend-cleaning the island with a tablecloth that had been left there—anything to distract me from the tension that was filling up this suddenly very empty and threatening house.

Nicholas laughed from the corner of his mouth. "Your words mean nothing to me now. You can no longer mold me into your obedient little slave boy, no matter how hard you try." He was looking at me with this piercing look of pure evil. I couldn't understand it. How was Nicholas showing up at our house, trying to spin this extremely messy divorce as something that only *I* did?

If it wasn't Nicholas, then it was Terrance. And before that, it had been Harrison. I was so sick and tired of the absolute crazy men that I had wasted so much of my life with, who had no clue how to handle a woman with her own mind.

"I know what you did," he spat, leaning in over the island to deliver his words. "You froze the accounts."

So that's why he was here. My lawyer had finally gotten permission from the bank to cut Nicholas off of any and all of our shared asset accounts until the divorce was finalized. His spending was so erratic that despite usual proceedings, the bank had accepted the temporary hold. There was no way of knowing how long this hold was going to last. But it had clearly gotten him into a crazy rage. I felt a fire burning inside of me as the battle against the man who had attempted to ruin my life was unfolding before me, whether I liked it or not.

"So that's why you're here." I grinned, getting momentary satisfaction at the idea of Nicholas discovering that he could no longer wire thousands of dollars to his gold-digger girlfriend. "Well, Nic, what are you going to do now? How are you going to keep your girlfriend interested without lining her pockets full of cash?"

"Don't speak about her. Don't you *dare* speak about her. She is *nothing* like you. She doesn't take and take and take until there is nothing left, until there is no reason for me to want to *live*." The veins in his neck were pulsating out of him as he spat out his words.

All that was between us was the kitchen island, the very island that I remembered falling in love with, back when we were buying our first house, and Nicholas's main goal was to keep his family and me happy and secure. *And now look at us*, I thought. At war with one another. There would only be one winner.

"Oh, grow up, Nicholas," I hissed. "This is so sad. Look at you. Showing up at your family home, trying to threaten your wife!"

Nicholas laughed slowly, walking around the island, trying to get closer to me, as I edged around it, avoiding him, without looking like I was trying to get away. The adrenaline was kicking in, and I was afraid that I would just freeze. But Nicholas wasn't the only one that had pent-up rage deep inside. He had given me a whole lot to be furious about.

"Who said anything about a threat?" he said. "I just want what is mine. Give me my money, Leila."

"What money?" I scoffed. "You seriously think that you're going to get anything out of this? You're fucking delusional. You're delusional if you think that I will not bleed you dry and cut you out of our lives, so help me God. You're delusional enough to think that a twenty-something-year-old would want anything to do with you. She is laughing at you, Nicholas. She thinks you're a joke. Your own family is laughing at you, wondering if you are sane. And she is laughing at you behind your back while you sit at home and cry about how horrible your life is—"

Nicholas plunged himself towards me and wrapped his hands around my neck, cutting off my air circulation. I looked back at him, frightened, in complete shock. He pressed his thumbs against my voice box and pressed his hands so deeply at the back of my neck that my vision started to blur.

The oxygen was gathering in my brain as I felt the effects of the veins in my neck being completely cut off from blood flow. His hands—the hands that had held mine when we said our vows together, when he had asked me to marry him, when he had held our babies for the first time—these hands were now preventing any blood or oxygen from flowing through my body.

I reached up with my hands and tried to break free. I scratched at him, and I dug my nails so hard into his skin, he roared in reaction, pressing harder and harder and harder into my neck. He bashed me against the wall of the kitchen and looked me dead in the eyes, so fixated on keeping me in his grasp, so fixated on ensuring that I would not draw another breath.

The fight inside me for life was weakening; my legs were buckling underneath me so that now, I was only being held up by his own strangulation. I felt the blood rush towards my head as patches of black started to fill my vision. Suddenly his face was replaced with the old Nicholas, the teenager who had pulled out the knife at the party, the one who had crept into my house while I was sleeping and slept in my bathtub. The man who would, on occasion, show signs of rage. Now, decades later, he was trying to steal my life away from me.

I tried to scream. I tried to yell for help. I tried to reach for somebody, anyone that could get me away from the maddened man who was trying to kill me. But there was nothing. Just the indescribable panic of my bodily autonomy trying to survive. With every millisecond that went by, I drifted deeper and deeper out of consciousness. My vision was disappearing, and everything around me was muffled with this cloak of serene darkness.

In this valley of pain and suffering, I could see the faces of my children, the sources of light, the very things that I lived for. I felt the physical breaking of my heart, and I watched as they looked out onto a lake, searching for pieces of my heart, fishing for parts of me to mend me back together. They were alone. They were too close to the edge; someone needed to tell them to get further back from the water.

'Get back from the water!' I tried to scream, but there were no words. There was no sound. Nothing could come out of me anymore.

For a brief flash, I was brought back into consciousness, and I saw the crazed face of my killer once again, putting all of his strength into ending my life. How could this be, I thought? Please don't let it end like this. I can't let it end like this. Please, what about my babies? Please, God, let me live for them. God, please let me live for me.

Uncle Daniel's face was before me. His heavenly form gave him a white and fragrant glow. He smiled with pain, welcoming me to the brutality of my fate. "My dear," he said, "I am so sorry. But I did try to warn you all those years ago...."

~

Nicholas

The gurgling had stopped. The gurgling noises—nowhere had said anything about the gurgling noises. The whimpering, it had sounded like an animal dying from a headshot wound. Her head now bowed before her, her tongue hanging out of her mouth, her body limp.

I hadn't thought about what it would feel like to hold her like this. Limp, lifeless. The blood in her body was slowly turning cold.

I peeled my hands away from her neck, terrified that she would wake back up. Her body collapsed on the floor, and I saw the purple markings of my hands imprinted on her neck. Then I looked back at my hands. I looked at the foamed cup of coffee underneath the machine that Leila had pressed moments ago.

It was just a moment. A moment of delusion, a moment of madness. Any minute now, and I would wake up from this. Any moment now, and the cup of coffee would be given back its purpose. Time seemed frozen as I looked around the kitchen. I tried to imagine what this house would look like without her.

I whimpered, pressing my fingers to her neck and looking for a pulse. Her body was cold. She had been out like that for—for I don't know how long. I stopped being able to see. I stopped being able to hear. There was this deafening thundering beating of a drum inside my head as I had pressed and I pressed and I pressed and I—

This was not my intention. Surely, anyone would be able to see that. I knew the type of guys that killed their wives. I had dealt with countless cases in the police force. Teary-eyed husbands who had been beating on their wives, claiming that she had fled the country, only for us to discover his fingerprints all over her bruised and battered body. I wasn't like those guys.

I would never do anything like that. I would never do anything-

I looked down at her. The bruises were forming, the bruises on her neck. How could that be? How could skin bruise after death? This was not real, I demanded. This was not real.

I whimpered, hearing it echo around this cold and empty house. "What have I done?" I whispered quietly enough that the voices inside my head couldn't hear me.

There was a creak from somewhere around the house, and I jumped, convinced that I would see her broken-necked body, staggering around the house after death, threatening me, threatening my future, my whole life.

"No," I said. No. I was not going to let her ruin this. I was not going to take the blame. This—her, like this—this wasn't my fault. She had driven me to do it. She had threatened me. She was going to take everything I had and not allow me to provide for Gabriella.

There wasn't much time. She had driven me to do it. Anyone could see that. I wasn't like those other husbands. I wasn't like those—

I thought back to crime scenes, countless crime scenes that looked just like this one. I needed to draw from them. I needed to think of an escape. Leila had already taken so much of my life from me, settling for me when she had no intentions of staying when she had never felt the same love that I had felt for her. Well, she wasn't going to take my future. This would be the last time I stepped foot in Florida. Now, I could finally be with Gabriella and be free.

'And now look at what you have done, Nicholas. Look at what you have done.'

I could hear her. Leila. I could still feel her all around me, dictating everything and trying to control my life, trying to keep me down so that I didn't experience any sort of happiness without her. There in front of me was her lifeless body, but all over the walls, all over this house, she was more alive than ever.

I had to get rid of her. I had to dispose of the body. Those husbands, all of those husbands that were teary-eyed and had been beating on their wives. Some of them had gotten away with it. Which ones? Which ones had been clever enough to beat the system?

I thought about leaving her. But the idea of my mother walking in—of the children...

The children. The children.

"Make it stop!" I yelled through gritted teeth, banging my fists against my skull. "Make it stop."

Her body was turning stiff. She would only become more and more difficult to move. I looped my arms around her shoulders and dragged her up the stairs. Her neck was hanging, lopsided. I must have broken it. The hands, those hands must have broken it. It wasn't me. It was the way she was struggling. It was the way she looked at me. It wasn't my fault. This was not what I had wanted.

But these were the cards that were dealt. I closed my eyes, walking backward with my wife's stiffening body, unable to look at her this way. I stopped on the landing and began to throw up. The vomit kept coming, and yellow stomach bile erupted out of me. I gazed back at my wife's limp body in the hallway from above the toilet seat. Just above us, there was the attic. I could place her there for now, in one of the large suitcases that we used for holidays. But the smell of the decomposition would leak out all over the house. Whoever the new owners would be, they'd recognize it instantly.

I thought of the garage, the freezer. The freezer! If I was able to lump a body up the stairs, then I could do the same with the freezer. We had a plug socket up there. It was built in as part of the new construction, in case we ever wanted to renovate it.

Time was running out, and I had to act. It was going to be a long night. I got up from the toilet and washed my face with some cold water. Then walked past her limp body to get down to the garage, preparing her temporary coffin.

BE CAREFUL WHAT YOU WISH FOR

*I*t had been far too risky to phone Gabriella. I didn't want any record of that on my cell. I would surprise her instead. She loved surprises. I was supposed to fly over there in a couple of weeks anyway, but weeks felt like centuries. There was no way I was going to waste another second of my life without her by my side.

I sat in my airplane seat, giddy at the prospect of what was waiting for me in Columbia. A woman beside me gave a side-eyed glance as I laughed silently. I flashed her a smile and ordered a rum and coke. It was time to celebrate.

The things that had happened, the things that had transpired between Leila and me, were unfortunate. I knew that the children would be confused when they read her note detailing how she left to pursue her greatest desire of having a career without the burden of being a mother.

My mother could look after the kids. Things had been so chaotic between the two of us, and now I was disappearing too. Maybe, in some twisted fate, they would imagine that we ran away together, deciding that the only way our marriage would have worked was if we didn't have meddlers and pests like the children and my parents and her family getting in the way all the time.

I chuckled to myself, thinking of all of the strange scenarios that people would come up with for our disappearance. Truth be told, I felt like I had just hit the jackpot. I was about to move to South America to be with the woman I loved and to enjoy the rest of our lives together, on white sandy beaches, sipping cocktails in the sun. It was like a fairytale. It was as if I had imagined it. And in many ways, I guess I did. Sitting there on our couch, day after day after day, wishing for a better life, and then it finally happened.

Just like magic, Gabriella had come into my life and swept me off my feet. She understood me. She listened to me. We spoke the same language. Love language. I got hard just thinking about her. She was magnificent. And the way she handled me in bed drove me wild. I was addicted to her. I couldn't get enough.

This was the life that I deserved. This was the reality that I wanted to live. I was finally getting to live my dreams and be with someone who could show me the type of love that I had been too afraid to ask for from Leila. Leila had been so obsessed with the kids, so obsessed with her career, so obsessed with education, so obsessed with herself. She would have been happier if I had just sat there, rotting away on that couch for the rest of my life. She just couldn't stand the fact that I had found someone who adored me. She couldn't bear that I was no longer obsessed with her, that this wasn't about her for once. Well, now, there was nothing she could do about it. Now, that problem no longer existed.

I got a cab straight from the El Dorado airport to Gabriella's new apartment. I was leasing a place for her in the city, somewhere closer to her friends and family. I'd gotten her parents an apartment a couple of blocks down the street. They were close, and Gabriella liked being near to them.

To me, this was all I had to know about her as a person. She was clearly family-oriented. She cared about the people close to her, and every single day, she reminded me of how much she loved me. She never stopped calling me pet names, telling me that she loved me, and sending me pictures of that perfect sculpted piece of ass. Who could have blamed me for what I'd done? If they could see Gabriella, they'd understand.

I gave the driver 10,000 pesos and got out of the cab, two bags with me to carry up the stairs. Gabriella didn't know this, but I had gotten my own key cut for the place to ensure I could always have access to her as soon as I landed in the country. This meant that I could completely surprise her; it was early enough, she was probably still sleeping. I could climb into bed and wake her up with gentle kisses. She'd groan and probably jump right on top of me as soon as she saw me. Gabriella was a fiend.

I turned the keys in the door and dropped my bags down on the ground. Then slipped my shoes off, getting ready to unbuckle my belt as I walked into Gabriella's room.

She shot up when I came in the door. "Mi—mi corazón, what are you doing here?"

I put my finger on my lips and smiled, letting her know that she had nothing to worry about. But then I saw him: a man, lying beside her with his back turned, a head of jet black hair on his head.

I clocked him, then looked back at Gabriella and back at him.

"Bello, is no what you think." She said. I backed away, staggering a little, feeling the ground slip from underneath me. I didn't know what to think. What had she done? A mistake, it was a mistake.

I couldn't blame her; she probably didn't think that I was going to be coming over at all. She must have missed me so much. Maybe she was expecting me to get back with my wife. It was a mistake. I made a mistake, and so did she. We were human. We could get past it. Of course, we could get past it.

"Gaby, I..." I began but didn't finish my sentence. I leaned on the wall for support as I lost my balance, weak from the shock of what I had seen. The man beside her groaned in his sleep and turned over to look at me, the bedsheets half off him, his body toned and in the perfect physique. He was young and handsome, the exact sort of man you would expect Gaby to be with. Except she had been with me. What had this fucker done to her to force her into bed like that?

This intruder grinned when he saw me, looking up at Gaby with knowing eyes and smiling.

"¿Es esta la perdedora que paga nuestras cuentas?" He grinned and Gaby slapped his arm.

"What the fuck, Gaby?" I asked as it became apparent that this was not a one-night stand. "Who the fuck is this guy?"

The man stood up in front of me, completely naked. "Me?" he said, with a thick Colombian accent. "I'm her fiance, you stupid fuck," he said in Spanish.

He smiled and laughed, and Gaby pulled the sheet up to hide her bare breasts, where she had been making love and lying in a bed of deceit. He walked out of the room and poured himself an orange juice from the refrigerator, completely unphased. This egotistical degenerate that was living off of my money and fucking my girlfriend. I could barely see straight with the anger that was pouring up inside of me.

Inhale Exhale.

There was red all around me as I took in the scenario. The love of my life had destroyed me; she had put a knife in my heart and ripped it out and stepped on it. The woman that I had risked my entire life for. I had killed my fucking wife for this woman. There were so many women I could have chosen from that website. And now here she was, lying in bed with another man who called himself her fiance?

"Gaby, how could you?" I breathed, looking at her straight in the eyes and demanding an answer.

She smiled at me like she was getting some sort of sick pleasure out of my humiliation.

"Oh, come on, Nico, you cannot be so stupid," she said. "What do you think? That a girl like me likes a guy like you?"

She had turned into the complete opposite of the character she portrayed throughout our relationship.

"But you—but we... You told me to come and be with you. I made love to you... you... you said that you wanted to be with me forever."

"I wanted money. I need a Visa," she said flatly, sitting in the bed with an expressionless face. I looked back at her, watching as my own fantasy was crumbling in front of my eyes.

This was a completely different environment than the one she had led me to believe in my head. And then, what had I done? I had risked everything for her. I had committed a crime that would ultimately change my entire life. I would have to live on the run for the rest of my life, all because this bitch told me that she wanted to be with me, she told me I was the best man, best bello alive, she led me to believe that I was finally in the right relationship with the right woman—but no. She had used and abused me, just like my wife, just like all of them had.

From the time I was a teenager to right now, these women had taken advantage of me and made a complete and utter joke out of me. They had never loved me. They had never wanted to be with me. They were just looking for a plaything to feed their sick and twisted egos. I felt the gun in my pocket. The gun that I was licensed to carry, even on an airplane. How many people in the world could say that? And these sick and twisted freaks think that they could mess with me? They thought that I wouldn't get even?

"Oh, Gaby," I said, my voice low and shaking. "You are so going to regret saying that."

I took out my pistol and shot a bullet straight through her skull, and she bolted down onto the bed, crimson-red blood soaking the bedsheets.

Of course, then her screaming, prissy bitch-ass fiance came running in after, screaming and crying for someone named Maria, shouting like a petty little child. He wasn't so brave now that I had a gun in my hand—and the idiot thought that I was going to let him off.

He looked at me, his entire body shaking with fear. He put his hands up towards his face and attempted to run out of the room, but I caught him and slammed him back onto the ground, putting three bullets into his chest and one into his head for good measure.

He lay there, lifeless, and I could smell the scent of burning flesh, the smell of the contact from the bullet, and the light stench of blood filling the room. It was a smell that seemed familiar because it was familiar. It was the scent of every crime scene and shooting I had dealt with in Miami, except this time, there was even less of a chance of the cops showing up. There in the middle of Columbia, no one would know what I was capable of. No one would know the empty pit of darkness that existed inside of me, except for my victims, except for my body count. *They* would know all too well.

I walked up to my corazón, seeing her beautiful face half drenched in blood as the bullet had hit her left temple, piercing right into her skull. She hadn't suffered, thankfully. I brushed a piece of hair out of her face and kissed her sweet, plump lips. "Ciao, mi corazón," I whispered before putting the sheet over her head.

There was only one thing left to do. I walked into the kitchen and searched for liquor. I found some tobacco and skins and a half-bottle of vodka. I rolled myself a cigarette and smoked it, listening to the unremarkable sound of a bustling street for the last time. I sloshed half a glass full of vodka in one gulp.

I would miss my mother. I would miss the smell of fresh coffee and pastries on a Saturday morning. I would miss the intoxicating feeling of being aroused by someone for the first time. I wouldn't miss the pain. I wouldn't miss the disappointment. I wouldn't miss the daily, mindless bullshit of trying to keep a woman happy that was destined to keep me miserable.

I walked over to a mirror that was in the living room and

took a look at my reflection. I laughed at what I saw. A maddened man with blood smeared all over his body and his third kill in a matter of hours. He was a monster. That's what this world has done to me. Behind my shoulder, I gasped like a frightened child when I saw Leila's face, her head dangling from her body like a rag doll, her mouth gagging for air like an animal hit in roadkill.

I looked all around me, expecting to see her there. All of the bodies that I had taken from this earth. All of the ghosts that were haunting me. I wanted to get them out of my head. I wanted to get *myself* out of my head. There was only one thing left to do.

I walked into the bedroom of the bloodied lovers, the piece of shit that I had put my love and trust and hope in.

I felt the cold mouth of the gun reach my left temple as I got ready to pull the trigger. I looked at Gabriella's stony, bloodied face. "This is for you, baby."

Even in heartache, even in death, I would make my way back to my corazón. If I couldn't have her in this life, then death was the closest second.

"I'll see you in my dreams, baby," I said. No matter how much she tried to get away from me, I was coming to find her. If I was going to hell, then she was coming with me.

ABOUT THE AUTHOR

Rose Curiel is a native of Port-de-Paix, Haiti. She moved to the United States as a young child.

So Many Women is her debut novel. She wishes to continue writing; her second novel is already in the works.

Rose currently lives in Florida with her family.

www.ingramcontent.com/pod-product-compliance
Lightning Source LLC
Chambersburg PA
CBHW052047240626
47153CB00006B/2247